A CROWN OF DESPAIR

A CROWN OF DESPAIR

JENNY MANDEVILLE

ISIS

LARGE PRINT

Oxford

Copyright © Janet Mullany, 2013

First published in Great Britain 2013
by
Robert Hale Limited
London

Published in Large Print 2013 by ISIS Publishing Ltd.,
7 Centremead, Osney Mead, Oxford OX2 0ES
by arrangement with
Robert Hale Limited
London

CIP data is available for this title from the British Library

ISBN 978–0–7531–9210–8 (hb)
ISBN 978–0–7531–9211–5 (pb)

Printed and bound in Great Britain by
T. J. International Ltd., Padstow, Cornwall

Katherine Parr

Katherine Parr was born in 1512 and named in honour of Henry VIII's first Queen, Catherine of Aragon, to whom her mother was lady-in-waiting.

Following the death of her father in 1517, Katherine's mother, a pious and determined woman, sought to secure the future of her eldest daughter through marriage, despite her tender age.

In 1526, at the age of just fourteen years, Katherine was forced to marry the aged and senile Edward Borough, 2nd Baron Borough of Gainsborough. She nursed the elderly peer for just two years until his death, leaving her a widow by the time she was sixteen.

In 1530, Katherine married for a second time to John Neville, Lord Latimer. Their thirteen-year marriage is said to have been amicable, with their time divided between Yorkshire and London, when visiting the court of King Henry VIII.

John died in 1543, a year after the execution of Henry's fifth wife, leaving Katherine a widow for the second time. It was then that she came to the attention of the bloated and increasingly tyrannical monarch.

This is where her story begins . . .

Prologue

Katherine Neville, Lady Latimer, 29 September 1541, Hampton Court Palace
King Henry VIII's Michaelmas Celebrations

My heart suddenly skips a beat as my eyes fall upon a man . . . I squint to get a better look, convinced that my eyes must be deceiving me. Oh dear God; it *is* . . . it is *him*, the man who I had that momentary encounter with at a summer celebration all those years ago; the man who I shared a strange, brief, forbidden moment with. *Oh Lord!* I take another quick look at him; my heart racing, and my face already flushed with embarrassment. He hasn't changed at all. He is still *exactly* the same; as handsome as I remembered. His face is identical to the man who has occupied my dreams on so many occasions; the man who I have punished myself for. Hated myself for.

I slowly sink into my chair to hide myself, lowering my head behind the people in front of me. In my concealed position, I watch him shyly through the gaps in the crowd. He is moving his body in time with the other dancers and laughing along with the people at his side. I notice a young woman to his left who is making the most of the opportunity by pressing herself against him and touching him . . . I look away as she does this. It troubles me somehow. It makes me feel uncomfortable. Surely this cannot be jealousy? How can it possibly be? I have barely said two words to the man, and have not laid eyes on him in years! It is a wonder that I even remember him at all! I force myself to return my gaze to the dancers and to sit up in my chair like a lady instead of hiding as though I were a common criminal. After all, it is certain that he will not remember me as I remember him. Why on earth would he? He is handsome by anybody's reckoning so it is likely that he has women falling at his feet wherever he goes. I try to laugh away my silliness, but it sounds strange; forced. Unconvincing. I very much doubt that I am the first woman whom he has smitten, and I can hardly imagine that I will be the last.

I find that the sight of Sir Thomas and his . . . *companion* has left a sour taste in my mouth, and I want to leave immediately, to go home and feel sorry for myself.

"Darling?" I turn to my husband, John. "Could we think about leaving soon? It is late and my head hurts from all this . . . noise." For effect, I bring my hand to my brow. *Holy Mother, please forgive this pathetic charade.*

"Oh, but I am enjoying the show!" he protests. "Maybe just a little longer." He squeezes my knee affectionately and returns his attention to the middle of the hall. I sigh and follow his gaze. The dancers have stopped moving and have huddled together in small groups, chatting and laughing, waiting for the musicians to start the next dance. I turn away and slump back into my seat. I have no desire to watch them being merry any longer; it is only making me feel worse. If I have to stay then I will turn my chair and sit with my back to them, and then I will not have to watch. Watch him. *Him.* Him and his pretty, young lady friend. Suddenly the violinist's voice rises above the chattering crowd and the clink of goblets.

"Your Majesties, my lords, ladies and gentlemen, if the couples would rise for our final dance!" Thank the good Lord. The *final* dance. Now *that's* music to my ears! He is skipping around gaily, gesticulating to sheepish couples, trying to persuade them to join the others on the floor. I look at John who is clapping his hands enthusiastically. For once I am not disappointed that he always refuses to dance with me; to twirl me around the room; to show me off to everyone; to make me feel young and alive. For once I am grateful that he is content to be a spectator.

I stare at the floor, feeling more sorry for myself than I did before. I feel fat and aged and dour. I am not quite thirty and yet I sit here like an old maid. Without warning two feet suddenly appear under my nose, shattering my melancholy thoughts. I draw a sharp breath but do not move a muscle, not even to look up into the face of the owner of those two feet. Like a simpleton I just stare down at the golden buckles, all the while my heart is pounding like a hailstorm. *Oh no!*

Oh no! Oh Lord! I don't know why, but without even having to look up I just know that it is *him* standing before me, willing me to raise my eyes to meet his. But I cannot! After a few awkward seconds the owner of those shoes coughs pointedly. My heart sinks; it *is* him! I can hardly believe that I recognize him after all these years through just his shoes and his cough! What in God's name is wrong with me?

He clears his throat again and I realize that I have no other choice but to greet him. As I raise my head slowly, I think a thousand different thoughts, all the while trying to second guess what might happen next, consumed by an urgent need to remain in control, whatever might happen. Should I show him that I recognize him? Shall I show John that I have met this man? Will he recognize *me*? Is he here to talk to John or to one of the other guests and if so . . . will he simply pass me by as though I were just another insignificant woman? Could I bear it if he did? If only I had paid attention instead of just sitting here, wallowing in my own self-pity, I would have seen that he was approaching and could have done something! I would have had time to prepare! I could have run! After what seems an eternity, I find that I am spared the painful greeting as Sir Thomas Seymour turns his attention to my husband.

"Lord . . . Latimer, I believe? I don't think that I have had the honour of making your acquaintance."

John turns to him and smiles broadly, rising from his chair to greet him formally. "Oh, yes, Sir Thomas, yes,

yes, we *have* met before. Some time ago, at court I think. But yes, pleasure, I'm sure."

I glance up at Sir Thomas hesitantly; his eyes are flitting between my husband and myself, despite the fact that it is John alone who is addressing him. My heart continues to race as our eyes meet and I quickly look away, blushing.

John turns to me. "Ah, my wife, Katherine . . ."

I feel as though I am about to die as I hold out my hand meekly before me.

"Katherine," he repeats, as he lowers his head and gently kisses my hand. His eyes bore into mine and he smiles at me. It is a familiar smile; a mischievous smile. A smile that I instantly recognize as being just for me. "Have we met, My Lady Katherine?" His eyes do not leave my face for a second, just as the smile never wavers. I had wondered if he would remember me . . . but I do not wonder any more. His smile and his pointed, teasing question tells me that he does.

"I . . . I am not sure, Sir . . ." Oh what to say! John knows nothing of our momentary encounter. I pull my hand from his, suddenly fearful that John may notice something amiss.

Sir Thomas turns to my husband once more, smiling broadly. Oh, that smile! "My Lord, it saddens me to see your beautiful wife not partaking in this last dance. May I be so bold as to have the pleasure?" *Oh no!* What in God's name is he asking? I cannot dance with this man. I *will* not dance with this man. I am already hating myself for these feelings; my reactions. I cannot allow him to dance with me in front of all these people;

in front of my husband! To touch me . . . to hold me in his arms. And yet . . . he called me *beautiful* . . .

I silently will John to refuse on my behalf, to say something — anything — to decline his invitation. I beg him inwardly to dislike Sir Thomas, and to announce our departure, but to my horror, he looks at me expectantly, almost as though Sir Thomas has asked him for the most innocent of favours.

"I am sure that she would like that. She loves dancing, don't you, darling?" John turns to Sir Thomas. "I am afraid that I am not one to dance." I look up at Sir Thomas, willing him to withdraw his offer. Pleading with wide, desperate eyes. He must see how I am feeling. He must know that he cannot ask this of me. Yet he continues to smile. His expectant expression has not changed, only now he is raising his eyebrows as if he is playing with me like a cat with a bird. I turn to John in a panic.

"Thank you, but no, I am afraid we have to go as . . . uh . . . I do not feel at all well." I try to speak as calmly as I can, and force a smile as if that will somehow conclude our conversation.

Sir Thomas looks at me sincerely, although the corners of his mouth are twitching a little with amusement. His soft, deep voice transports me back to our first encounter, making me feel a little dizzy. "Must be something in the court air, eh?"

Oh Lord, he remembers our meeting! He remembers how I had tried to excuse myself back then under the pretence of being ill. Despite myself, this revelation lifts me. He remembers my pitiful words all these years later. He and John share a brief chortle; his pointed remark thankfully wasted on my husband. John pats my knee again.

"Go on, Kate, I should like to see you dance! And *then* we will leave, I promise!" I stare at my husband, my mouth gaping open, frantically trying to think of some other excuse. But what can I do? I know that I must not dance with this man. I must not have contact with him.

Before I know it Sir Thomas's hand is wrapped around mine and he is pulling me from my chair. I look down at his large warm hand, and without meaning to, I find that I have locked my fingers with his; already enjoying the feel of this innocuous, apparently innocent touch. I look back at John, still silently pleading with him to intervene, and yet all the while desperate for him not to. Not *now*. Not now that Thomas is already holding my hand. John taps me cheekily on the backside as I am pulled from the table, and claps. I feel like a lamb to the slaughter; like a girl about to be kissed for the first time.

Sir Thomas leads me towards the other dancers and pulls me to the centre of the crowd. I feel relieved that we are not on show, and yet frightened by our anonymity as we merge into the masses. I look around hesitantly, fearful that someone I know might be watching. Thankfully there is no one. I take my place in line with the other ladies, feeling awkward and embarrassed as Thomas stands opposite me, facing me, among the other men; his eyes never leaving my face. I

9

try to hold his gaze for longer than a second, but I cannot. It is too familiar, too intimate. It is as though he can see into my soul; as though he can read my thoughts. My guilty thoughts. The violinist strikes a short note with his bow and on the third count the men take two steps towards us. My body is shaking, but I force myself to move with the other ladies, and step towards the line of gentleman; towards Thomas. I walk around him as he stands motionless. My bare shoulder accidentally brushes against his as I pass, making the hairs on the back of my neck stand on end. As I walk behind him in a close circle I find myself leaning in, moving my body nearer to his than I need to. I shut my eyes for a second, enjoying this closeness, feeling his eyes upon me as he looks over his shoulder. I tilt my head back so that my face brushes against his thick, brown hair and I breathe deeply, as though trying to drink him in. He smells so good. He steps to the side and I walk a pace towards him and take his hand in mine. It feels strange taking his hand, even if it is part of the dance. Me; initiating contact. He wraps his fingers around mine tightly, the intensity of his grip making me breathless.

He twirls me forcefully, once to the right, then again to the left and finally around the back of him. I find myself laughing spontaneously, feeling resolutely alive. Still his hand is in mine and I am aware of how sweaty my palm is and how firm his hold has become. He grips my hand tighter in his, his fingers pressing into the back of my hand, and his thumb stroking my thumb. I grip his hand in return, which seems like the most natural and yet most dangerous thing to do, and my heart races as I press my nails into his palm. I turn to face him again as the music changes and we draw our bodies together as the dance dictates. I look up into his eyes to try to read his expression. He looks back at me; he is serious; unsmiling; passionate . . . It is just he and I now in this room. There is no one else. This time I find that I can hold his gaze. I don't care if he can read my thoughts. I *want* him to read my thoughts. Our faces are now just inches apart. I look at his mouth and back into his eyes again. I notice that he is looking down at my mouth. There is a hungry look on his face that excites me. He pushes me away and draws me close again, taking both of my hands in his this time, holding me tightly. Are we in time to the dance? I don't even know any more.

The beat of the drums and the sound of the violins seem far, far away, as do the dancers, who are all around us, enveloping us. Hiding us. All I am aware of is my body pressing against his; against his chest, his shoulders and his hips. Every small movement excites me. He pushes me away for a moment, still gripping my hands, and I am overwhelmed with a need to feel his body against mine again. Thankfully, he pulls me towards him for a third time, and holds me so close that I can feel his beard tickle my forehead. He lowers his head until his mouth is level with my eyes. His breath is hot. We separate and he twirls me repeatedly in front of him. I can see that his eyes have dropped to my body and that he is looking at my waist, my hips, my breasts, my bare shoulders . . . I pretend not to notice, but his gaze, so full of yearning, is enticing. I suddenly feel more invigorated than I ever have before.

The music changes and we form two lines again. We ladies twirl in circles together before meeting our partners in the centre. I hold my hands out towards him, desperate for him to take them. He smiles and reaches for me. He wraps his fingers around my wrists and slowly runs his hands over my hands, along the length of my fingers before locking them into his own. This one small act, so easy to miss, so innocuous, is so sensual that I feel I could burst. Our gazes lock once again as our bodies move in harmony with the music. According to the rules. And yet I know that we must be breaking *every* rule. His hands, his grip, his gaze tell me that, and my responses to him tell me the same. I feel so different with this man; so alert, so aware of my body; of how my heart is racing, how my face is flushed, how my chest is heaving and the sweat that is running down my back. Here, with him, in the privacy of these dancers, it is as though I have become a different woman. I am not Lady Latimer when I am in his arms. I am just Katherine; young, passionate, alive.

At the change in tempo he stands still again and watches me intently as I dance around him, raising my skirts slightly. Our eyes never leave each other. His arms are folded behind his back and he stands with his chest puffed out beneath his dark blue doublet. He looks so handsome, I can hardly believe that he is dancing with me. I will this part of the dance to end quickly so that he can hold me close to him again; so that I can breathe in his scent once more, for one more forbidden moment; to feel his chest rising and falling against mine. Soon enough, he takes my hand, and pulls me towards him but this time it is my back that is pressed against his front. He wraps his arms around my chest until his hands are touching each shoulder. He lowers his head slightly and I can feel his breath tingling in my ear, making me tremble. I turn my head so that my cheek is almost touching his and I close my eyes. It is all I can do to not throw my arms behind me and wrap them around his waist. Suddenly I hear his soft voice over the music as gently as a feather caressing my ear.

"Katherine . . ." He whispers my name. "What it is that you do to me?" His words make my heart race anew. I do not know what to say in return, so I concentrate on moving my body as the music ordains, in keeping with the other dancers, my eyes facing the couple in front. *If I do not reply then I am not doing anything wrong* . . . . He takes a deep breath, and my heart continues to race with anticipation at what he might say next.

"If we were anywhere but here, where we were not known, people might think that we were lovers . . ." His final word is drawn out and sensual, and makes me gasp aloud. His words shock me and I pull away. I suddenly don't know what to do. There is no more ambiguity; the words have been spoken. It is as though the sin has been committed, realized. I turn to face him, not knowing what to say, but all the while knowing without hesitation that this dance must now end. It is ruined. My betrayal has become tangible. He has gone too far. He has reminded me that *I* have gone too far.

For a brief moment we stand looking at each other; my eyes are wide and suddenly full of fear. His expression is desperate and I can see that he is sorry for his words. I want to embrace him. I want him to hold me and to kiss me and to tear this dress from me with all the passion that I know he feels. But he cannot. We cannot. This is wrong and I must end it immediately.

Thankfully, the music ends seconds later, and, according to expectations, he bows; I curtsey. We hold each other's gaze but we do not smile. I am too afraid to smile. He reaches down and takes my hand in his. This time his hold is gentle. It is no longer passionate, and I do not grip his hand in return. He stoops to kiss it and my heart breaks as I know that this wonderful, strange encounter is over. It can never happen again. His face is red with heat and his chest is still rising and falling as though with a great effort. He smiles at me softly and I manage to smile weakly in response before turning and walking slowly away from him; my head held low, fighting back the tears. As I approach my husband's table, I do not look back. I cannot. I cannot look into his face again; his beautiful face.

I fight the urge to cry out loud with a new sorrow as my eyes latch onto my husband's. He is clapping and beaming with pride. I force myself to smile at this dear man who deserves so much better than me.

14

"Wonderful, my darling. Couldn't see much of you, but what I could see was very impressive! You looked like an expert, I'd say!"

I force myself to continue smiling as broadly as I can, to hide my feelings of confusion and shame. John stands and wraps his arm around my shoulders and we walk towards the door. No doubt he is keen to keep his promise that we could leave as soon as I had finished dancing. I feel safe and protected in John's arms, even if I have no right to them any more. I say little as we leave, which my husband thankfully accepts as a sign of my aching head. My emotions are stark and conflicting, confusing and exhilarating. I feel empty and yet complete. Excited yet listless. Alive and yet dead.

CHAPTER ONE

Then He Will Have Me

His Majesty, Henry VIII,
March 1543,
Whitehall Palace, The King's Chambers

Oh yes, I like her very much! And I think she likes me too! There is a chance for happiness yet after my beloved Jane. And happiness for her too, dare I say it! Women are such fickle things, I know better than most. But Katherine . . . I have thought long and hard about a woman who is truly worthy of being my Queen, standing proudly at the side of the people's beloved sovereign, and I suspect that she is the one. And to think, she has been right here, under my nose all along! I have made my mistakes, and as a consequence, the people have been deprived of the Queen that they deserve, but Cromwell had his hand in much of that, corruptly meddling time and time again. Yes, we all know where *his* true motives lay, but he will burn in hell as a result — I have seen to it! These dreadful advisors who have been cursed upon me; some worse than the evil women they themselves have blighted me with.

"*Ouch!*" Buffoon. Can't anyone change a simple bandage without tearing off half my leg! Thinking about Katherine these days actually helps me to forget my pains. Why, at times I almost feel my old self again. Perhaps I should ride once more, to help me get back into shape. Yes, love truly is the best tonic! I have no doubt that as a woman she finds me very attractive; but a man can never be complacent — not even the King!

The useless doctor continues to peel away the bandages, apologizing profusely and annoyingly as he does, but I ignore him, lost in my own world. I have better things to think about! Why, if I were to ride every morning again, nay, *hunt* every morning, just as I did when I was courting that whore Howard, I could easily become the man I once was. It wouldn't take much for me to return to my former glory! A bit of jousting and archery in the afternoon too, that will help. Why on earth did I ever stop? My broken heart, that's why. Torn to pieces, blackened and infected like my poor legs, sending poison through my veins. And now look at the state of me! All these wicked, immoral people who have wronged me, *wounded* me, and deprived me of the happiness and contentment that I deserve! But *she* will be different. Ha! This time I have chosen my Queen myself, and who better than me!

Katherine will feel such pride on my arm, and I expect that she will be grateful to have a proper man at last! I remember Borough, that ancient invalid her mother made her marry when she was just a child, and then that spineless lump, John Latimer. A real fool, if I

17

remember correctly. One of those who would have died in the gutter long ago had he not inherited his fortune. Both quite unworthy of Katherine, who, they say, has proven herself to be learned and scholarly on many occasions. She will enjoy a few debates with me. Oh yes, I'll be able to keep her on her toes! I expect she is looking forward to that!

"My God, man, why does it smell so?" I curl my lip in distaste. "What have you done to my leg?" The doctor quickly pours warm water over my wound and places my foot in a bowl. I flinch as it leaches its way into every painful split and crevice, and I turn my head away in disgust. Blasted, darned doctors; they are useless, every last one of them, and make no jot of difference at all. "Just hurry up and bandage it so I don't have to look at it any longer!"

There is nothing standing in my way, which in itself must be a sign from God that she is the proper choice. Indeed, I would say that she is most resolutely and undeniably right for me. For the Kingdom. Why, she has proven herself to be virtuous beyond doubt, as well as pious to a fault, and kind too. I do not heed the rumours about that Thomas Seymour either; wicked whispers in my ear from those who wish me to remain lonesome and unloved. Seymour may be the brother of my dearest Jane — my one true love — but I don't trust that scoundrel for an instant, and neither, I'm sure, does Katherine. I've been told that he has set his licentious sights on the poor woman — as though she would ever look twice at such a peacock of a man! The vain, supercilious and boorish fool! How he could think for a single moment that a woman such as she would ever give him a second glance. Nonetheless, true or otherwise, I have no desire to look at that effeminate face any longer, so I will see to it that he is well and truly out of harm's way.

My sniggering has incurred the doctor's raised eyebrows. I shall ignore him. I think I will send Thomas off on another of those diplomatic missions. And perhaps not such a *restful* one as before either, just to remind him of his station!

I shall ask my men to find me a new horse. A big black stallion I think; strong and muscular, like me, able to carry the weight of a King. In time — but not too much time — I will be fighting fit and robust again and we will have lots of hearty sons! I chuckle again, feeling aroused at the thought of what is to come. I picture her slim waist and petite bosom, and imagine how delectable they might feel. The doctor looks at me and asks if everything is all right. I laugh some more. Everything is certainly *all right* now! I shall send her another gown, in the French style that ladies like. And maybe some rubies. She will certainly approve of those, after all, intellectual or no intellectual, she is still a woman. She must have finished mourning for that idiot by now, so it won't be long before she writes to me and accepts my gifts in the manner that they were intended. Perhaps she will visit and show her appreciation in person . . . I like the thought of that! But no; that is not her. She is not a harlot, not like Howard. Not like Boleyn. She is a lady; upstanding and moral and that is why I have chosen her. That is why I am certain that she is the perfect choice.

Oh, lucky, lucky Katherine! The envy of half of the Kingdom. How excited she must be at the thought of becoming my Queen! My consort!

One month later . . .
Katherine Neville, Lady Latimer,
5 April 1543, London

I am thirty-one and I have buried two husbands. I am a widow once more. I thought that I knew what it was like to be alone, but I was wrong. *Now* I know what it is like to be alone. The man whom I adored, who amused me, irritated me, supported me, loved me and entertained me has gone. My John; my reason for leaving court those nine short years ago who turned out to be so much more than I could ever have imagined has gone. The man who lifted my spirits, who made me laugh; the man who made the sun shine, he has gone. He has left me and I am now truly alone.

Who will cheer me with silly magic now? Who will delight me with tall tales? Who will find animals in the clouds and give voices to the horses? Who will bring me hope when I am sad and remind me of all the wonderful things that God has blessed me with? The London house is missing more than just one man; one simple mortal. It is missing a great, optimistic light; an infectious energy that no one could escape; a larger-than-life character whom we all adored.

The house is devoid of warmth, of happiness, now that my John has gone. I am grey. I wear black, but my soul is grey. There is nothing to smile about now, nothing to laugh about, nothing extraordinary or strange to entrance and amuse me. His clothes look ridiculous without him to wear them. Food tastes bland now that I eat alone and the house feels cold like an everlasting, cruel winter without his presence to warm me. I have occupied my mind with the practical matters that a dutiful widow must concern herself with. I have organized his funeral, I have arranged his affairs and secured his daughter's education. I have busied myself and distracted myself until there is nothing else to distract myself with. There is nothing left to do and nothing else to think about. I am forced to inhabit this miserable, bleak world without him, with nothing to think about but him.

It is only now that I am beginning to truly accept that he is gone, and that he is never coming back. I don't know when the dreadful truth finally sank in, but it did, and, without warning, I just stopped expecting him. I no longer brace myself when entering rooms for fear that he might leap out at me from behind a door. I no longer purse my lips a little crossly as I walk into my chamber, fully expecting to find my things missing or rearranged. It is only now that I have stopped inspecting the stuffed animals that line the corridors in case he has turned them to face the wall or has dressed them in my gowns, and it is only now that I no longer search under my bed sheets before falling asleep at night for small objects that he might have hidden there to amuse me.

Five days later . . .
Katherine Neville, Lady Latimer,
10 April 1543, London

I cannot stay in London forever. I hate it here. But I cannot decide where else to go. I do not want to return to the country without John; it would be too dreadful. Too lonely. The dear man has left me two manors and an annuity. He has seen to it that I will be a very wealthy widow. Again. If only he could have left a little happiness in his will as well. That would have been more welcomed than all the wealth in Christendom. Just a little piece of him to help me cope would have sufficed; just a tiny fragment of his busy, eccentric optimism to help me understand what on earth I should do now and how I am supposed to carry on without him.

My maid, Bessie, is outside my chamber door. I know that it is her as I recognize the sound of her footsteps on the wooden floor. She hasn't knocked yet but she will, just as soon as she has thought of an excuse to disturb me. The knocking comes earlier than expected — she must have something in mind already, or perhaps she feels that after all these years she doesn't need an excuse. I try to force myself to respond, to invite her in, but I can barely bring myself to open my mouth. All I want to do is lie here, to be left alone in my bed with the sheets pulled up high around my throat and the curtains closed. After a few moments, she opens the door gently and walks in. I can see her squinting as she stands in the doorway, trying to adjust her vision to see beyond the darkness in the room. I hear a deep sigh as her eyes find me lying in my bed. She is sad for me, but also a little impatient, I expect. I think that she is disappointed in me. She walks quietly to the window and opens the curtains, turning her face from the sharp morning sunshine that streams in. I, too, avert my eyes from the offending light; the dreadful reminder that there remains a world outside, and that life — my life — cannot stand still forever in this dark, silent chamber. As much as I might want it to.

"My Lady, you can't stay here all day . . . you must eat."

I lie still with my back to her, willing her to go away and allow me to sleep. She just doesn't seem to comprehend how tired I am! I will get up when I have properly slept. I don't know how long it will take but I need to rest. Surely she must understand that?

Fifteen days later . . .
Katherine Neville, Lady Latimer,
25 April 1543, London

Last night I dreamt of Sir Thomas. I dreamt that we were riding together in the grounds of my childhood home, Kendal. I was galloping my grey mare through a vast, lush field, with Thomas slightly ahead of me on his bay stallion. We rode for miles, effortlessly jumping logs and streams, racing each other up and down steep hills with the wind streaming through our hair. I dreamt that we left the horses and had lain together in a clearing in the woods. I was not in my mourning garb when he placed his large hands around my waist and pulled me forcefully towards him; I was wearing a dress of sumptuous purple, and cared not a jot when he tore it from my body. As I woke I could still feel his hot breath against my throat as he kissed me passionately, and the heavy weight of his body as it pressed urgently against mine. It was the most beautiful and exciting dream, and I woke in a sweat with an eager smile on my face, as though I had been released from all of my woes.

Although I felt ashamed of myself, it wasn't until later, when Bessie helped me into my black gown, that I forced myself to stop rehearsing each sensual scene over and over again in my mind for fear that I might lose such a precious dream and escape, for a moment, from my misery. It was only then that I allowed myself to acknowledge the impropriety of my thoughts for this other man.

I haven't heard from Thomas for several months. He visited me shortly before John's death, and sent me a brief note soon after. There were few words in his note, and yet they affected me deeply. My dearest husband had barely left this world yet I found that I could not destroy Thomas's letter; his declaration; his invitation. I placed it securely in a drawer in my chamber that night, far away from prying eyes. I don't know why, but in these last few days I have found myself reading it over and over again in secret. I have pored over his words through the hot tears that have streamed down my cheeks for the loss of my John, and yet, despite my grief I have allowed myself to study the inelegant stroke of his quill, each line and curve of his letters and all of his words; all the while trying to picture his face and his body as he wrote it. I did not throw his letter on the fire when I received it, as I know I should have, no matter how inappropriate it was. I could not allow his words to disappear forever as my conscience bade me. His letter was a summons; a call to me to summon him; to summon him to my heart. He said that he was waiting for me. I think about those words now. They are etched into my mind along with all their possible meanings. I still don't know how I am supposed to feel about this man, and yet I cannot deny that he is often in my thoughts. If only I knew what I should do next. I know that I long for Thomas in a way that I have never longed for another man; and yet I long for John more, in a way that one wishes for a heavy fur wrap on a cold day or a hearty meal after a long and exhausting hunt. I long for the familiar; for John to bring back the laughter and merriment that he brought to my life, the certainty and the security. But despite this, I find that I cannot stop thinking about Thomas.

Two days later . . .
Katherine Neville, Lady Latimer,
27 April 1543, London

There is a knock at my chamber door. Bessie walks in quickly and without being invited. I am sitting in my window seat, watching the spires in the distance as they

25

reflect the morning sunshine. Bessie is wearing an anxious expression and is wringing her hands together as she often does when worried about something. She approaches quickly, an urgent look in her eyes that startles me.

"My Lady, there is a gentleman downstairs. He has just arrived." My heart misses a beat and I look up at her expectantly. Is it Thomas? "He says he is one of the King's advisors or something like that," she continues, "and is demanding that he sees you immediately."

I gasp at the mention of His Majesty, and feel a sickening panic wash over me. Our eyes lock for a few seconds; our faces mirror each other's in worry. We are both aware that this cannot be good. My heart races at the thought of whoever might be downstairs, waiting for me; unannounced, unexpected and uninvited. "What does he want?"

Bessie shakes her head and swallows deeply. "He wouldn't say, My Lady. I tried to tell him that you are not receiving visitors, but he was quite adamant that he should see you. He said something about having given you 'sufficient time'."

Oh dear God! Sufficient time? Sufficient time for *what?* I have prayed that His Majesty's unwanted attentions would have fizzled out by now; that he would have lost interest in me; that he would have recognized my silence for what it was, or that he might have simply found something new to distract himself with. Some*one* new. I have even tried to persuade myself that I misread the intentions behind the letters and the gifts that he sent to me after my dearest John passed, telling myself that he was only being generous and kind to the widow of one of his own peers. But *this* . . .

"What shall I do?" I whisper, my heart still pounding. Bessie's face is etched with concern. She shakes her head, clearly not knowing what to suggest; anxiously looking over her shoulder every few seconds as though this unwelcome visitor has followed her to my chamber and is listening to our frightened words outside the door.

"My Lady, perhaps he is here to pass on the King's condolences?" Her look is desperate; she doesn't believe what she says. I try to nod my agreement, praying that she is right, and rise hesitantly from my seat knowing that I cannot refuse to meet this man nor delay him any further. She takes my hand in hers as we make our way towards the door, no doubt fearing, as I am, that he might bring news of the King's continued interest in me.

He stands in the hallway, puffed up and pompous; tall and intimidating. Cruel. His hair is black and oily and his skin is sallow. Peter, John's manservant, is offering him a cup of ale, which he refuses, and he taps his foot impatiently whilst waiting for my arrival. I watch him as I silently descend the dark stairway, taking in his mannerisms, his movements, in the hope that I might divine the purpose of his visit before we meet and prepare myself. I watch with a heavy heart as he turns a small box around and around in his long fingers. My eyes fix on that box with terror as if it contains my death warrant, and I slow my pace, hoping that I can delay this meeting forever.

Eventually he notices me approaching, and turns. He bows deeply, smiling broadly, showing a mouthful of long, stained teeth. His smile is insincere. He reaches for my hand as I near him and kisses it. The feel of his cold, wet lips upon my flesh revolts me but I do not remove my hand from his grasp. I know that I cannot possibly offend one of His Majesty's own men.

"My Lady! How simply lovely you look today!" I curtsey low to him and force a small smile of gratitude. "I am Sir Francis Ballard, a close advisor to His Majesty. I have been sent here especially by the King to see you."

He pauses as though he expects me to throw myself on the floor and giggle like a girl, like an excited Kathryn Howard. I do not giggle. I do not even smile, I am too terrified, and so I simply nod once to confirm that I have understood his words. He frowns at my lack of enthusiasm, narrowing his eyes as they meet mine in evident disapproval. He lowers his gaze to my dress, sneering as he takes in my heavy, black, sombre outfit. His expression strikes me as terribly rude and unpleasant, but I know that I can say or do nothing to express my dislike. I stand before him; awkward and upset, praying that he quickly take his eyes from me and leave. After a few moments of silence he stares into my face and pouts. It is horribly disingenuous.

"I see that you are still in mourning for the late Lord, My Lady."

"Yes." I tell him forcefully and without hesitation. "I am still very much in mourning for my dearest husband." I swallow heavily, trying to pluck up the courage to say something — anything — which might convince him that I am not in the least bit interested in any form of attention from His Majesty. His expression changes in response; he frowns and his cold eyes narrow menacingly. I take a deep breath and choose my words carefully so as not to offend or incite trouble, and say as calmly as I can manage: "I think, Sir, that I will be in mourning for . . . for quite some time."

He looks a little startled, and tilts his head to one side as if he does not understand. He peers over my shoulder at Bessie and then at Peter, searching for an explanation. I notice that both of them are staring back with a mixture of fear and determination on their faces; yet neither of them dare utter a single word. The man returns his gaze to me and smiles. He leans forward and pats my elbow a few times, making strange cooing sounds. I do not allow myself to move away or to wince at his touch — his flagrant and insincere gesture — as much I would like to. I simply smile so as not to appear ungrateful.

"It won't be long, My Lady, until you are out of that miserable black, and back to your pretty old self and thinking about the future!"

The smile drops involuntarily from my face. How very presumptuous! He lowers his voice and leans towards me again, ignoring my changed expression.

"That is certainly how His Majesty sees things, anyway!" He winks conspiratorially, which turns my stomach, and he glances down at the object in his left hand. I follow his gaze hesitantly. It looks like a trinket box. It is beautifully carved and clearly expensive. He holds it towards me and smiles again, lifting his arm until the box is almost level with my face before fumbling with the latch. Again, I resist my desire to flee from the scene, to be rid of this man and whatever horror that may be lurking in that box. I want to turn away from him, to scorn the gift, to push it from his hand, to throw it to the floor, but I know that I cannot, and so I stand mutely and watch with fear as he opens it slowly, dramatically, as though presenting me with a most treasured and coveted prize. It contains a small, silver, heart-shaped locket, studded liberally with tiny rubies and attached to a long silver chain.

My heart races the moment I catch sight of the shape and the intricate engravings that circle each of the small gems. I try to control my breathing for it is shaking audibly. His widening smile tells me that he must think that I am excited by such an extravagant gift. There is no mistaking the intention of this object; there is nothing ambiguous about this. I could fool myself about the other gifts, but this is quite different. It is something that one would give only to a sweetheart. I look up at the man, who is gazing down at me intently, his arms beginning to shake from the effort of holding them aloft. His expression is confident and expectant; he clearly believes that there is no question of my showing anything other than delight at this poisonous, dreadful thing. I force myself to smile in return, not knowing what I am supposed to do next, and all the while praying that he will soon lower his hands and take it away from my face so that I can breathe again.

He turns and tilts it slightly towards Bessie and Peter. I watch them as they force small, awkward, timid smiles in response. They look afraid, as, like me, they can understand its terrifying significance. He turns back to me and holds the box to my face once more and instructs me to remove the locket. With a shaking hand I obey his command and reach in, suppressing the urge to wince the moment that my fingertips brush against the cool silver. I would rather reach into an angry beehive. I carefully lift the small locket by its chain, holding it in front of me at a safe distance, trying with all my might to look pleased and impressed. It is heavy, despite its diminutive size. The man is now looking at me strangely; his smile is no longer as broad. Perhaps he is able to read my hesitation.

"Open it," he commands.

I look at Bessie for support, and she returns my gaze with fearful eyes. She knows that there is nothing she can do to help me. I am completely alone. I grit my teeth and fight the urge to cry as my fingers clumsily battle with the clasp. There is no eagerness in my actions; no impatience; only fear. I am simply obeying an order. As the locket finally snaps open, I turn it slowly in my hand so that I can look at the picture inside. I catch my breath at the image. *Oh, Lord!* The sight of the tiny portrait of His Majesty leaves me nauseous. His chin is raised imperiously and he is looking at me with his small, pig-like eyes. His red beard covers his many chins, and his skin has been painted a ghostly white. The sight repulses me. It is all that I can do not to drop the locket onto the ground as though it was a hot coal scorching into the flesh of my palm.

One day later . . .
Katherine Neville, Lady Latimer,
28 April 1543, London

My collection of unwanted gifts grows. I place the locket at the very back of a small drawer in my chamber along with his other gifts: the bracelet with his initials etched into the side, the pearl necklace and the jewelled trinket box. The pink dress that he sent to me whilst my husband had lain dying has been folded away in the bottom of my wardrobe beneath a large linen sheet. I do not want to look at it; at its shocking lascivious colour. I do not want to look at any of it.

His intentions are becoming startlingly clear and his persuasion is growing stronger. Yesterday, his advisor refused to leave until I had secured the locket around my neck. It wasn't enough that I had thanked him for it. It wasn't enough that I had promised to write to the King to thank him personally. He was adamant that he had to see me wearing it; to see it close to my heart, where, he said, it belongs. I had fought back the tears as he awkwardly secured the clasp behind my neck with his icy fingers, feeling violated by his touch, by his mere presence, by everything that he represented. I hated myself with a passion for not standing up to him and insisting that he take his hands off me and return the gift immediately. But how could I? How could I have dared to offend His Majesty?

Does he want me to be his wife or his mistress? I could not bear either. Nothing has been formally asked of me yet, thank God, but I know that I do not want to be anything to him other than a subject from afar. I do not want to be his Queen, and I am certain of that fact with every fibre of my being. I cannot envisage anything more awful. I shudder at the thought of him near me, as my suitor, as my lover and husband, and I despair that he has set his sights upon me. Why me, for heaven's sake? I have done *nothing* to encourage his advances. Nothing at all! I am not a harlot, so why would he choose me as his mistress? I do not have affairs with men, and I am nothing like the wives that he has chosen for himself either: I am not passionate and vivacious like Anne; I am not sweet and innocent like Jane and I am not coquettish or flirtatious like Kathryn.

Why oh why is God allowing this cruel injustice to happen? Why is he punishing me yet again? I just do not know how the King might imagine that I would welcome his advances. I have never shown him any sign that I might want to be his Queen or mistress. I can barely stand to be in his presence; I can hardly bring myself to look into his cruel and repugnant face. We have nothing in common; he is a tyrant, a brute, a monster . . . and not only with traitors and heretics but with his own wives as well — the women he once claimed to love. I cannot allow it to happen. I will do anything to stop this insanity. God forgive me, but I would rather die than be anything to that man.

If I am to marry again I know that it will be to just one person; the man whom I have guiltily desired for so long. The man whom I barely know and yet who holds such an unnatural spell over me; who has ensnared me and has captured me so willingly in his web. I reach into the back of a small drawer at the bottom of my dresser and carefully retrieve his well-worn note. I sit in my chair next to the fire and read it over and over again with longing, my head still a little dizzy at the thought of his choosing these very words and forming these passionate sentences, just for me. He tells me that his heart is mine . . . I fold the letter carefully and hold it to my heart. It is comforting and reassuring, and soothes the invisible stain left by the locket that had been so rudely forced upon me yesterday. I suddenly know with utmost certainty that it is time for me to call on Thomas; this man who has offered me his heart. He is the man that I must marry; no one else.

I shall write him a letter, a short innocuous letter in case it falls into the wrong hands, and I shall have a messenger deliver it to him at his London home immediately. With my heart pounding, I cross the chamber to my desk and hastily scribble him a short passionless note.

Thomas,

*You offered me something precious. I wholeheart-
edly accept and can offer similar in return. Please
come to me in haste.*

Katherine

I hold the letter lightly between my fingertips,
blowing on the ink gently so that it will dry. I hope that
he will see through my emotionless words and accept
this as a declaration of my need for him; of my
continued longing for him. I pray that he will still feel
the same and will come for me soon, before the King
does.

Two days later . . .
Robert Caskell, Groom of the Stool,
30 April 1543, Whitehall Palace

I peer around the privy chamber doorway towards His
Majesty's bed. He is sitting there puffing and wheezing,
trying to catch his breath having slowly made his way
up the stairs. His hands are pressing into his enormous
knees, his head is held low and his chest is heaving. He
looks to be managing for now, and is even able to bark
an order at a servant for something to drink. Even so;
poor fellow, he looks exhausted! I turn back to the task
in hand, eager to finish in good time in case His
Majesty suffers from another bout of urgency.

As I scrub the wooden surround to the royal
chamber pot I realize that I will have to light the
candles soon, for it is already getting dark in here.

Humming to myself, I lift the lid covering the chamber pot and carefully inspect the inside; it must be spotlessly clean in readiness for His Majesty's use. Listening to the panting from the adjoining room, I smile as I think of how very fortunate I am to be here in the royal favour. Who else can say that their work takes them this close to the King and to the hope of great riches and fortune? It makes me so very happy! I have held this coveted position for seven years now, since I was seventeen years old, and I must say that I have mostly loved every minute of it. In many ways my role brings me closer to His Majesty than almost anyone else in the entire Kingdom. Oh-ho!

My father is most proud of me, as he might be. I chuckle as I think of how, after all these years, he still tries to persuade me to reveal His Majesty's deepest, darkest secrets. As if I would! I intend to keep hold of this most respected role until the end of my days, thank you very much. I am sharp enough to know that discretion is an absolute must when it comes to a King such as ours.

As I run a cloth around the rim of the chamber pot lid to scrape off the remnants of the dried royal urine, I chortle as I think of one of my predecessors, Sir Henry Norris, and his unfortunate fate. Now, there was a man who had no discretion! And didn't he pay the price for it! Fancy becoming romantically involved with your master's own wife. And not just any master, but your master the King! And not just any wife either, but Queen Anne Boleyn! It is really quite laughable when you think of how foolish some people can be. The poor fellow lost his head for his crime, which, frankly, was nothing short of what he deserved.

I haven't been so foolish, oh no, and neither will I be. All these years I have made sure that I have kept a very safe distance from all of them. You never can trust a woman, that's what I say, even if she is the Queen. I was but a lad when Jane was on the throne, so I was never tempted by her, and that poor Anne of Cleves was hardly ever here. Not that anyone would have looked twice at her, of course! Poor cow. And as for the whore, Kathryn Howard, well, I made sure that I stayed well and truly out of her way, given her reputation. I certainly wasn't going to be sullied by her wanton ways. If you ask me, I had a very lucky escape from that one, as I am sure that once or twice I felt her harlot eyes on me. What a silly, silly girl to risk her life and her soul for such a cheap dalliance.

And now there is his new love interest; a woman called Katherine Neville, née Borough, née Parr. Hmm . . . I'm not sure that I approve of any woman who has already killed off two husbands! Ha!

I laugh at my joke and drop to my knees to inspect the rushes around the chamber pot. I replace them regularly, of course, as more often than not they bear the brunt of His Majesty's poor aim. They feel dry, thank goodness and do not overly smell. I crawl around the back of the large wooden frame that houses the pot and try to recall this Katherine. I think that I have seen her at court once or twice. In fact, I am sure of it. I seem to remember that she is quite pretty, in a wholesome, freckled sort of way — not beautiful like

Anne or Jane or Kathryn, of course, but pretty enough, and we all know how important that is to our King. It is very high on his list of essential requirements and no mistake; just ask that poor Anne of Cleves — she'll tell you! I chuckle again. Now, this Katherine . . . I don't know much about her other than that, apparently, she was schooled here when she was a child. That would make her rather bright, I suppose, which His Majesty will most probably like. Hmm . . . If you ask me, she sounds ideal. A right good choice indeed!

A loud grunting shatters my thoughts and I quickly look up, banging my head on the chamber pot surround. *Ouch!* Lord knows what a clumsy idiot I can be at times. What was that noise? The grunting becomes louder and I quickly realize that His Majesty is making his way to the privy. I scramble to my feet and stand to attention. I hadn't counted on his needing the chamber pot so soon! I try to make myself look presentable by quickly wiping away the strands of long hair that are plastered to my face with sweat, and brush down my rush-covered doublet.

"Make haste, Robert!" His Majesty bellows, panting as he squeezes his great bulk through the doorway. "It comes!" The urgency in his booming voice is enough to make me leap into action and I hastily drop to my knees before him and begin to unbuckle his belt. He shifts his weight from one leg to the other with discomfort, tutting impatiently. *Oh Lord!* I fumble with the many buckles and laces and silently pray that I will be quick enough. "Faster, boy!" he barks. His voice is strained and he is clenching his fists. I can tell that he must be struggling to hold it in.

"Sorry, Your Majesty, I am going as fast as I can." I tug with all my strength until finally — mercifully — his belt unfastens and I can free his great belly from its prison. I quickly tug his hose over his mighty backside along with the many layers of undergarments, and struggle to my feet just in time as the King lowers himself onto the pot. I thank the Lord silently for the reinforced strength of the frame as it creaks under the might of his considerable weight. His Majesty, now sweating liberally, shifts his buttocks until he is comfortable and doubles his body over in an effort to push. I shout to one of the servants, who is hovering in the bedchamber, to bring some warm water so that I will be able to cleanse the King properly when he is finished. I turn my back to His Majesty, offering him a little privacy whilst I wait patiently for him to purge himself.

"Have you had any word from the Lady Neville, Your Majesty?" I inquire nonchalantly, trying to take his mind from his obvious discomfort. The poor man. Of late, he has suffered terrible trouble with his bowels. It takes such time and effort these days for him to fully evacuate the royal stool, but I don't mind waiting; I've nothing else to do.

"Hmph?" I twist around to see him looking up at me quizzically, his face creased from the effort of straining. "Nay. Darned woman is playing hard to get." Well, he has certainly changed his tune! It was only a few weeks ago that he was gushing about how lucky this Katherine

is and how she is going to be the happiest woman in
Christendom!

"Ah, but you must be mistaken, Your Majesty," I
protest, "for she is obviously smitten with you!" I smile
and turn my back to him again.

"Of course she is!" He bellows gruffly, with utter
certainty. "Obviously playing the minx isn't she?" He
gives a deep throaty laugh. Oh good, he is relaxing.
That should speed things up a little. "Well, just wait
until she comes to court, m'boy, and then I will make
her an offer she certainly cannot refuse! The lucky girl
. . . *Oh!* . . . . Wait . . . yes! Here comes the last of it." I
suppress the urge to giggle as the royal bowels noisily
rid themselves of their collection, and I hold my breath
for a few seconds as the familiar stench engulfs the
room. I do not allow him to see my expression. Any
hint of disgust would be the height of rudeness, and
knowing His Majesty, would probably cost me my
head! "Help me up, would you."

I turn, and offer His Majesty my arm. He grabs it
with both hands and heavily prizes himself from the
wooden throne. My muscles strain in agony as they
bear the full force of his weight, but I do not mind. A
few aching joints are but a small price to pay to be this
close to royalty. As I pull him to his feet, I call to the
servant again, who scurries in with a dish and a pewter
jug that is filled to the brim with warm water. He places
it next to the chamber pot, and I dismiss him quickly
with a jerk of my head; this business is mine. The King
turns his body to me and folds himself over the back of
the seat, proffering his backside for my careful

attention. This part of the job, perhaps seen by some to be the height of revolting, is anything but to me. To have the opportunity and the right to touch this royal and divine body can never be underestimated. I pour a little water into the dish and use it to dampen a linen cloth. I fold it carefully in two before proceeding to clean His Majesty's substantial behind. My, the smell is quite potent today! I wipe the cloth with some force across his buttocks. Certainly not one of his better movements! I hum quietly to distract myself from the stench; God forbid that His Majesty might think that I am offended by any of this.

"Stop that fucking whine!" he growls after a few seconds. Well, somebody is in a foul mood today! I can't think why that is, especially with such a lovely young lady on the horizon. Perhaps I should remind him of that, to help soften his fiery temper.

"Do you have any more gifts in mind for the Lady Neville?" I ask as I rub the cloth repeatedly over the slick of faeces that wets the insides of his buttocks until he growls. I soon give up my efforts, resoak the cloth, and try again.

"She needs no more gifts, boy, I have given her more than enough. Besides, what greater gift could there be than to have me for a husband? And to be England's future Queen?" He shifts his weight. "Can you not hurry, for pity's sake? I need to rest."

"I'm getting there, Your Majesty," I reassure him, rubbing the cloth into the folds of his upper legs. "Rubies!" I blurt out.

"What?"

"Rubies, Your Majesty. For Lady Neville. If she is not already in love with you — which I am sure she is — then rubies will certainly make her fall into your arms. After all, *every* lady loves rubies!" I drop the dirty cloth into the dish that is now overflowing with stinking, murky water, and grab a fresh dry cloth from the table. I can hear His Majesty muttering to himself as I pat his backside dry.

"Yes . . . rubies." He shifts his weight again. "Can't hurt, I suppose, can it, boy?" He tries his best to turn his head, to look over his shoulder at me, but the girth of his neck prevents him from doing so.

"There we are. Fresh as a daisy!" I declare, and stand to help His Majesty back into his clothes. He seems in better spirits already, and he even jokingly tries to hold his great belly in as I fasten his belt. When everything is tucked away neatly, he pats me on the back appreciatively. What a marvellous man!

"Thank you, m'boy." He squeezes back through the door, and strides purposefully towards his bed. I shake my head with sadness as I watch him slowly and painfully lower himself onto the mattress. I have grown very fond of His Majesty over the past few years, despite the foulness of his moods, and although I would never admit it to anyone, a small part of me quite pities him as well. It is no secret to anyone how much he has suffered thanks to all those dreadful women, and it is no secret how much he continues to suffer with his poor legs and his great weight. I do hope that he marries this Katherine soon, for his sake. Perhaps she will be the tonic that he so desperately needs.

That evening . . .
Katherine Neville, Lady Latimer,
30 April 1543, London

I give my messenger strict instructions. He is to deliver my note to Sir Thomas in person; to place it in his hands and his alone, and to wait in case he wishes to reply.

An hour later I greet my messenger as he canters his horse into the courtyard. I am nervous; fearful of the news that he might bring. We speak in whispers, in secret, and he tells me that Thomas's response was short and simple. After reading my note, he instructed him to relay just one word to me: *Tomorrow*. The messenger assures me that he will tell no one of his impending visit, and I, similarly, will tell no one. I could not bear the humiliation if he changes his mind or if his visit comes to nothing.

One day later . . .
Katherine Neville, Lady Latimer,
1 May 1543, London

Somehow I must prepare myself for him; for whenever that might be and for whatever his visit might bring. I barely slept last night in anticipation, and in fear that this may all go horribly wrong. I try to banish the feelings of guilt and shame that accompanies my thoughts of seeing him again as I can't help but feel that our meeting is a betrayal of John. I wonder if I am acting improperly? Should I be writing notes to a handsome stranger, asking him to visit me? Should I be offering my heart so freely and so soon to someone I barely know? I do not know the answers. All I know is that I am both frightened and elated by the prospect of being near him again. Perhaps it is wrong, but the thought that he might take me freely in his arms without reservation or shame is almost overwhelming.

Bessie helps me dress this morning. She is pleased that I am in better spirits, and is delighted that I have chosen to wear a colour other than black. I have not told her the reason for my sudden change of heart. She thinks that I am simply moving on. I wear my hair long, beneath a blue bonnet that is adorned with small pearls. I know that it is immodest wearing my hair free like this, as though I were still a maiden, but I don't care. I want Thomas to see me as I feel when I am with him; young and alive and free. God forgive me, but I do not want him to think of me as a mournful widow or to pity me for my loss. I couldn't bear that. Bessie approves of my choice of a blue velvet gown. She pulls my corset in tightly, lacing it securely at the back, and compliments me on the smallness of my waist. My shoulders are bare and my dress is cut low, but I am not cold. I am too excited to be cold. Too restless. She brings me a small plate of cold roasted beef and bread for my breakfast but I find that I cannot eat anything. If she notices my agitation, she does not show it; she does not question my distracted state, my fidgeting or my preoccupation over the slightest sound that comes from outside. Perhaps she knows that I have called Thomas to me; perhaps the messenger has not been as discreet as I had instructed. She will know soon enough.

An hour passes and he has not arrived. It is still morning and so I am not worried yet. I sit in my chamber, in front of my looking glass, gazing intently at my reflection and wonder whether he will still find me attractive. I run a comb repeatedly through my hair until it shines, and select a string of pearls that I fasten around my neck with slightly trembling fingers. The anticipation is growing so strong now that I can barely stop myself from breaking into a sweat every time I hear footsteps pass my chamber door, or the slightest crunch of stone under foot from the courtyard. I am frightened of his visit; I do not know what will happen, and that uncertainty scares me. I try to imagine what he might say and what I might say in response, but I simply cannot. Part of me is so afraid that I want him to change his mind, or to postpone so that I can better prepare myself . . . and yet I know that I could not bear any kind of rejection from him.

Another hour passes. Perhaps the weather is delaying him. There have been persistent showers all morning. Perhaps that is the reason. Perhaps his horse is lame. Perhaps he has changed his mind about me now that there is nothing to stop our being together . . . Perhaps I was only exciting to him when our few meetings — our precious encounters — were forbidden. Perhaps he no longer thinks of me as desirable.

I am unable to eat or to read. My nerves are frayed and on edge and I am short-tempered with the servants as though his absence is their fault. I brush my hair again, change and re-change my jewels; I try to decide whether I should wear gloves. I debate whether to select a different gown or whether to arrange my hair more formally. Perhaps I should pray. No, I cannot pray, I am too nervous to concentrate, and I don't know if God would understand or approve. Perhaps I will call Bessie again and speak with her. She has known me my entire life so surely she of all people will not judge me. Surely she of all people will recognize my craving for this man and my need for happiness.

A few moments later and there is a knock on my door. Bessie walks in. Thank God she is here. I resolve to tell her everything; all about my expected visitor and about the feelings that I have kept hidden for so long. I feel as if I might explode if I keep this to myself for much longer. But I quickly realize that I will not have the opportunity to disclose my secrets; her expression tells me that she is not here to indulge in small talk or matters of the heart; her expression tells me that she is about to announce something important. My stomach churns as she turns her head to the door. Dear God, is he here?

"There is a gentleman downstairs, My Lady. It is Sir Thomas Seymour, that rude man who barged his way in when the master was unwell. The one who brought you flowers."

I gasp and my eyes widen in shock. But I didn't hear him arriving! I'm not ready! Oh dear God, he is here! Oh, but *thank* God, *thank* God that he has not changed his mind! I resist the urge to cross myself gratefully in front of Bessie. My forehead begins to perspire in a panic as the reality of the situation suddenly dawns on me. He is downstairs waiting for me! He is *downstairs*! I can hardly contain my terror at the thought of him being here, so close to me, in my home . . .

"I told him that you were not expecting visitors, My Lady," she continues, cutting into my frenzied thoughts, "but he was quite insistent that he see you." She is looking at me quizzically, awaiting instructions. Awaiting answers. She is probably hoping that I will turn him away.

Her expression changes to one of concern as she notices my flushed cheeks and my rapid breathing. I try to suppress the excited and anxious smile that I can feel playing on my lips. She approaches me and lowers her voice.

"My Lady . . . is everything all right?"

I meet her gaze and fan my face fiercely with the book that was lying unopened on my lap, well aware that I must look quite a sight. Our eyes meet and she frowns; she looks worried about me. Does she suspect my feelings for this man? Can she see in my face how fearful I am about meeting him again? And yet, how happy I am? I take a deep breath and force myself to stand and walk towards her purposefully. There is no time to explain; I must go to him.

"Bessie, I have *asked* this gentleman to visit me." There! I have said it! I try to ignore her startled expression and rush past, keen to avoid more of her questions. I dart along the corridor and run my hands across my gown and along the length of my hair to check that everything is in place. I take a deep breath to steady my nerves before slowly descending the narrow stairs to greet him.

Thomas is standing in the doorway with his back to me. He is wearing his riding clothes; dressed from head to toe in black, with long, polished boots covering his hose, and a simple doublet that accentuates his broad back and muscular shoulders. Peter is standing next to him, looking up at him accusingly. Thomas turns his body the moment he hears me approaching and, for a second, I am unable to move as his eyes lock onto mine. My heart races as it always has when he is near, and the sight of him looking up at me with those big brown eyes makes me suddenly giddy with excitement. His face is as rugged and as beautiful as it ever was; his mouth and his well-defined cheekbones are so alluring that I can hardly bear to tear my gaze away. He looks flushed as though he has ridden fast, and his hair is hanging messily over his eyes. Suddenly he breaks into a wide grin, transforming his countenance from serious to unmistakably happy. I mirror his wide smile with my own. It is exhilarating to see him looking so pleased to see me, and I sigh in relief as my worries about him having changed his mind evaporate into thin air. We walk towards each other slowly, our smiles unwavering; never taking our eyes from each other.

Not knowing what else I can do, I hold my hand out a little hesitantly. He reaches down and gently wraps his fingers around mine, instantly awakening my senses with his touch. He raises my shaking hand to his mouth and brushes his lips against my knuckles before planting a single, tender kiss on the back of my hand. The feel of his mouth upon my skin renders me breathless, and I find myself weak with longing for him to kiss every inch of my body. As much as it pains me, I force myself to take my hand from his. I know that I must, for appearance's sake and for that of the servants.

"Thank you for coming, Sir," I whisper.

"It is my honour." His voice is as I remember. I do not know what to say in return. There is an awkward moment, where no one speaks. All eyes are on me, waiting for me to decide how this should progress. I look out of the window onto the courtyard and notice that it has finally stopped raining. It seems more respectable and more appropriate if we walk in the gardens; more fitting than inviting a stranger into my husband's home. And if we are outside, we can be alone, away from prying eyes and offended looks. I voice my suggestion and he smiles and nods his agreement. Bessie anxiously insists that she fetches me a robe to keep me warm, but I decline her offer. If it is cold, something tells me that I will be too distracted to notice.

That evening . . .
Katherine Neville, Lady Latimer,
1 May 1543, London

I lie in my bed; a happy, contented smile playing across my lips. It is late but I am under no illusion that I will be able to sleep tonight. Besides, I do not want to sleep.

I want to stay awake and rehearse every single blissful second of this wonderful day, until the memory is so engraved in my mind that I will never forget it.

I sigh deeply as I picture us walking through the gardens together just a few hours ago, my arm locked in his as though it was the most natural thing in the world for me to do. I smile as I remember our making small talk as we passed the old monastery; of him telling me about his daring adventures in foreign lands, and of his hopes and fears for the Kingdom. It was all very civilized, very formal and yet extremely gratifying. I loved listening to him talk; I loved his tales and his recollections, and I found myself agreeing with his every opinion on matters of politics and religion.

I grin widely into my soft pillow as I remember how all of a sudden the skies had opened, cutting short our conversation, and how we had sprinted, hand in hand, to an old oak tree for cover. We stood expectantly for a few seconds, waiting for shelter from the leafless branches overhead, and when it did not come we held our faces to the heavens in defiance, laughing like children as we accepted the full blast of the downpour. I recall with excitement how he became suddenly serious and how he had leaned his back against the ancient oak, pulling me close to him with an eager determination. I remember the wonderful anticipation for the touch that I knew would soon come, and how I had felt uninhibited as I had never felt before, holding my face proudly aloft and willing him to kiss me. I remember that we looked into each other's eyes for a few delicious seconds before he gently brushed the hair from my face and kissed me softly on the mouth for the first time.

At that moment the rain had streamed through the branches with a great ferocity, drenching our faces, our hair and our clothes; but as his kiss became deeper, more passionate and more intense, I found that I barely noticed it. I pressed my body against his with an unreserved passion and wrapped my arms around his neck with longing. I delighted in the feel of his broad shoulders beneath his sodden doublet and the soft, wet skin of his neck. He placed his strong arms around my back, holding me so close to him that I could feel every movement of his body as it rubbed against mine, all the while running his hands across the back of my saturated gown. I remember the sensual feel of his mouth and his tongue, and how the stirring of his hungry body had enflamed me, thrilled me, making me long for him all the more; for his entire body, for his naked skin, such as I have never felt for any man. It was the most rousing moment, the most passionate embrace that I have ever experienced, and as my fingers clawed through his thick, drenched hair I prayed that it would never come to an end.

Alas, we knew that it could not last forever, and that he must leave me. But whilst it did last, whilst our fervent embrace continued, I felt truly happy. I felt happier than I have ever been. At that moment I forgot about my past worries and about my concerns for the future. At that moment I experienced complete joy and contentment. As he held me so tightly in his arms I knew that every hope I had about this man could be realized, and that every fantasy could be surpassed.

21 days later . . .
Katherine Neville, Lady Latimer,
22 May 1543, London

Sir Francis Ballard is waiting for me in the reception room. He is joined by another; one Sir Thomas Wriothesley. I do not know this man, but I can tell that he is cut from a similar cloth just by looking at Peter's frightened expression. Bessie is with me in my chamber when he rushes in and tells me that I have been summoned. Summoned in my own home. Bessie and I set to work quickly and silently, both of us of similar minds; changing my green gown to one of black, and securing my hair beneath my widow's dour bonnet. I remove my jewels so that I will look as plain and as unappealing as possible. I do not know whether our efforts will be to any avail, but we are desperate, and we will try anything. I do not need to practise a doleful expression; it is all that I can do to stop myself from sobbing by their mere presence in my home.

I walk into the large room that we use to greet visitors at the front of the house. Peter has tried his best to insist that they speak to me in the hallway just as Ballard did a few weeks ago, but apparently this new man, Wriothesley — this *Risley* as he calls himself — has other ideas. He has clearly something more formal in mind. The two men are already standing, waiting for me in silence, with broad smiles. They bow deeply as I walk into the room. Wriothesley is similar in appearance to Ballard. He is pale with black hair, and sports a long black beard that ends in a neat point at his throat. He is tall, as Ballard is, but thinner, with pronounced elbows, and immaculate, effeminate fingers and wrists. His steely blue eyes are cold and menacing, just like Ballard's.

Wriothesley drags a high-backed wooden chair to the centre of the room for me to sit on, and places it in front of theirs. I watch him closely as he does this; taken aback by the audacity of his actions, by his unquestioned right to arrange the furniture in my own home just as he sees fit. He places the chair a mere foot from his own and Ballard's, and gestures for me to sit. It seems horribly intimate to be so close to them, and my immediate response is to protest and to drag my chair a respectable distance away. But there is something about his assured, confident manner which tells me that there is little point in trying to fight him. As I slowly lower myself, I notice that my hands are shaking in anticipation of whatever dreadful token they might have for me this time.

Peter brings them wine. He places it on a small table between them. They do not thank him. The only words spoken instruct him to go. He catches my eye as he leaves the room, but I do nothing to contradict them; I know that they will undermine anything that I say. It doesn't matter that this is my home and that Peter is my servant; these are the King's men. Wriothesley clears his throat as he lowers himself into a chair next to Ballard's. It is so forced that I can barely bring myself to look at him.

"Finally, we meet, My Lady." His smile broadens. "I have heard so much about you lately. A real honour!"

I force myself to smile in return before lowering my eyes to the floor. The sight of his pale eyes are already repulsing me.

"I hope you will forgive our impertinence for coming here unannounced. I trust that we haven't disturbed you. I know that you have already had the honour of meeting my esteemed colleague here, Sir Francis. He speaks very highly of you. Quite an honour, really. Sir Francis is *quite* discerning!" He smiles as Ballard lowers his eyes with mock modesty. "I am another of His Majesty's most loyal advisors ... just like Sir Francis."

Wriothesley takes a deep breath. "You will forgive me if I get straight to the matter at hand, My Lady, I have never been one for dry pleasantries, I'm afraid. More of a woman's thing. You see, Sir Francis has had the privilege of bringing you gifts from His Majesty, which I am sure have gladdened your heart in no small measure, but I, *I* have been entrusted with the privilege of bringing you something far more pleasing, and I know that you will agree!"

My heart pounds as I try to imagine what dreadful gift he is referring to this time. I look down at his long, bony fingers, fearful of what he might pull from the folds of his coat. But he does not move. His hands remain perfectly still in his lap. I shift my gaze to Ballard, certain that it must be he who is carrying whatever gaudy piece they are alluding to, but he doesn't move either. Like Wriothesley, he simply smiles and stares back at me.

"My Lady," Wriothesley's tone is nasal and sickeningly patronizing. I can feel myself beginning to sweat. "You are clearly a bright woman, that fact is well established, and so I very much doubt that His Majesty's gifts and the intentions behind them will come as any real surprise."

I shut my eyes firmly, trying to contain my panic as I quickly realize that this gift is likely to be far more sinister. This gift is to be spoken. I take a few deep breaths to prepare myself for the words that I know are playing on his lips. The words to *explain* the gifts. The words that I had prayed I would never have to hear.

"You see, His Majesty is alone, My Lady, he is lonely after that hateful Jezebel . . ." He stops speaking and swallows heavily as though his words have caused him a great distress. "We do not have to drag up old memories that are best left forgotten, do we?"

Ballard shakes his head, tutting.

"No," Wriothesley continues, "I think we all agree that we need to move on; to look to the future! You see, it is well known that the King has been very unfortunate in his wives and in the heirs that they have given him. As you are aware, Lady Katherine, our dear and sainted Queen Jane bore him but one son, God protect him, but the others . . . well . . ." He sighs deeply, shaking his head. "As I said, old memories and all that."

There is a pause. I raise my gaze tentatively. He smiles as he catches my eye and runs his long fingers along the length of his beard. I feel so dizzy; so very, very afraid, so fearful of how I know this will progress.

"Well, let's just cut to the chase shall we?" Suddenly his voice becomes animated and his smile widens. "Of all the women in the entire Kingdom, My Lady, of all the women, he has chosen you!" I purse my lips together, and lower my head once again until he is speaking to the top of my bonnet. "You! His Majesty has recognized a quality in you that has not been noticed before — if you pardon my forwardness. He thinks of you as a Queen! As *his* Queen! You; wife and consort to the King! How few are ever honoured so!"

A silence descends upon the room. I keep my head low, fighting with all my strength to contain the tears that are brimming in my eyes. I take short, sharp breaths and wring my hands together tightly to prevent them from shaking. I hear a faint muttering from the men. With my eyes lowered, I can only assume that they are watching me and trying to gauge my reaction.

"My Lady Neville . . .?" Wriothesley accentuates each part of my name, drawing out the vowels and turning it into a question. A challenge.

I cannot bear to listen to his dreadful voice and his condescending tone any longer. What in God's name does he want me to say? How am I supposed to respond? I try to order my thoughts; to quickly think of something appropriate to tell him; to somehow impress upon him that I cannot, will not . . . that I would rather die than accept the King's offer.

I look up and meet each pair of cold eyes in turn, hoping that they have noticed my distress and the tears in my eyes for what they are. With my quivering lips and my trembling hands, I implore them to recognize my reluctance and to free me from their impossible demand; to let me go; to give up now and to move on to someone else. Someone willing. And yet they sit and say nothing. They just look at me with disdainful expressions; their lips curling in disbelief. I quickly realize that my display of emotion will not be enough. I see that it does not matter a jot to them how I feel. My wishes are nothing to them; a minor hurdle to overcome; a battle that can be won with the flick of a wrist or a hangman's noose. I do not know this Wriothesley, but I am certain that he will soon demand that I answer him, and so I take a deep breath, and try to summon my final reserves of strength. I must think of *something* to say! What else can I do? I cannot sit here any longer whilst their eyes bore into me. God forbid that they mistake my silence for gratitude and acceptance. God forbid they mistake my expression for apprehension, and God forbid they assume that I am so overwhelmed with happiness that my tongue has been stilled and that I cannot bring myself to speak. Lord give me the strength to say something to save myself. Give me guidance to find the right words.

"But I am still in mourning!" I announce with sudden conviction, grabbing my black skirt as if they were not already aware of my sombre attire.

Wriothesley smiles lightly as though my comments are of as little importance to him as the state of the weather.

"Ah, but it has been . . . what? Five months, My Lady? I think that His Majesty has been very considerate in giving you such time to grieve."

Ballard leans forward, mirroring Wriothesley's patronizing smile. "There comes a time," he adds, "when we must all move on in life, hmm? Yes, I think so."

Ballard's tone stings my senses. I look away; I cannot bear the sight of his insincere expression or the sound of his high-pitched whine. They sit in silence with their hands clasped in their laps like little boys, expectant and unperturbed, assuming that the matter is resolved. Their demeanour tells me that there is nothing left to discuss and so I quickly try a different tactic, one that I pray will have an effect. I take another deep breath and will myself to be strong.

"I am to be married to another man!" There is no reason to lie, I have committed no sin. I have not promised myself to the King. Surely *this* will work; surely if they know that I have given my heart to another man? They would not expect me to marry the King if I am in love with another! Would they? A sneer plays across Wriothesley's mouth.

"So much for being in mourning, My Lady!" He throws his head back and laughs.

Ballard tuts at me disapprovingly. I lower my head in shame having been so stupidly caught out. How could I have allowed my panic to so easily confuse my thoughts?

"And if you are referring to that ridiculous Seymour, My Lady," he continues, "a man who, quite frankly, does not deserve to bear his family name, then *no*, My Lady! *No*, you are not to be married to him!"

My eyes widen in terror as he mentions Thomas by name. How did he know about Thomas? How did he know that I was referring to him? I have told no one! Oh dear God, I can only assume that Thomas must have shared his feelings with others and that his words have travelled to court.

My emotions become too strong for me to contain and I cry openly. I do not care about masking my reluctance any more. Let them be under no illusion about what it is that they are asking me to do. Let them see how much I do not want this.

"Didn't you know, My Lady, your *betrothed* is in foreign lands!"

Wriothesley smirks as my eyes widen with shock. I quickly tell myself that he must be lying; another tactic to trap me. He *has* to be lying . . .

"You see, he is a soldier, a commander, and His Majesty needs his skills elsewhere. It was all very sudden, of course, but you will not be seeing him again for quite some time, if at all, I can assure you of that! But I wouldn't worry about him; we can keep him safe if that's what this is all about. He is quite one for the ladies, don't you know, being a soldier. Famous for it, in fact! It won't be long before he finds himself a pretty young thing and you are all but a distant memory! So you really mustn't worry. Yes, a long, safe and happy life can be his if you so wish . . ."

"Here, here!" snorts Ballard, cruelly.

"So you see, My Lady," Wriothesley's voice becomes quiet and serious. "There is nothing at all standing in your way." He sighs heavily. Dramatically. "You are long past mourning, and there *is* no other man, is there? Oh, My Lady, I know that it is all very sudden, even with the gifts. Who on earth could ever prepare themself to be the Queen of this magnificent realm? I know that it must have come as quite a shock, and I know that this . . . this *silliness*, is no doubt due to your gratitude towards His Majesty, and that your humility has confused your thoughts. Yes, you must be feeling very overwhelmed, but my Goodness —"

"I am not good enough for him!" Suddenly a thought enters my head. I will denigrate myself. I will make them realize that I am not worthy and then they will come to the conclusion that this is all a terrible mistake and that the King has been saved from an unsuitable and unworthy bride! I grasp at this last straw with every fibre of my being, this last vestige of hope. "His Majesty must know, Sirs, that I have been married twice before . . ." They look at me, nodding, their expressions unchanged. I lower my voice as if revealing a scandal. "Sirs, I have known two other men . . ." Their expressions do not waver. "Sirs, I have *known* them, biblically, and often as befits a good wife."

Wriothesley's smile broadens. "My Lady, you need not worry about having had two husbands. My goodness, let's not be shy here, we are among friends."

He lowers his voice to a whisper and leans forward. "If we are to speak on the subject of spouses, don't forget that His Majesty has had five!"

Ballard laughs and slaps his knee as if in an alehouse.

"But surely," I implore, ignoring Ballard's amusement, "the King does not want a woman who is . . . *used*?" The word sticks in my throat. I hate debasing myself like this in front of these horrible men. "Surely," I swallow, and turn to Wriothesley, certain that of the two it is he who holds the real authority, that it is *he* whom I must convince, "surely he deserves someone who is pure . . . a virgin. Someone untouched by another man. Someone clean. Only a virgin is fit for a King!"

"Nonsense!" scoffs Ballard firmly. "What matters to the King is the person. He is well aware of your late husbands, but still he has chosen you! What a privilege that you do not need to be a virgin!"

"I cannot have children!" I spit out in desperation. A silence falls upon the room as my voice breaks in sorrow. I put my hand over my face to console myself, and sob deeply. I do not know how many years I have been holding those fateful words inside, but they burst out like an avalanche, and I hate them for making me say it. I weep from the pit of my stomach as I think of how unfair it is that I have been reduced to using this dreadful curse as a weapon against them. As a weapon to save myself. I cannot bear to hear the words spoken aloud, even by me. I cannot bear to hear them in case they might actually be true. Wriothesley looks a little sad for me for the first time, as though finally he is able to recognize my distress. Perhaps I am just imagining it; perhaps he is not such a monster after all . . . perhaps there is hope yet.

"My Lady, I am sorry to hear that you think you cannot provide His Majesty with an heir, but really now, your first husband, he was not a well man, was he? If truth be told, he was probably too unwell — too old — to give you children . . . yes?"

I stare at him in disbelief, amazed by his knowledge. Surely he is not about to contradict me on *this* as well? Surely he cannot think that he knows more than I do about the emptiness of my womb?

"And the Lord Latimer, well, perhaps his body just stopped working as well as it once did. I know it sounds silly, but that's what the doctors are beginning to say! So, My Lady, I think that you have simply been a victim of dire circumstances, that's all. You have endured a cruel and unjust set of events, which no woman should be made to endure, but I am confident that with His Majesty, there will be no more disappointments. This is your chance to finally have a child! A child with a real man; a virile man! The child that I am sure you have always desired. You must see that?"

Ballard nods in agreement. I look at them in utter bewilderment, at their raised eyebrows and at their hopeful expressions. How can they think that such nonsense is true? My God, do they honestly believe that we will have a child together? Lord, let me die right now if I am ever expected to lie with that beast. I shake my head in disbelief. I can see that they are certain of their arguments, of their flawed reasoning, and I soon realize that my efforts have only lowered me further into their trap. Every defence that I have is being cruelly twisted and used as an excuse for marrying him.

"But I do not *want* to marry the King!" I don't know where my words come from, but they are spoken passionately. There is no ambiguity about the sentiment or the tone this time. Even to them. Their eyes widen in shock, their smiles disappear and the room becomes oppressively silent. Their expressions tell me that they may have expected tears and confusion from me, but they had not prepared themselves for an outward refusal.

Wriothesley narrows his eyes and leans forward, bringing his head close to mine. I do not allow myself to flinch, and somehow I manage to hold his accusing gaze defiantly.

"I am going to ask you a question," he says calmly, his breath washing over me, "and I would like you to think very carefully before you answer." He closes his eyes as if he is about to blaspheme. "Why do you *not* want to marry the King?"

My mind races in a desperate attempt to think of the right words to say. A single word against His Majesty, about his person, his character, his reign . . . anything, no matter how mild, could well amount to treason, and God knows that I could be carted off to the Tower for it. I sit in silence with my mouth ajar, looking desperately from one angry face to another. *Why* must I explain? Surely my refusal is enough!

"My Lord," I whisper through my tears, "surely the King would like a wife who wants to marry him? Surely the King does not want a wife who has been forced into marriage? What pleasure could a man have in marrying a woman against her will?" It is a desperate attempt to save myself; a final crack of an already broken whip.

"*He* wants to marry *you*! You have been blessed, as if by God Himself and yet you choose to disrespect him like this!" Wriothesley's voice rises in anger, masking my sobs. "You have *no* reason to not want to marry him! None at all! Do you hear?"

I try to think of something else to say. I feel so weak with the effort of trying to defend myself; as if battling with an unconquerable foe; a beast with many heads.

"The only reason that I can think of ..." Wriothesley's whine interrupts my thoughts like an arrow. I look up at him with pleading eyes, in the hope that I might have awoken some shred of humanity in his soul and that he will stop this now. He sits back and fingers his beard again. His voice becomes measured and his tone quizzical. "Well, I'm sure that this is quite untrue and I'm sure that you will set the matter straight, My Lady, but as you will not tell me exactly what it is that so offends you about His Majesty then you leave me with no other choice but to guess. Now, the only reason that I could imagine that any woman in her right mind might reject such a blessed offer would be if someone had poisoned her thoughts ..."

I look at him, frightened by his menacing intonation. What in God's name is he talking about this time?

Ballard turns to him, nodding slightly, his eyebrows raised and a hint of a smile playing across his lips."

"Poisoned them with treasonous words against His Majesty," Wriothesley continues, glancing at Ballard. "Yes!" He turns back to me with an urgency that makes me jump and he raises his finger in the air. I look at him and try to anticipate where this might be leading.

"There are people at court — dreadful people, My Lady — who do not wish to see the King happy." His voice is now animated and excited. "There are people who, for some unknown reason, would wish to see him ill. Believe it or not, My Lady, but some people hold *him* responsible for things that were done in the past. Things done in his name. Important things that some people did not understand! Can you think of any such people, My Lady?"

I stare at him mutely. I do not move a muscle in fear that I might give the wrong answer and somehow incriminate myself.

"Some people still dare to question the wisdom that sent the whore Boleyn to a deserved death . . . just as an example."

"Dreadful, dreadful," Ballard repeats, shaking his head in exaggerated disbelief.

My heart begins to race. What in God's name is he saying?

"Can you think of anyone who might be so perverse and disloyal, My Lady? Someone who might bear the King malice, who might share their treasonous thoughts with you? Perhaps someone close to both you and the King; someone who could poison your mind against him, and make you not want to marry him?"

I shake my head. No one has uttered treasonous words to me! They don't have to! I know exactly what the King is like without having to hear it from anyone else. I have spent much of my life observing him; the way he acts around other people; the brutal way that he has treated all but one of his five wives.

Wriothesley loses his smile and looks deep into my eyes. "Let me think . . . ah yes, your sister Anna, for example. She comes to mind. Now, she was very fond of the Boleyn woman, I believe, being one of her ladies-in-waiting. Her most *faithful* lady wasn't she? Quite *devoted*, some said. Yes, whilst you were away, married to Latimer, she remained at court, didn't she, and served that harlot so very loyally? Yes . . . if I remember correctly, she was *very* upset at her death."

I gasp, sitting back squarely in my chair. I feel like I have been winded. Dear God, did he just say what I think he said? Did he just drag my dearest, most innocent sister into this dreadful hunt? They stare at me. Their expressions are suddenly triumphant. They know that they have won.

Wriothesley smiles and strokes his beard. "Yes, thinking about it, her continued devotion to Boleyn even *after* her wicked crimes were revealed, may in itself have been treasonous . . ."

Slowly I lower my head into my hands and allow myself to quietly weep as the implications of his vile words become clear. With a heavy heart, I realize that they have me.

They do not say any more. They do not need to. They have allowed themselves to stoop this low. They have beaten me with the most contemptible, the most cowardly and base card that they could play. They have threatened my dearest Anna, and have all but accused her of opposing the King. I know that they will have her head if I refuse, and probably mine too. There is no need for this to continue any longer; there is no need for me to even remain here in their vile presence. I rise from my chair and walk slowly to the door as if in a nightmare. Each step becomes more numb and more distant as my hopes for Thomas and for the wonderful future that I had imagined for us slowly drains away. I turn to them just before I leave, with a blank, deadened expression.

"Then he will have me," I whisper, shrugging weakly. What else is left to say?

14 days later . . .
Katherine Neville, Lady Latimer,
5 June 1543, London

I have had no word from Thomas. Dear God, was Wriothesley telling the truth? Surely Thomas would have told me? Surely he would have sent word. All I know is that I miss him with a sorrow that I have never before experienced, and that every time I picture him in an unknown wilderness my heart breaks as though I am bereaved once again.

I wonder if he knows of the King's intentions towards me? He must by now if he has been so cruelly banished from his own land. Does he blame me for this unjust punishment? Does he think that I am in any way complicit in this horror? I can only pray that he knows me well enough to realize that I would never betray him by succumbing to another had I a choice.

If only my dearest Anna was not so exposed then I would have refused the King's offer without a moment's hesitation, whatever the consequences might have been. I would have said anything — *done* anything — I would have willingly gone to the Tower dungeons as if I were a lowly criminal than ever have accepted this dreadful fate. At least that way there might still be hope that one day we would finally be together as I know we were supposed to be. Perhaps Thomas tried to tell me? Perhaps he has tried to write? Perhaps he waits for a reply from me that will never come? Does his heart break anew every day, just as mine does, when no word arrives? My dearest, darling Thomas! I can hardly bear the thought of him suffering all alone, thinking that I have forsaken him!

The King has made his choice, and so once again, my destiny lies in the hands of another. But I will never forget the way that Thomas held me in his arms and told me that he loved me, and nor do I want to. I will rehearse each and every memory so that I never forget him and the way that he made me feel. Just the knowledge that he is out there, somewhere, thinking of me with longing; dreaming of me as I dream of him consumes me with an utter despair.

The injustice! I know that I could never be a good wife to the King. God must surely see that, and yet He continues to punish me! I know that I will always be a fraud, for as long as I shall be married to another, whilst Thomas is on this earth, however far away he might be, my heart will unreservedly belong to him. The King may be able to rob me of my freedom, he may be able to use my body like any other part of his property, but he will never steal my dreams or the precious memories that I have of the man whom I wanted to marry. If it is adulterous to think of another, then I am surely nothing less than a harlot, for every night when I go to my bed I will dream of none other than Thomas.

One day later . . .
Sir Thomas Wriothesley,
6 June 1543, Whitehall Palace

I am not one for an inordinate amount of sleep. Never have been. The Kingdom isn't going to run itself and so I cannot afford to lie in bed when there is plenty of work to be done. Besides, the earliest hours of the morning and the latest hours of the night are by far the most productive for concentrating on important matters. No damn interruptions, for a start! I clap my hands loudly, and my groom, Phillip, comes scurrying into my chamber, looking bleary-eyed, and yawning. I shake my head when I see him. For heaven's sake! It is only a few hours past sundown and the fool is acting as though it is the middle of the night. One would think that having been in service to me for all these blasted years that he would keep himself lively and alert. But no.

"Light some more candles would you, it's getting dark in here. And look alive, for God's sake!" I snap at him irritably. He bows halfheartedly before lumbering off. I turn back to the task at hand and squint through the dim light that fills my chamber. I move my head closer to the pages that are scattered across my writing desk, trying to read the words in the dying light cast from the small flames of the candles.

The wedding preparations have already begun in earnest, thank goodness, and His Majesty has bestowed upon me the considerable honour of personally overseeing each and every last detail. No greater compliment could have been paid. Needless to say, it is essential that his instructions are followed to the letter, as nothing can be left to chance. I have spent the last few days writing to all manner of merchants, from tailors and jewellers to the finest cooks in Europe, not to mention searching in earnest for the best entertainment that the Kingdom has to offer. I have instructed my most trusted men to secure only the finest produce for the celebratory feast, and woe betide all of them if they disappoint me in any possible fashion. There will be no second chances, mark my words. Nothing must stand in the way of His Majesty marrying again, and in style.

I am in the process of organizing a special heretic burning in honour of the occasion; something that I would not wish to leave to anyone else. Quite a delicate matter are these burnings: too many can be over-egging the pudding and really quite vulgar; too few and . . . well, you lose the spectacle. I do not foresee any real difficulties in arranging it, of course; there are so many heretics to choose from these days that I am practically spoilt for choice. The damned Protestant fools, every last one of them; a stench upon this valiant Catholic Kingdom, and they deserve nothing less than to feel the might of the flames upon their heathen skin. Who knows, maybe it will prepare them for the everlasting torment that awaits them in hell if they don't recant.

My chuckle turns into a hearty laugh. Why shouldn't we enjoy their suffering? There's absolutely nothing wrong with that. I wonder if the lovely Lady Katherine will appreciate the justness of their punishment when she sees them all lit up and bathed in flames? It should gladden her heart when she hears their cries as their flesh smoulders and the fat drips from their bones. Now, I appreciate that a good burning is not exactly a traditional way to celebrate a marriage, but she had better learn to enjoy it if she is to please the King. She will if she has any backbone, that's for sure, and she certainly will if she is a good, true Catholic as I am. As is His Majesty the King. That will be a test in itself. Well, if for some reason she doesn't appreciate it, then she had better act as though she does, that's all I can say. The King will not take too kindly to an ungrateful wife, or worse, a wife who is sympathetic to heretics, God forbid. And she can rest assured that neither the hell will I.

They met for the first time earlier today, the King and his betrothed. I wonder how it went? I have not seen His Majesty since his return from dinner, for as soon as Katherine left he went straight to bed complaining of a headache. I hope that doesn't bode ill. He has been in such high spirits ever since she accepted his gracious offer of marriage, and all going well, he will be even happier tonight, despite his many ailments. If she behaved herself, that is. I trust that she was agreeable and that she did not show any outward sign of hesitance as she did with me — for her sake. Of course, they have met on many occasions before, but never like this. Why, the last time she visited court she would have been married to that Latimer fool. Now there was a proper imbecile.

The King's wedding ceremony will be a private affair at Hampton Court, for which I am thankful, given the bride's reluctance. We wouldn't want her to be too overwhelmed, or risk her saying or doing something that she might later come to regret. The King wants nothing spared when it comes to the later celebrations, however, and quite right too. After all, this is hardly a marriage between a pair of lowly farm hands. One of the former wives, that Protestant heretic, Frau Pig-face of Cleves, has been summoned by His Majesty to be a witness, no less. How absurd! I will have to ensure that she is kept as far away from his new bride as is possible. God forbid she tries to corrupt Katherine or poison her mind against the King with her course German tongue.

I curl my lip, picturing the bloated sow's face. No, this union shall go without a hitch, I will see to that.

I frown as I picture Katherine's small mouth and narrow eyes and her obvious lack of manners. She will not make a pretty bride. I wonder if she will be capable of providing the King with many more sons? One, even? I shake my head. Unlikely. Of course, he has the young Prince Edward to succeed him, praise the Lord, but the legacy really needs to be more secure than that. There needs to be at least two male heirs if the Tudor line has any real chance of surviving. An heir *and* a spare. Besides, and may the Lord forgive me for thinking such thoughts, Edward is a little sop, much like his weak milky mother was. Not a great deal of strength in either one of them. What His Majesty really needs is a strong wife to give him a strong male heir . . . but is that Katherine? Oh, she seems to have *some* good qualities, with her upbringing and alleged intellect, but who knows? If you ask me she doesn't even have common sense in her favour. Why, she acted like a damn fool when I met her, tripping herself up at every turn. But then, that's women for you.

Just as I reach my arms up and allow myself a good, long stretch, Phillip re-enters my chamber with two fat burning candles that cast the room into a new and welcomed light. Ah, that is better! I dismiss him with a wave of my hand and try to decide what to do next.

Now, I wonder what His Majesty sees in that scrawny woman; after all, the good Lord knows well enough that she is getting on and can hardly have many more years of childbearing left — assuming, of course, that she had any in the first place. I scowl as I think of how she tried to use her childlessness as an excuse to not marry the King. The cheek! Of course, I filled her mind with nonsense about it being her late husbands' fault, of all things. Well, what else could I do? The King has his heart set on her so I had no other choice. I was quite impressed with the quickness of my response, of how well I had managed to think on my feet, and so was Ballard. Oh, there are no flies on me and didn't she soon realize it! Ha! She believed my every word, and who knows, perhaps they even offered her a little hope? I scoff loudly. And people say that I am not charitable! Pah!

But nonsense it was, of course; I am under no illusion that if a man can stiffen he can sire children if the vessel isn't flawed. But we shall see soon enough. I will be there to witness the consummation. And awkward it will be, I'm sure, for all concerned. I can't imagine either one of them will steal the show that night! I snigger at the thought. Queen she may be but I will be watching her like a hawk for the slightest hint of reluctance, and God help her if she does not satisfy him.

I shake my head in wonder as I think of how His Majesty's standards have fallen so very low in recent years. And now he has gone and chosen someone who doesn't even like him! Well, thank the good Lord that he has not chosen another Howard; that's one blessing, at least. Katherine's reluctance to marry him is a major concern to me, I cannot lie, and one that I cannot ignore either. God forbid the King should ever suspect that she does not want him. But then I will be there to remind her of her sister's safety should she need more reasons to be happy! And I will not have her rising above her station either; not like the Boleyn witch did. No, Katherine will not be making any real decisions in this court — big or small — not without my say-so, anyway. If she really is as clever as they say, then she will quickly know her place and will not cross me. Oh yes, I am confident that we will be able to mould her into just what we want her to be: a good wife, God-willing a good mother and, most importantly, a good, Catholic Queen.

I think back to My Lady, the sainted Catherine of Aragon, God rest her soul. Now *that* is the sort of England we need to return to. One of piety and devotion. That is what we must strive for. A God-fearing Kingdom governed by the Holy Catholic Church! Nothing could be better, in my mind. The Kingdom has taken a notable turn for the worse these past few decades and it is high time that we restore it to its former glory, with a strong, united leadership and one religion for all. His Majesty was insane to rid this land of its one true Queen; and for what? For that reformer trollop Boleyn who used witchcraft to entrap him, and almost succeeded in bringing the Kingdom to its knees.

Well no more, and not with this Queen, and certainly not under my watch. I have learned always to be wary and never to take anything for granted, so I am not going to sit back and assume that this Katherine is of the true faith like myself. No, one always needs to hold a certain amount of suspicion, because that way, one will never find oneself surprised. *That* way, one will always remain firmly in control. I have never heard anything to suggest that she is anything but a good Catholic, but this does not in itself warrant my trust. Oh no. My trust must be earned. From now on, her actions and words will be scrutinized very closely for any hint of a reformist leaning, God forbid. And if she shows even the slightest sympathy towards the Protestants — just the slightest — then I will be the first to know and the first to act. Queen or no Queen, she will find herself in the Tower quicker than you can say "traitor" if I ever get a sniff of anything untoward.

I smile contentedly at the fruits of my labour, and allow my mind the pleasure of idle drifting; a very rare indulgence! It doesn't take long before my thoughts turn to a different kind of satisfaction; one that will not require such a high degree of fastidious mental concentration . . . Now whom shall I call upon at this late hour? Whom shall I grant the honour of performing this service? And what an honour it will be! I smile as I think of all those at the mercy of my most personal and intimate whims. Ah . . . such power, such entitlement! This is what I have worked so hard to achieve!

My need becomes unexpectedly urgent and so I call to Phillip again, who appears in the doorway within seconds. I smile with some satisfaction at his sudden promptness and how, finally, he seems to be making an effort to appear more alert and less like a ragged whelp.

Why, standing there in the half-light, looking up at me sheepishly with his fair hair falling over his big blue eyes, one might say that he looks almost delicious . . .

"Come in, Phillip. I have a need for you."

I glance up at the window and out at the clear, starry night sky. It must be about six hours until sunrise yet; plenty of time for my enjoyment, and time enough to sleep after that. I run my eyes across his chest, his belly and his hips as he stands in the doorway, and I smile as I think of the pleasures that await me. Naturally, I could call upon my wife if I had a need for her. After all, it is my God-given right do so whenever I choose, regardless of how she might be feeling, but sometimes I crave alternative pleasures that only a man can fulfil. I've never had a need for the whores who pollute court so wantonly, who entice my fellow peers with their painted faces and their frilly gowns. And why would I? They could never satisfy me. If truth be told, sometimes all a man needs is a quick, hard, uncomplicated fuck that only another man can provide. And I'm not the only one either, oh no. I'm in very esteemed company. I am well aware of what goes on behind church doors at the very highest levels, so there will be no guilty thoughts here. No reprisals here, thank you very much. Now that's not to say that my wife isn't obliging when the need takes me, and she is pretty enough and from good stock too. But as for now, my need is greater than her. Phillip knows what I want; he knows my expressions by now, he recognizes that tone. He closes and secures the door behind him and smiles before walking towards the bed and unlacing his hose.

CHAPTER
TWO

To Be Useful In All That I Do

Seven weeks later . . .
HRH, Queen Katherine Tudor,
27 July 1543, Hampton Court Palace

Dear God, will they not leave me alone? Is a Queen to be harried by every lady of the court like a beast of prey? I slam the door to my privy chamber and sit heavily on my bed. I lower my head into my hands and close my eyes. Why, even as a girl at Kendal I was granted more privacy than this. *Just a few moments, oh Lord . . . a few quiet moments to gather my thoughts is all I ask.*

So much has happened in the last few weeks. So many frightening things. I have been swept along as though I have been riding a dangerous and unruly horse that has no regard for its rider. I have been granted almost no say in anything that has happened, despite my being at the very heart of each and every event. And at the end of it . . . well, I am now married for the third time to a man whom I do not like, and have become, as if a mere afterthought, the Queen of England.

It all started when I was summoned to court to dine with my then future husband, the King. It pains me to think of the word *husband*, even now, even after all that has happened. It was a small and intimate occasion with just the two of us present, and as I had feared, he formally asked for my hand in marriage. Naturally I had no choice but to accept. We were served nothing less than a small feast, for which I had no appetite, and yet somehow, for fear of appearing rude or ungrateful, I managed to force down a few morsels of the rich foul fare that was placed before me. We ate in a small, quiet room adjoining his lavish chambers, almost as though he did not want to frighten me by too much attention or fuss; and for that, at least, I was grateful.

I remember feeling so very afraid at the prospect of meeting him, given his intentions and the inevitable proposition that I knew awaited me. I did not want to go to the palace; I did not want to have to pretend to like him; to put on a show and to make him believe that I would ever want to be anything to him, least of all his wife. I don't know how I managed to ready myself; how I managed to overcome the feelings of nausea, the panic, and the crippling megrim that I had endured since that dreadful visit from Wriothesley all those weeks previously.

I remember how I had struggled when deciding how I should present myself. Naturally, I had wanted him to not like me and for him to change his mind and to realize the grave mistake that he had made in thinking

79

of me at all. So I chose to wear a sombre outfit as I did when I met his advisors; not at all lavish or in any way provocative, in the hope that he would find me undesirable. I had pictured Kathryn Howard as I prepared myself, that slattern whom the King had found so very appealing. I wanted to present myself as unlike her in both appearance and manner as I possibly could. It sounds so naïve now that I believed I could manipulate his feelings and escape my fate. And yet, in all honesty, I did think that I might show him the error of his judgement, and that he would simply change his mind and choose another. So I donned a rather staid blue gown; an outfit that was so very unflattering and old fashioned that it would have looked more fitting on one of his upper servants. It was certainly a dress that I would never have allowed Thomas to see me in. And my manner was no less rehearsed either; it was as far from my predecessor's character as was possible. I was both quiet and courteous as I picked at my meal; restrained and awkward. Not once did I giggle, nor did I gesticulate overly, and neither did I clap my hands or throw my head back in response to his jokes as she did. But despite this; despite my being as unlike her as possible, my efforts proved to be of no consequence at all.

The King was polite and courteous in return and did not appear to be dismayed or surprised by my actions. At all times he was respectful and gentlemanly in his conduct, and yet still he remained determined to have me. With every passing moment it dawned on me that

His Majesty had no intention whatsoever of withdraw-
ing his offer of marriage, however dull and uninteresting
I might have proved. And nor, alas, did he give me any
inclination that he might change his mind at a later
date. Strangely, he actually seemed to enjoy my
company.

After an hour or so I realized that my attempts to
dissuade him were not working as I had planned, and
so I decided to adopt a rather bullish and matter-of-fact
style of conversation. I had thought of Anne Boleyn,
who was so very forceful and unrestrained, and I
reasoned that if I could emulate her at her worst, then
perhaps he might find my manner equally as unnatural
and unbecoming for a woman. I must have surprised
him no end when out of the blue I began to discuss
politics of the Realm, and how I volunteered to debate
with the most learned at court regarding his own
Kingdom and his relations with foreign princes.

Regrettably, I was wrong. He responded to my
change in approach with relish, as if I had pulled an
extravagant and unexpected gift from beneath my
gown. He listened to my arguments, and no matter how
forcefully I put them, he suggested an alternative
perspective to my own. He laughed when we agreed,
and he challenged me gently when we did not. My
heart sank when it finally dawned on me that it was
almost as though we were already husband and wife! I
could have screamed at his excitement when he said
that he was looking forward to many more such
discussions once we were married! I smiled in response
to the gallantry of his compliment, but inside I wept as

once again my efforts to discourage him had merely strengthened his resolve.

To his credit I saw no display of the lecherous vulgarity that I had witnessed on so many occasions in the past. Thank God I was shown that mercy at least, for I do not know how I might have endured any groping or mauling. Had he dared to place his hands on me in the lewd manner with which he did with his last Queen then I do not think I would have been capable of keeping my true feelings to myself, regardless of the aftermath. There is only so much that a woman can endure.

"Joyce, please! I'm not yet ready. Please close the door. Just tell them I won't be long."

The door is shut a little too pointedly for my liking, but at last I am alone again with my thoughts. I close my eyes and allow my mind to wander back to that fateful evening all those weeks ago . . .

After dinner the King had inquired about my feelings when I had first learned of his intentions, and whether I had found the proposal of marriage in any way unwelcome. I was quite taken aback by his unexpected concern for my interests and what appeared to be a moment of self-doubt. Why, it had not occurred to me that he would ever have questioned my response, or ever assumed that I would have greeted the news without celebration. I remember thinking long and hard before replying, as I was well aware of his expectations and of the answer that he demanded from me. I remember gulping for air as I wondered how I could respond in a way that would sound both sincere and heartfelt.

With a great effort I informed him that I had been surprised by his proposition, quite overwhelmed in fact, but flattered too. I told him that I had naturally been unprepared, as never had I imagined such a fate for myself, and that in truth I was anxious that I might disappoint him. I went on to reveal with some hesitation that it had never been my ambition to hold any form of high rank and that I was not sure how well I would adjust to being a Queen, or indeed whether I was even worthy of such a position.

Alas, my words served only to hearten him as he told me that the modesty of my revelations exposed a deep and trustworthy side to my nature. Again, it dawned on me that by humbling myself, I had served to strengthen his resolve still further. How stupid of me to be modest! How stupid of me to think that after Anne Boleyn and Kathryn Howard he would not want to avoid another disastrous union with an aspiring wife!

I raise my eyes as the door slowly opens and Joyce tiptoes in with all the delicacy of a cart horse. A bitter laugh escapes my lips as I watch her efforts to move noiselessly. I dismiss her again and return to my thoughts. How in God's name did it get to this?

I remember that I asked him politely the reason why he had chosen me above so many others. I had to bite my tongue to stop myself from adding that I was hardly his type. He told me that I had always struck him as a good and caring person, and a pious and moral, God-fearing Catholic. I almost laughed out loud when I thought of my Bible that had been translated from Latin into English, which I had acquired during Anne Boleyn's reformist campaign, and of how John and I used to enjoy reading it aloud to each other without the need for a priest! Needless to say, I kept that particular thought to myself.

He went on to tell me that one of the reasons that he was so attracted to me, and why he thought I would make such a worthy Queen was that I was the complete opposite of his previous wife. I almost spat a mouthful of wine across the table at him upon hearing his words. Oh, stupid, stupid me! What on earth was I thinking? I remember clenching my fists tightly under the table until my knuckles turned white, and chastising myself bitterly for not having smothered my face in heavy powder and danced on the table as I imagine that she would have. He *never* would have married another Howard, the woman that he had beheaded, for God's sake! How could I have been so foolish?

At times he seemed so very reasonable. He came across as intelligent, polite and charming, and for a moment a small part of me contemplated telling him of my true feelings about his proposition. At times I could barely believe that sat before me was the man whom I had labelled a tyrant on so many occasions and who had proven me right almost without exception. For a split second I honestly thought that he might have

84

changed with old age and that he might have understood my feelings and taken pity on me.

I remember searching for the right words to say, and when finding them, holding them at the tip of my tongue for so long, waiting anxiously for the right moment to utter them. But I held my tongue. I quickly realized that I could not risk trusting him based upon a few moments of uncharacteristic kindness. I came to my senses when I cast my mind back to the man that I had known of old. I thought of the King who had so cruelly cast his first wife aside for a younger and more attractive woman; of the man who rejected his fourth wife for the plainness of her face and her independent manner; and of the man who sent two wives — wives that he once purported to love — to their deaths. I quickly recognized that I could not risk offending such an arrogant and unpredictable brute lest he show his true colours to me as he did to them. Thank God I came to my senses in time, as He alone knows what the King might have done to me.

I shift my weight and lean back until I find a more comfortable position on my new uncomfortable bed. I am conscious of my waiting guests, but I allow myself a few more moments of reflection.

I watched him regretfully that evening as he ate; as he spoke to me with that wet mouth, chewing his vowels along with his food. I studied his greying beard that glistened with grease, and the pink-rimmed eyes that leaked rheum at the corners each time he smiled. I tried not to show my disgust as I stared at his short, pink fingers and at the coarse red bristles that coated their backs. He waggled them at me from time to time whilst impatiently waiting for another bird to pick clean. The very sight of him across the table from me, stuffing himself with an insatiable appetite was almost overwhelming; it was only then I realized that by taking my hand in marriage he would have my body as well, and as often and however he wished. This revolted me to the point where I was forced to look away each time he wiped at his greasy mouth with the sleeve of his gown. If only I could have blocked my ears to the roar of his belches, and my nose to the stench of his wind.

I was summoned to the palace again several days later; but by this time I was invited as his *official future wife*. We watched a play performed by the Mummers in the great hall of Hampton Court Palace along with a small group of guests who had been chosen to congratulate me on my apparent good fortune. I sat at his side on the dais, unmoving like a statue, as all his other wives had done in their turn. I sat in a ridiculous chair, wearing a ridiculously elaborate dress that he had instructed me to wear, trying desperately to control my feelings of panic. The guests were sickeningly reverential, and paid me such unreserved attention that at one point I thought I might become completely overwhelmed and faint.

This time the King was a little less restrained in showing his affections, for he insisted on moving his great chair as close to mine as possible and whispering in my ear at every given opportunity. I remember how he ran his gaze slowly and obviously across my body in front of everyone before leaning across and complimenting me on the fit of my dress. I remember the elaborate and embarrassing show that he made of staring at my hair before nodding in satisfaction, and how he leant towards me and complimented me on its feminine style. Worst of all was when he reached his damp, pink hand towards me, how he gripped my chin between his thumb and forefinger and turned my face to his; how he stared into my eyes for what felt like a hellish eternity before passing comment on their *pleasing blueness*. I exhaled the second he pulled his body away; so relieved to be free of his clammy touch and his repulsive, showy attentions. I refrained from correcting him, for had he really cared to look he would have seen that, actually, my eyes are green.

He introduced me to his guests as *England's future Queen*. It made me feel very uncomfortable to hear those words spoken aloud and in public, especially in front of those who, for the past decade, had known me as Lady Latimer; wife to the gentle, sweet John. I couldn't help but wonder what they must have thought of me sitting above them on my miniature throne, all trussed up like some ridiculous peacock. Did they think me scheming? Did they think that I was privy to this charade? Could they sense my deep reluctance? God forbid they thought that I might want this!

I quickly became aware of a new and very noticeable divide between myself and the guests; one that naïvely, I had not anticipated. How overnight their conduct towards me had transformed from one of equals to that of master and servant. No longer were they warm and welcoming, relaxed and keen to share stories and exchange jokes. They had become formal and hesitant, as though suddenly wary of me. Fearful even. Their behaviour made me feel that I had become a different person, which of course I had not!

I tried to converse with them as I used to, but in the King's presence I could say very little. I was unable to reassure them as I too was uncomfortable and afraid. I thought that perhaps I should make an effort to respond appropriately to their reverential bows and curtsies — like a Queen would — but I did not know how I was supposed to behave! I did not know how a Queen was supposed to act! And as far as I was concerned I was surrounded by my friends, not my subordinates, and certainly not my subjects! What they did not know was that I would gladly have changed place with each and every one of them in a heartbeat.

The following few weeks are little more than a blur of frightened and panicked memories. So many people visited me at my London home to prepare me for the wedding day, and to move my belongings to the palace; to my new and unwanted, elaborate chambers. I was fitted for a gown of white and gold with ermine; my fingers were measured for my wedding ring and my head was measured for my crown . . .

Part of me felt as though I was a child again, being made ready for my marriage to Edward by Mother. I never thought that after all this time, after all these years I would ever have experienced a greater terror than I had felt before my first betrothal. I remember shutting myself away in my chamber, not two weeks ago, far from prying eyes, and how I had retrieved my two precious letters from my beloved Thomas from their secret hiding place. I remember how I held them to my heart as though they were a part of him and read them slowly and bitterly for the last time. In my final moments of privacy I cried deep and bitter tears of regret for the man whom I had dared to imagine might one day become my husband. I knew all too well that I could never risk taking those precious reminders of him with me for fear that they might be discovered, and so with the greatest reluctance I threw them into the fire. I watched as each cherished stroke of the quill disappeared into nothing more than a pinch of ash, as though they had never been written; as though they were nothing more than a figment of my imagination. It is true that each word has been committed to my memory, but even so, the loss of something tangible that had come from the hand of my beloved tore open anew the already festering wound.

The King and I were married several days later at Hampton Court Palace. Thankfully, it took place in the small closet next to the Queen's chambers — my chambers — and so I was not forced to perform in front of hundreds of courtiers as I feared I might. The dreadful Wriothesley was present, of course, watching my every move, as were all the members of the Privy Council. The King's former wife, the German lady, Anne, was also present, much to my amazement. I had never met her before, but I must admit that I did not like her very much. I swear that as the Archbishop asked the King if he would take me to be his wife, she shook her head as if she pitied me. The last thing I wanted was her pity, as it served as nothing less than a reminder of my dreadful fate. The fate that she had been spared! And besides, I had enough pity of my own.

I remember saying very little to anyone during the feast that followed. Naturally I smiled throughout and offered my thanks as custom dictated, but I saw no need to exaggerate my pretence any more than was absolutely necessary. The deed was done, wasn't it? I spent the rest of the day in a trance; my hand encased in the King's eager grip, trying to contain my tears and suppress the ever-present fear of the consummation that lay ahead of me; the prospect that had hung over my head like an executioner's sword from the first moment that we had dined together. The realization that I would soon be forced to endure it for real was almost too much to bear.

That evening I waited in my new chamber to be escorted to the King's bed. I remember that there was much pacing, many tears and many desperate attempts to think of a way that I could escape. Once again I felt like a child, being forced to do something that I so desperately did not want to do; something that I knew was fundamentally wrong. I remembered how I had been forced to lie with Edward all those years ago, and the crippling dread that had preceded it. But that evening as I waited to be called to the King, the fear that I had experienced as a child somehow paled in comparison. It didn't seem to matter that I was a grown woman and nor did it matter that I was well aware of the act of consummation and what I would be expected to do. No, that evening, as I waited for my summons, it felt as if I was about to be escorted to the scaffold.

Wriothesley had the *privilege* of calling for me, which only served to increase my panic. With his caustic jeer, he informed me that I should join the King immediately wearing only my nightgown. I remember how he had smirked cruelly as he told me that I would have no need for *superfluous clothing*. That horrible man! I had suspected that there might be others present during the "act" to confirm that the consummation had indeed taken place, but somehow, until that very moment I had managed to suppress those particular fears. But that evening, as that dreadful serpent bowed and smiled in his sickening way, the full significance of the humiliation to follow finally dawned on me. I remember thinking that I did not know which would be worse: being intimate with the King, or being watched whilst doing so in front of an audience of prelates and ministers.

At that moment, as God is my witness, I prayed with all my heart that I would die rather than face either. I remember suddenly feeling short of breath; I remember how my heart had raced and how my knees almost gave way beneath my weight. I had to call for Bessie, who held me tightly in her arms as though I was an invalid. I already felt naked in front of Wriothesley despite the fullness of my nightgown. How, I had wondered, could

I possibly allow him to see me naked? How could I allow *anyone* to witness my being violated?

I don't know how I managed it, but somehow I found the strength to tear myself from my maid's arms. I followed Wriothesley mutely as if in a nightmare, clutching the heavy robe around my shoulders tightly for protection. I remember that my feet were bare and cold as they pressed against the cool stone floor of the narrow corridors and the spiral stairway that divided our chambers.

I didn't say anything to Wriothesley as we walked; I didn't have to. He knew very well how I felt and I had no intention of showing him my fear any further. He uttered just one thing to me as we reached the King's chamber door. He leant towards me and whispered in my ear that I *knew my duty* and that I was *not to disappoint the King in any way*. He added grimly that I would be *very sorry* if I did . . . *as would Anna*. I remember that I pulled my head away from his in disgust and how I had glared at him. I did not return the false smile that spread across his face; I simply held his gaze defiantly and told him to keep his distance as his breath offended me. It was my one last, pointless, pathetic rebellion. I could not help myself. I simply hated him and everything that he was making me do, and I didn't care that he knew it.

The King was sitting in a large chair in the centre of his privy chamber, dressed only in a giant white nightgown that fell to just below his knees. To my horror, surrounding him on all sides were seven men: four members of the Privy Council including Wriothesley, a priest and two of the King's grooms. I remember that they halted their conversations mid-sentence as I entered, and how the King turned to me and smiled. I curtseyed to him and willed myself not to vomit as my eyes turned involuntarily to the great bed next to where they had congregated. The King struggled to his feet and approached me. He took my hand in his and we all stood in silence whilst the priest quietly blessed the bed. I remember how the nine of us — *nine!* — then joined together and how we lowered our heads in a communal prayer. Wriothesley, that wretched man, had the audacity to ask the priest to pray for a son.

The King instructed me to wait for him on the bed and to make myself ready to receive his attentions. I was shaking almost uncontrollably by then but I did as I was instructed, mutely and as though I was in a trance. I kept my nightgown on, of course, and tried not to look too ashamed as I sat awkwardly on the far side of the bed, as far away from the onlookers as was possible. I dangled my legs over the edge and lowered my head with embarrassment. Noticing my discomfort, the King instructed one of the grooms to hold aloft a sheet to protect my modesty. I must have sighed so audibly that he chuckled aloud, causing a ripple of mirth to spread across the group.

He then joined me on the bed, climbing between the bottom two posts and moving his great body on all fours as though he was a large, predatory cat. His groom, Robert, was at his side the entire time, assisting him as he moved awkwardly and slowly towards me, and showing no sign of leaving us alone. The King asked me to turn around and to crouch on all fours, which I did quickly, thankful, at least, that he had not insisted that I undress. Suddenly he raised my nightgown to my waist, exposing my most intimate parts to the two of them. I remember clearly how I had screwed my face up in anguish and how I had lowered my head between my shoulders in shame. I shook my head furiously so that my hair fell across my face; that way no one could witness my tears.

Robert was duly instructed to lift the King's nightgown and to hold it aloft around his chest. The King shuffled forward a final time, leant over me and pressed his fat, clammy hands into my shoulders to support himself. I remember holding my breath and closing my eyes as tightly as I could in anticipation of his entering me. I waited as he pressed his groin against my naked backside ... and yet ... I barely felt anything at all.

The King moved himself across my buttocks and kneaded my shoulders with his hands as he began rocking forward and back. I remember having to use all my strength to keep my body from collapsing under his colossal weight. I endured the unpleasant rubbing for several moments, my eyes still tightly closed, waiting patiently until he was ready. But still ... nothing happened. Confused, I looked over my shoulder and saw that his eyes were firmly closed, and that he wore a look of deep concentration. I nervously peered over the top of the sheet and into the faces of the onlookers. I remember wondering if they knew what he was doing and if they realized that our marriage was not being consummated.

The King continued to move his flaccid member across my buttocks as if trying to stimulate himself, but it was to no avail. I lowered my head again and grimaced at the feel of his giant belly that was pressing into me like a mound of cold, damp dough, ripping across the small of my back. Suddenly the King began to moan loudly, and started rocking his hips to and fro at speed. I felt him stiffen a little as he roughly squeezed my shoulders in time with his movements, but still he did not penetrate me. Did he not realize that he was simply rubbing my buttocks? Did he have no feeling below?

Thankfully it took but a few moments, until, damp with perspiration and wheezing for breath, he sat back on his heels and fell against Robert for support. I remember wondering what I should do next; whether there was more to come; whether I should wait for a second instalment . . .

Even in my horrified state I realized that I could not continue to expose myself to them like a mare in season, even in the low candlelight that surrounded the bed, and so I quickly pulled my nightgown down to hide my shame. I felt very afraid of how he might react to his failure, and feared that he might take his inevitable frustration out on me.

Without warning, he smacked me hard on the bottom and let out a mighty roar. I turned to face him in surprise, and he grinned widely the moment he caught my eye. He asked me over his panting how I had enjoyed being *serviced by a King*. I remember smiling back at him hesitantly, trying to understand how he felt; trying to decide whether this was an attempt to trick me. And yet, strangely, his expression remained nothing short of jubilant.

Not knowing how I should respond, I quietly thanked him for the honour and bowed my head. Suddenly the King's men and the grooms began to clap to congratulate us on our good fortune. Praise the Lord, as they seemed not to have noticed the King's inability. As Robert assisted me from the bed, we caught each other's eye. He gave me a reassuring smile and a look that can only be described as knowing. I don't know why, but I knew that, like me, he would hold his tongue on pain of death that the marriage was by no means consummated that night.

As the King's language became coarse, and I heard myself described in words that neither John nor Edward ever used, I curtsied and left the chamber. I remember walking as quickly as I could along the cold dark corridors, desperate to escape the laughter and whistling that followed. Naturally, there were tears when I reached my chamber, and thankfully Bessie was there to console me. But despite my ordeal I was secretly relieved. I was relieved that I did not have to bare myself in front of all those people; I was relieved that the King did not maul me or physically humiliate me; and most of all, I was relieved that he seemed incapable of violating me in that most intimate and most feared way. It was a small mercy, but a significant one, and for that I thanked God repeatedly. It hadn't really occurred to me until that moment that it would be one thing to be his wife, but entirely another to be his lover.

Two months later . . .
Robert Caskell, Groom of the Stool,
29 September 1543, Whitehall Palace

Ugh! How can she stand it? How can she bear to be near that dreadful thing? How can she look at it without wincing, without retching, and how in God's name can she bear the rancid stench of his decaying flesh as though it is nothing more than a sour whiff?

Now, I love my King dearly, but as much as I try, there are certain things that I just cannot do for him. Certain things that he must leave to others. Thankfully, he has his new wife now, and she is proving to be someone whom he can rely on in no small measure, especially in the tasks that I have no stomach for. He has, of course, countless physicians and herbalists to treat his leg ulcers, but for some reason he prefers the ministrations of his new wife. And quite frankly, who can blame him? After all, she seems to be doing an awful lot more good than they ever did!

I glance at them, at the newlyweds. They look more like nursemaid and querulous patient if you ask me! I chuckle quietly to myself. Well, they *are* a sight to behold. His Majesty is lying in bed in his undergarments, his giant mound of a belly unashamedly exposed in its pasty glory and his four pink limbs splayed out like great sausages in all directions. He is struggling to look in Katherine's direction, as his many chins are forcing his head back onto the pillow. I have to stop myself from laughing at the sight. Lord, if His Majesty were to read my thoughts, then I would be for it!

The lovely Katherine, my new Queen, is perched on a high-backed chair next to His Majesty's bed. His right leg is resting heavily on her lap, and she is bending her body over the ulcer that stretches all the way from his kneecap to his ankle. I try to make myself busy by sorting through the rushes at my feet with my toe. It is a pointless and unnecessary task but it saves me from having to look at that dreadful leg of his.

His Majesty has instructed me to help Katherine in any way that is needed, and so I have no other choice but to be here. I just hope that "help" will necessitate little more than carrying a few bowls of water for her to wash him with; any more than that and I don't know what I will do. Perhaps I should be pleased that His Majesty allows me to witness the decay of the royal flesh? But if you ask me, the less privileged have had a very lucky escape indeed, for there is nothing fortunate about that leg in the slightest.

I wrinkle my nose as the stench wafts across the room. I know that smell very well by now: it is offal, putrefaction and death. I try to blink away the tears that fill my eyes as though they are being poisoned. I am more than aware that the Queen must smell things as I do, but whenever the royal leg is freed from its bandages, my stomach churns and I fear that I will pass out. Nevertheless, I know that I must pretend, for God help me if His Majesty suspects my revulsion. But the smell is so very strong today! So potent!

I have to breathe through my mouth to lessen the effect, but I can taste the stench as it finds its way over my tongue and into my lungs. I feel as though my mouth has been stuffed with mouldy, rancid cheese; cheese that is so tainted that even the poor will not eat it! No . . . it is even worse than that; it is like mouldy cheese mixed with the bodies of dead criminals as they rot on the gallows! I swallow deeply at the thought and will myself not to retch. If only I could be more like Katherine. Never have I seen her gag or wince, or even avert her eyes from the offensive sight. Solid as a rock, that woman, and no mistake.

Katherine looks up and calls to me. "Robert, please could you fetch some fresh water?" She smiles as she speaks and I can't help but smile back at her innocence. She is by far my favourite Queen! Always so polite and courteous, even to the staff. I am at her side in three long strides, holding my breath as the smell intensifies. She hands me a bowl of murky reddish-brown water from a small table next to the bed. I take it with as much good grace as I can muster, retaining my fixed smile the entire time. I walk to the fire with the bowl in my outstretched hand and turn my head in disgust as I empty the putrid contents into a large pot. Ugh! I will instruct one of the lower servants to take that filth to the moat later, where it belongs. I won't do it, oh no. God forbid I spill it on myself; that stench would never come out.

I plunge a heated rod into a second pot of clean water that is resting over the flames, and smile at the reassuring hiss. That will do the trick! Nice and warm, just as she likes it. I ladle it into Katherine's empty bowl and hurry back to her, glancing at His Majesty's face as I do so. He is staring out of the window, and so I can only imagine that he does not want to look at his dreadful leg either. He is wearing one of his cross expressions, which means that he is most probably in a sulk. As usual. Well, I suppose I can't blame him. After all, it must be awfully painful having somebody prodding at your great wound as though it were a pin cushion. Rather him than me.

As Katherine takes the bowl from my hand, I force myself to take a quick peek at his leg. The sight makes me wince and I almost spill the water over both of us. Oh, it is worse than I had imagined! How can she just sit here so calmly with it festering away in her lap? The Queen watches me closely; not unkindly, but expectantly. It is as though she expects more from me; as though she wants to see a little courage!

I sigh and turn my eyes slowly back to the horror that rests on her lap, willing myself not to act the fool again in front of her. This time I am ready. This time, I hold my breath in preparation. Nonetheless, I cannot help but curl my lip in disgust as I take in the sight, for it looks so unnatural, so unlike anything that I have ever seen before; as if some kind of evil has burrowed into His Majesty's leg and has eaten away the flesh from the inside. I shake my head sadly. I hadn't realized quite how ill he was until this moment. Poor, poor man.

I take a closer look, feeling a little braver now that the initial shock has passed, and take in the colours and the textures of the wound. The ulcer is crudely outlined with black skin as though it has been burnt. How in God's name could that have happened? Surely burning isn't one of the doctor's latest cures? Good God, I hope not, for His Majesty's sake. I notice wet green pustules pooling in the centre of the ulcer, shining under the light of the candles, and streaked with blood. Oh, this is nothing short of horrific! I had only ever imagined that His Majesty had been plighted with a stubbornly infected cut; that's all. I had always imagined that the skin would grow back and that it would heal in time. But this . . . this surely cannot heal! There is barely any skin left, and most of the flesh that surrounds the wound is simply rotten.

Now, I was too young to remember, but I have heard people talk about his injury. It was a nasty jousting accident, apparently; an unfortunate fall from a horse which resulted in a deep gash across his shin. And somehow, for reasons known only to God, that gash has turned into the ulcer that lies before me; the ulcer that has blighted him for so many years and which refuses to heal. When in a good mood, His Majesty likes to tell everyone that he was sent flying by the stumble of his horse and not by the lance of his opponent. He also says that the reason he suffers so is to set an example of bravery to less courageous sportsmen. But I can only assume there must be some other explanation for his continued plight, for sporting injuries heal. Everyone

101

knows that. Why, he must have had these wounds for years, and the good Lord alone knows how many doctors have tried to treat them.

Katherine looks up at me and smiles kindly. She dips a corner of the cloth that she holds between her fingers in the bowl of warm water and dabs gently at the edges of the ulcer. "You see here, Robert?" she says gently, pressing the cloth against the blackened edge, "this is dead skin; skin that cannot heal."

I nod my head automatically, dumbfounded. How can she utter these words so calmly?

"And this . . ." she dabs at the congealed lumps with such nonchalance that one would think she was polishing the fireplace. "Robert, we need to rid His Majesty's leg of this; we need to separate it from the living tissue so that the wound can recover." She carefully wipes away a tiny fragment of the green mess with the cloth.

I watch as His Majesty winces. Poor man. I can't blame him for swearing under his breath. She takes a deep breath before turning her attention to another area. She is so careful that she barely touches him. Is she afraid of hurting him, I wonder? Goodness, I would be!

"But it is difficult, you see, because as much as I need to remove this diseased flesh, it will cause His Majesty an inordinate amount of pain. So to do this, Robert, we need to apply warm water, and then we can lift away what we need."

She looks up to check that I am paying attention. All I can hear is the word "we". Surely she does not expect me to have any part in this? I nod mutely, trying to conceal my growing panic.

"Anything you see that is pink is good, Robert, for that means it is new skin. There is much more pink skin than there was last week, so I think that My Lord is well and truly on the mend!" She smiles and looks genuinely pleased with her work.

I watch as she continues to lift away the decayed flesh, bit by bit, in tiny amounts using just water and her cloth. With each new dab, His Majesty becomes more agitated, and it isn't long before he is crying out and thrashing his arms across the bed in pain. Even so, I can't help thinking that this is all very restrained for him. I have heard greater outbursts for the most trivial of misdemeanours. I can only assume that he is holding his tongue for his new wife's sake.

"Your Majesty, should I fetch you some ale or some wine?" I ask, feeling rather useless. "To take the edge off?"

The reply comes in the form of a bark. "Need a fucking lot more than that, boy!" I look at Katherine, hoping that she will tell me what I should do. She shakes her head, indicating that I should leave him alone.

As I watch her, so diligently tending to the King's ailments without hesitation or complaint, it strikes me that she would make a most dutiful and loving mother. God only knows why He hasn't blessed her already, after all she was married twice before she married the King. I smile at the irony, as both she and I know there is little chance of that happening now. Not unless a miracle occurs. But she will make a wonderful stepmother to those children of his; especially to the little boy. That at least is a blessing, for he must need a mother as much as she must need a child. And she is already such a wonderful Queen; I am not the only person who thinks so either, for most of the staff here are quite delighted by her presence. Why, she seems to have returned normality to court, just as it used to be under Queen Jane's reign. Oh yes, I think we all agree that it is quite impossible not to like her.

I think back to her first few days at court, when she was so very awkward and uncomfortable around everyone. I don't think that anyone really minded; after all, we recognized that it must have been quite a shock. I remember how her face had reddened with embarrassment when I first referred to her as "Your Majesty". It was almost as though she didn't believe me, or that she didn't want to hear it. In my opinion, she didn't like the attention one bit. It must have been difficult, having all those people who were once her friends fawning over her, trying to impress her and shower her with unwanted gifts. Personally, I would have loved it, but poor woman . . . she was such a mouse. Now, I am nothing short of thrilled that His Majesty decided to marry her, but sometimes I can't help but wonder why on earth she ever agreed to be his Queen.

I suddenly realize that I have been staring at Her Majesty for a few moments, completely lost in my thoughts. She is looking up at me questioningly. I smile and quickly return my gaze to the King's poor leg.

"It is important that it is cleaned every day, Robert," she continues, "for the last thing we need is more infection. We need to take great care of the healthy skin if it is to grow." She turns to the King. "My Lord, this may smart a little. I am going to wash the wound. Do you mind?"

I sit back and shake my head in admiration. My God, I have never known a Queen to behave like this; to want to learn from the doctors and to do their work! Are such ministrations not beneath her? She carefully folds a dry cloth in her lap and tucks it under his leg. I brace myself as she tips the bowl and slowly pours a stream of water into the ulcer itself. Lord only knows how much this must hurt! It doesn't take long until His Majesty is crying out in pain. His massive hands are balled into fists and he is gripping the sheets so hard that his knuckles have turned white. And yet . . . something is preventing him from screaming his usual obscenities and lashing out as I would expect him to.

The water trickles from deep within the ulcer and onto the cloth in her lap. I watch in horror as the dirty yellow liquid stains the material and seeps onto her dress. But she does not seem to mind. She waits patiently until the wound has emptied before drying it with another cloth. His Majesty continues to writhe in agony. I don't know where to put myself; I know that I cannot help and so I sit uselessly at the Queen's side, waiting like a fool for instruction. Her Majesty remains seated, watching her husband with great concern. She purses her lips together, as if trying to decide what she should do next. Suddenly she speaks:

"Have you had a chance to read any of the books that I gave you, My Lord?"

Books? At a time like this? Surely she should be asking after the pain. Surely she should be asking if there is anything else that she can do. Suddenly it dawns on me: she is trying to engage him in conversation to take his mind *from* the pain! The last thing she wants to do is remind him of it! Very clever!

"Hmph?" His Majesty grunts. "No, no." He shifts his hefty weight a little so that he can look at her.

"One of them," she tells him lightly, "*The Ninety-Five Theses*, absolutely reinforces your views about the Pope, My Lord." She ignores his brusque reply. "It is written by a German theologian, a Martin Luther, who has quite interesting opinions about the Holy Church of Rome. I think that you would find it extremely interesting reading. It offers a philosophical insight into the nature of prayer and the manner in which the Church watches over the souls of the ordinary people."

I frown. What on earth is she talking about? I didn't think that we were allowed to discuss religion any more . . .? Not since Cromwell lost his head, anyway. Well, whatever she is doing, she seems to be walking on risky ground, that's all that I can say.

"Martin Luther? Pah! I am no Lutheran." His Majesty growls, his voice rising. "And neither are you, wife!" Crikey, I don't know what that means but it doesn't sound good!

I brace myself for an argument, but instead the King simply lies back and sighs heavily. Her Majesty frowns and bites her lip. Suddenly her face lights up again and so I can only imagine that a new idea has sprung to mind.

"Have you given any more thought to the children's tutors, My Lord?" She smiles and continues to dab his leg dry. I can't help but smile too. The mention of his children is guaranteed to catch his attention. His Majesty replies emphatically, through clenched teeth.

"Damned reformists, teaching my blood kin! I'll not have it!"

Katherine grins to herself. She looks suddenly very pleased. Even so, I can't help but stifle a yawn. If this is going to turn into any kind of religious or academic discussion then I will have to think about making my excuses.

"Dr Langley and Dr Staple come highly recommended, My Lord," she continues. "I would not suggest them otherwise. Besides, I think it is important that the children gain a wider view of religion, as well as politics, languages and other forms of academia. Wouldn't you agree? If they are ever going to obtain a superior knowledge such as your own, we need to think carefully about their tutoring."

The King mutters something in reply, and as I turn towards the door I catch sight of him crossly snatching his leg from her lap. I tut quietly and shake my head. So much for gratitude! How easily that man forgets! Well, she certainly seems to have distracted him from his woes, that's for sure; but if that is all she is trying to do,

107

then she is going about it in a very dangerous way indeed.

Six days later . . .
HRH, Queen Katherine Tudor,
5 October 1543, Hampton Court Palace

My husband the King is standing in front of my chamber window blocking out the light. He is staring at me from across the room, watching me intently as I sit at my writing desk. His gaze makes me feel uncomfortable. He marched in a few moments ago to inquire after my *state*. He looks rather concerned. Or irritated perhaps. I am still not confident in reading his expressions. I am, of course, perfectly well, as always, although I must say, I do feel rather excited, thanks to an inspired idea of my sister's. She suggested that I use my influence to return our dearest friend Princess Mary, my husband's firstborn, to court. Naturally, I jumped at the idea and was amazed that I had not thought of it myself. After all, what is the point of being the Queen if you can't make important decisions from time to time? We haven't seen her for so many years, not since we were children at court. Not since my husband and her mother's successor Anne Boleyn sent her away so cruelly. Well, as I am now officially her stepmother, my opinion must count for something.

It suddenly occurred to me when planning her return that perhaps I should invite Elizabeth to court as well; my husband's second discarded child; the sole surviving fruit of Anne's womb. And maybe his precious heir Edward too; the King's only surviving son. I almost dismissed the idea the moment it entered my mind as I pictured the five of us sitting awkwardly together in one room: the tyrannical, unforgiving father, pouting and scowling with his arms crossed over his chest; the unhappy Queen, frightened of saying the wrong thing; the damaged daughters of two unwanted wives, both of them trying to make sense of their being unexpectedly summoned; and the delicate, mollycoddled son who is too precious and too important to be anywhere near any of us. One big happy family indeed! But then I thought: Why on earth not? If the truth be known, I expect that they would all welcome the opportunity to be with their father and each other; to be with those whom they should be closest to, whether they admit it or not. It didn't take me too long to reason that the fates may indeed be against us, but, as the Queen, it is my duty to think of others, and so that is exactly what I have done.

Unbeknown to the King, I have spent the day composing three very different letters to each of them. To Mary; to my long, lost childhood confidante whom I have not seen in over a decade, naturally, I wrote of my deepest regret for her many years of abandonment, and how I have missed her greatly as though she were my own sister. I told her that as I now occupy the position that once belonged to her sainted mother, Queen Catherine of Aragon, I will strive to use my influence to return her to court, where she belongs. I only hope that she accepts.

Poor Mary; God only knows how these long years of estrangement have affected her. I can hardly imagine how such a cruel and unjust denouncement might have taken its toll. There was talk of her returning under Queen Jane's reign, but it was a slow and arduous process, frustrated in no small measure by the King's pigheaded insistence that Mary debase herself by declaring herself a bastard in front of everyone. I don't blame Mary for turning her back on him after that; she would never deny the sanctity of her parents' marriage and her own God-given right to be his heir. And he knew it. Naturally, I kept these thoughts very much to myself when composing the letter. Anything written or spoken aloud must convey nothing but respect and admiration for my husband the King. God forbid I am accused of treason!

And as for Elizabeth; that little girl with the most regretful lineage; that unfortunate child who was harshly cast aside the moment that her mother, Anne, fell out of favour and lost her head. Now the last time I saw her she was a happy and healthy toddler, full of energy, adored by everyone and oblivious to the rising turmoil that engulfed her mother. As with Mary, I can only imagine what the last seven years have been like for her, living in the heavy shadow of one who became so thoroughly despised. I hope to God that those who care for her treat her with a mother's warmth and kindness, such that every child deserves. No matter who they are. From time to time the King forces himself to inquire after her health and well-being. When I ask of her, he tells me that she is a very bright child, with a voracious appetite for reading, and pretty too, with his vivid red colouring. It concerns me that there is only indifference in his voice when he speaks of her, despite his complimentary choice of words.

In my letter to Elizabeth I naturally conveyed my wish to see her. I told her that I had heard much about her passion for learning, and of her love of languages and poetry. I expressed my hope that she might one day join me in my household, and perhaps accept my offer of guidance and tutelage in scholarly matters. I decided to adopt a matter-of-fact approach in fear that any display of warmth would be viewed with suspicion. In truth, I expect that she will be confused if anyone tries to mother her. God only knows what her vision of motherhood is. Perhaps she will dismiss my efforts entirely? I hope not. But whatever her response, I am certain that the greatest opposition will be from her father. Oh yes, he remains a very bitter man when it comes to his past wives and their offspring. Whether he will forgive this unfortunate child for the crimes of her mother is anybody's guess. Whether she will forgive *him* for sending her mother to the block is another matter entirely.

And lastly, there is Edward, the child whom I have never met; the late Queen Jane's only son. My husband's pride. Unsurprisingly, his letter is proving to be the most difficult of all. How does one write to a six-year-old child? To a little boy who is destined to great things, who will one day become the most powerful man in Christendom and command two mighty Kingdoms? Which words should I choose? How can I tell him that he now has a mother? I expect that in truth, just like Elizabeth, he has no real inkling of what a mother is.

However I decide to make contact with him, I know that it will be very difficult persuading the King to allow Edward to visit. He is understandably anxious that the little boy may contract some terrible illness if he leaves the safety of his closeted country home. God forbid that my efforts only result in weakening him. I have heard rumours that he is not the strongest of children, so I understand his fears; after all, he has but one son, just one real chance of continuing his dynasty. It is a sad fact, but I think that the King and I are both well aware that unless he finishes me off soon as he did the others, and is blessed by God in his nether regions, then one son is all he will ever have.

"My dear, you look pale." The King shuffles towards me as I sit at my desk, my quill still in my hand. I quickly place a leaf of parchment over the letter to Edward. I do not want him to see what I am doing until I have finished. I want to catch him in the right mood if I am ever to persuade him to agree with my plans. He places his giant hand on my shoulder.

"My Lord, I have a headache," I tell him firmly, hoping that he will leave me alone. It is a very rare pleasure these days for a few moments of privacy, and I have no desire to surrender it to him. "I will be in perfect health once I have rested."

The King looks down at me and I catch his eye for a second. He frowns with concern. I can see that he doesn't believe me. I grit my teeth. What does he want from me now? I obey him like a slave; I do everything he wants me to do and always with a smile on my face. Why can't I be tired from time to time? He is ill often enough!

"I think that perhaps you have spent too long indoors, my love . . . serving me."

The King squeezes my shoulder. I can't help but raise my eyebrows in surprise at his words.

"We shall go for a lovely ride tomorrow, in the palace grounds. Just the two of us. We shall canter across the fields as though we were any other husband and wife! What do you say to that? And we can leave all the boring duties to Wriothesley! Ha! What do you think, my dearest Katherine?"

I look up at him again, a little taken aback by his suggestion. I very much like the thought of being outside in the gardens; well away from the oppressive confines of the palace; away from all those subservient people and all those dreadfully tedious chores. Even if I am forced to be alone with him. The truth is that I have not ridden for many months and I miss it terribly.

"I should like that, My Lord," I say quietly, the words unexpectedly catching in my throat. I smile at him with uncharacteristic sincerity. The King is pleased. I watch him as he waddles across the room, and as he turns his body awkwardly so that he can fit through the doorway. It suddenly occurs to me that I must send a message to the stable grooms immediately. I must inform them to fetch the largest carthorse from the fields in readiness for the King. Good God, I hope they have something strong enough or it will be back to the chambers for me, for another day of drudgery.

One day later . . .
HRH, Queen Katherine Tudor,
6 October 1543, Hampton Court Palace

The sturdy steed is strong enough. Just. Its heavily feathered legs do not look particularly secure under the King's weight, but I think it will hold him. The King seems embarrassed and is snapping unnecessarily at the groom who is trying to help him into the saddle. He isn't used to riding a beast of burden. Thank goodness it is so sturdy.

The feel of the young black mare as she moves impatiently beneath me has instantly lifted my spirits. Oh, how I long to indulge her and gallop her across the fields with abandon, but one look at the poor animal that carries the King, and I know that there will be nothing more than a sedate trot today. At best. Still, at least we are outside on this fine autumnal day, even if we do have to be together.

We set off alone, just as he promised, through the palace grounds. We ride side by side, and must look quite a sight to anybody watching. My mare is at least four hands shorter than his mount and less than half as wide around the girth. She prances as she walks, keen for excitement, throwing her head around and pulling against her bit. Her upward impulsion is invigorating; it reminds me that I am alive. Like me, she is desperate to flee, to escape the hold of the great beast.

114

The King looks down at me from time to time and smiles warmly. He must see how much I am enjoying myself already, even at this slow pace. He looks happy. We walk onwards in silence for a few moments, enjoying the feel of the sun on our faces. I glance up at the King and notice that he is riding awkwardly, as though in discomfort. He is trying to hold his legs aloft; to keep his calves away from his horse's sides. I can only assume that he must be in pain again and that the friction is affecting his dreadful ulcers. Still, he doesn't say anything. Perhaps he is suffering in silence for my benefit? I notice too that he doesn't seem particularly balanced in the saddle. Perhaps it is because he is not gripping with his legs as he ought. Perhaps it is because he has hunched his body over his horse's withers. Does his back pain him too? God forbid he falls and blames me.

"Are you enjoying yourself, Katherine?" he inquires, looking down at me from his unnatural position.

"Oh yes, this is most pleasing. It gladdens my heart to be riding once again."

"A lovely mare she is. You must take her for a gallop later and I will watch you from this hairy great brute!" He pats his gelding on the neck. I look up at him, my mouth slightly open in surprise. I cannot believe that he would allow me to ride on without him. Surely that would be a sign of utmost disrespect. Surely the last thing he wants is for a woman to remind him of his own limitations. Perhaps he is toying with me . . . testing me.

"No, My Lord, I am quite content to be at your side." It is the right thing to say, but a blatant lie nonetheless.

"I insist. I wouldn't want to stand in the way of a little well-earned fun. It is the least that I can do after all that you have already done for me."

I am shocked by his selfless reply. His words sound genuine. I raise my eyebrows as a request for him to continue; for him to persuade me that he is serious. He nods emphatically in response, holding my gaze and mirroring my eager smile. I turn my attention to the deserted lawns that lie ahead of us and grin at the prospect of indulging my young mare. How I love to be outside! Away from all those dreadful sycophants, and oh, how I long for my old life!

"Katherine, it is of no secret to either one of us that I am not the man I used to be. I am prone to such illnesses, as you know. My poor legs . . . my blasted megrims. Sometimes I think that I have been cursed by God."

I purse my lips together regretfully. His health is a pitiful state of affairs, there is no denying that. He smiles as he catches my eye.

"But then God blessed me with you! How could I have been more fortunate? At my greatest hour of personal need, you came along. Divine intervention, I would say. How very lucky I am!"

My face blushes with embarrassment. I cannot bear these overt displays of affection, which almost always end in some form of dreadful embrace. He is always so eager to compliment me whenever he is feeling sorry for himself. Why does he do that? And still I do not know how to react. Still he makes me feel sick to my stomach. It is strange that he feels such obvious warmth towards me. Oh, I have been nothing less than dutiful in the short time that I have been his wife, but never have I gone out of my way to do anything other than that which is expected of me. Although I do not shun him in any way, I neither initiate warmth, nor encourage his affections or attentions. And yet, here he is, complimenting me once again as though I am the most loving and attentive wife.

"Thank you, My Lord." My voice is suddenly quiet. Despite myself, his sincerity makes me feel a little ashamed. Perhaps I am too harsh? Perhaps I am wrong to assume that his words are always loaded with malice or deviance?

"Ahhh . . ." The King winces and reaches down to rub his left calf. His legs are too delicate to be contained within his long riding boots, and so he wears heavy bandages beneath his short hose to offer some protection from the horse's movement. I watch with sympathy as he turns the tips of his toes outwards so that he can shift the pressure to a different part of his lower leg. I keep a tight hold on my reins as my mare throws her head around in frustration.

"My Lord, perhaps we should return if you are in discomfort?"

"Absolutely not. We will ride to the end of the grounds and then Titan and I will watch as you two fine young fillies entertain us with your daring feats!" He laughs, despite his obvious pain. "I want to see you

117

leaping hedges, and nothing less! Oh yes, I have heard all about how you used to enjoy your hunting!"

I laugh along with him, suddenly feeling more relaxed in his company and relieved that we will not be returning to the palace so soon. "I could tell you a story or two about hunting, My Lord!"

"Bugger, bet you could!"

We continue for a few moments in comfortable silence before commenting on the vivid colours and the heady scent of the late flowering roses that were planted by his father when he was King. We pass the great fountain, and the giant beech trees, and ride on towards the sparse palace fields. I tilt my face to the sun and close my eyes as the warmth washes over me. It seems as though I have spent an age shut away in the dark confines of the King's many palaces, each darker and more suffocating than the last. I cannot remember the last time that I was able to go about my business freely; when my every move was not watched and scrutinized as though I was itching to perform some heinous act of treason.

"My Lord . . ." I take a deep breath and choose my words with caution. "My Lord, it saddens me, as your wife, that you do not have your family with you." There! I have said it! I cannot think of a better moment! My heart quickens as I try to anticipate his reaction. The last thing I want is for him to think that I am criticizing him. I take long, slow, deep breaths to calm my mare. She is clearly aware of my excited state.

He looks down at me again, frowning and shifting his great weight further forward in the saddle. "I have you. You are my family. Edward must be kept away from London for his own protection, as you know. God forbid we have another outbreak of the plague! It would be the death of him. It would be the death of me if anything were to happen to him."

"I know that, My Lord, but whilst there is no outbreak, I think that perhaps it would be beneficial for you both if he were to visit from time to time. He should know what a remarkable man his father is . . . and you should be there to influence him so that he will be a fine King one day. Just as you are."

He nods slightly in agreement. I can see that he is pondering my words. "But I trust the men who are responsible for him," he argues. "They are good men. They will protect him. They will teach him well."

"I'm sure they are, My Lord, and I'm sure that they will protect him against any ill . . ." I am encouraged by his lack of overwhelming opposition and feel confident enough to continue with my efforts. "But I would dearly love to meet and to get to know my own stepson. I hear that he is the most delightful little boy. I can only imagine that he is desperate for a mother's love as all little boys are." I sigh deeply for effect. "As good as your men are, My Lord, I fear that he will receive no such warmth from them."

He smiles and grips the pommel of his saddle for support. I can see that I have pleased him. He reaches across and I place my hand in his.

"Then perhaps we shall arrange for him to visit. You are right. He should be with us more often. But I must think about his health, Katherine. That is paramount. His survival is of utmost importance."

"Yes, My Lord, but his mind is of similar importance. If he is to be a good and wise King then he must also be a balanced and well-rounded young man. He must learn tolerance and discipline; the skills that will help him command great armies one day and win the hearts and minds of the people who serve him. For that, he needs you."

"I will think on it, Katherine. You may be right."

I can't help but feel a little taken aback. That was easy! Of course, it was no definitive agreement, and he may simply decide that the child is best kept far away, but at least he has agreed to give the matter some thought. I can't help but smile at the prospect of meeting the little prince! I suddenly have an irrepressible desire to hold him in my arms as though he was my very own child!

"You know . . ." I take a deep breath, "I was wondering whether perhaps we should invite the princesses to court as well?" I say it lightly as though the thought has just occurred to me. I glance at him hesitantly and notice that the smile has dropped from his face. I pat my mare's neck gently to calm her and I stare straight ahead. I choose to ignore his petulant expression.

"It seems so terribly unfair," I continue, praying that he will not be angry with me or think of me as impertinent. "They have known such sorrow because of the actions of their mothers. Just as you have, My Lord! No one has suffered as much as you!"

I have already learned that flattery and sympathy are the only tactics to use with my husband if I want something.

"It strikes me as so unjust that these innocent children have been hurt because of the failings of these women." I shake my head solemnly. "These women who should have been their protectors!"

It is very easy to blame the dead, even when they are blameless as they cannot defend themselves. God forgive me, but I would never admit that to the King.

"These girls have suffered just as you have, My Lord. Just as you have lost your daughters, they have lost their father, and it is through no fault of their own. Just as it has been no fault of yours! But you can change that now. Leave the past behind, where it belongs. Do not deny them a father and a home. And, My Lord . . . do not deny them the love of a stepmother."

"Never." He mutters, pulling his hand from mine impatiently. He breathes deeply, clearly trying to control his temper. "Never will I allow the spawn of that witch into my home. Never will I allow her to pollute the sanctity of this court as her mother did."

He is of course speaking about Elizabeth. "Our parents are not of our choosing, My Lord." I keep my voice low and measured. I do not wish to ignite his volatile temper. "She is but a little girl! She will have no recollection of her mother. Why, she has been apart from that dreadful woman for the majority of her short life. She will remember nothing." The King juts his jaw forward in defiance at my words. I reach across and touch him gently on the arm. "I am only ever trying to think of you, My Lord, of your happiness."

"They are of the same heathen blood, Katherine —"

"She is of your blood, My Lord! And surely your blood is stronger than hers ever was. You are anointed by God no less! Does that not make your blood pure? There can be no trace left in the child after all this time. There will be nothing of that woman left in her."

"Mary, I will consider," he concedes, reluctantly. "But not Elizabeth! Never Elizabeth." He lowers his voice and looks at me. I can see that he is making a pained attempt to be conciliatory. "She is cared for very well, Katherine, I would never allow her to be treated with cruelty, but this you cannot ask of me. This is too much. I cannot be reminded of her mother! Of how she hurt me. Of how she almost ruined me."

I slide my outstretched hand from his elbow to his hand again. He raises his eyebrows. My assertiveness has clearly surprised him. "I am your wife now. I am the one who loves you. I am the wife who will never do you harm. I will never allow anyone to hurt you again."

He allows himself a small smile in response. He must wonder what on earth has come over me.

"But right now, My Lord," I continue, my blood suddenly rising as though the fate of the child is resting in my hands, "she is just a little girl. A frightened little girl; a little girl whom you once adored! Whom you took in your arms and loved with all your heart. She has done you no wrong, and yet she is separated from the only people who can truly love her: you, Mary,

Edward, and, My Lord, me! I will be her mother. I will be the influence that she must so desperately need."

He looks ahead; he does not want to listen to my words. I stare at his profile pointedly and wait until I have his attention once more.

As a heavy silence fills my ears, I realize how impassioned my words are, and how my tone has become nothing less than pleading. If only I could tell him how much I suddenly want to unite this family! I look away in embarrassment and will myself not to cry as my emotions unexpectedly get the better of me. Does he not understand what I am *truly* fighting for? *Who* I am truly fighting for? Can he not understand my desperate and irrepressible need for my own children? For better or worse, this is my only hope for a family.

"Like it or not," I say, "she is your daughter, and she bears the Tudor name. She is your heir."

I take a deep breath to steady myself and pray that I have not gone too far. His hand remains in mine although he does not reciprocate my grip. I lower my voice, feeling suddenly exhausted.

"There are no more corrupting influences here. There is just a good and decent family now, and I know that a family is what you all must desire. Not just your children, but you too. Tell me that it isn't true?"

The King shakes his head and offers me a reluctant smile. "You are certainly a most persuasive wife, Katherine, I'll give you that!" His face becomes serious and his hand finally grips mine. "For my sins I am a bitter man, I know that. I do not find this business easy.

God forgive me, but I do not know how I can forget the actions of her mother —"

"Of her mother, yes, but not her! Not Elizabeth's actions. Her mother's actions! No one expects you to ever forgive Anne. She was a dreadful, dangerous, wicked woman, but Elizabeth has done you no wrong. She is just a child. An innocent child who surely, My Lord, surely has been punished enough . . .?"

"I will give your suggestion thought, Katherine." His tone tells me that we have reached the end of the matter. "But I cannot promise anything, and I think that you must prepare yourself for disappointment. But for you, my dearest, I promise that I will give it thought."

CHAPTER
THREE

Most Dear and Beloved

Four months later . . .
Mary Tudor,
10 February 1544, Whitehall Palace

Is it a sin to pretend to love one's own family? Is it a sin to hate them? I don't know. Surely it cannot be a sin to question their motives and their judgement when their past actions tell us all too plainly that they are not to be trusted. No, the search for the truth is always justified, and is always in the interests of the Lord God. He has returned me to court, and so in His name I will watch them and I will study their every move. I will be the eyes and ears of the Holy Catholic Church and I will do everything in my power to ensure that no more sin is committed here. Not now and not ever.

Oh, but this feels so very wrong! If I am ordained to be here then why does this feel so unnatural; sitting here with them as though we are just an ordinary family? Does God really want me to join in with their pathetic pretence at being normal? No, of course He does not, for such pretence is a lie, and lying is a sin, no matter the reason. There can never be an excuse for

125

breaking one of His sacred commandments. Let us sin no more; let us stop pretending that this farce will ever heal old wounds. This charade will lead to nothing but greater heartbreak and even greater folly if my father has anything to do with it.

But I cannot reveal my reservations, not if I wish to remain at court. After all, it is where I belong. It is my God-given right to be here, as an heir to the Tudor throne; as the legitimate child of my father's first Queen. It is only a shame that it has taken so very long for him to finally come to his senses and invite me back. But I'm no fool, I realize that this is not really his doing and that it was only at the prompting of his latest wife; my old friend Katherine. My latest stepmother. Shame on him! This family reunion comes from *her* need for children of her own, and nothing more. I am no idiot, and neither will they treat me as such, for I know very well — just as well as she does — that whilst she is married to my father, this is the best that she will ever have. This is the closest thing to a family that God will ever allow her. Perhaps for my sins this is the closest thing to a family that He will ever allow me too. I must go to confession before I retire for the night and seek absolution if I am not to be damned.

"More wine, dear Mary?" Katherine raises the jug in my direction and smiles. Has she become a serving maid now as well as a Queen? I force myself to smile, and shake my head. I am grateful to her, of course I am, but I have no need for her to baby me. She is not the only person who has grown up during the years of my banishment. And I am not an invalid either. I do not need her protection, nor her care. My years alone have taught me to be independent; to be resilient and to take strength from God alone, just as my mother did when she too was cast aside.

"Oh, yes please!" I wince at the whiny voice that interrupts my thoughts. It comes from the mouth of that child who is sitting across the room from me. She is looking up at Katherine with that injured puppy face that she pulls. I can't help but smirk as I look at her, with her long red plaits and her fussy red gown. Red for sin. She will not say "no" to anyone, that one. She will just take, take, take; just as her mother did. I can barely bring myself to look at her; at that spawn of the whore who bewitched my father and sent my sainted mother and me into the wilderness. The rancid fruit of their sin.

"Mary, you look tired." The King catches my attention. He is trying to distract me from the abomination. He is perched on his great chair to the right of the child, with his hands resting on the vast mound of belly that protrudes so revoltingly in front of him. How can he bear to be so near that spawn of perdition? I shake my head and run my eyes across his body in disgust. When did he become so utterly grotesque? He is a beast and a glutton; an affront to God.

"I am perfectly well, thank you," I lie. "Just a little tired. I shall depart for my evening prayers shortly, Father." And there I will ask for the Lord's forgiveness.

He frowns like a spoiled child. He is acting as though I am about to ruin his fun. I frown back at him.

"You may join me, brother, if you wish," I say, turning my attention to Edward, who has chosen to sit on a cushion on the floor by my side in front of the fire. He has barely said a single word all evening. Is he ailing? I look at him with sadness, at the perfectly domed head, the fair ringlets and at the lace collar and cuffs. He too is a child born of our father, but unlike the girl, he is not a bastard.

"No, Edward will stay with us, thank you, Mary," the King answers quickly on his behalf. Damn him! He is so protective of that child. He treats him like an invalid. If only he had paid me just a shadow of that attention! I look at Edward again with sympathy. His little face has flushed a deep red and he has dropped his eyes to the floor as though he is about to weep. Dear God, what have they done to the boy?

I returned to court two weeks ago, at the request of my new stepmother. After so long, I was delighted to hear from her, as she and I were so very close when we were children. I have such vivid memories of her during those long, dark years, of how she tried to support and protect me. I also remember how she used to despise my father for all that he did to my mother and me, and for how he changed the lives of so many for the worse.

Her mother was my mother's lady-in-waiting, so she was privy to all the hurt he created, and just as her mother tried to support mine, she tried, in her own way, to support me. I was shocked when I discovered that they were to be married. No, *shocked* is too mild a word. I was horrified! Why did he not just take up with another trollop rather than force this ridiculous match with my friend. Is there nothing left for me? Oh, how I hate him!

I turn my head away so that he cannot see the fury in my eyes. Poor Katherine. I do not think that she wants to be his wife. I have watched her these past few weeks and I have seen how she winces at his touch and how she tenses in fear each time he approaches her. Of course, he is too stupid and pig-headed to notice it for himself, but I see her shiver with disgust at even the slightest show of affection. It is as though she is utterly repulsed by him. And yet, to her credit, she hides it well. I can only imagine what is going on inside that head of hers, for she will not tell me.

In many respects Katherine still seems much like the child I knew all those years ago. If I close my eyes I can see her as she was when she was forced to marry that wretched old man, Borough. He needed a nurse too, if I remember correctly, just like my father does, so it is no wonder that she is so adept at tending to him. To marry two decrepit invalids with a buffoon in the middle — if rumour is to be believed — how cruel life has been to her!

I have watched her carefully with my father and seen how cleverly she turns to debate and discussion when his words become amorous. Perhaps she did that with her first husband? Who knows? Her efforts are quite admirable in one respect, but disturbing in another. I know that she does it to distract him, but I do not like to hear some of the words that spill from her mouth, especially those that concern the Holy Church. She goes too far; way beyond the provocative, in my opinion. I have heard her speak heresy! What use to save her body from his touch if it costs her her soul? She should know that religion is not a subject for debate, and that truth is revealed through the Church alone. May God keep her safe and protect her from dangerous thoughts.

I take a deep breath. I cannot bear the silence a moment longer. *They* may all be putting on a pretence of affable comfort, with their lounging around on their snug chairs, huddled around the fire, reading their books and sipping their wine, but I am not fooled.

"My Lady —"

"*Katherine*," she corrects me firmly, looking across the room and smiling. "Always just *Katherine*, Mary. Just as we used to be." I watch as she turns her attention back to the children. "That goes for all of you. There is no formality here."

Fine, "Katherine . . ." I force myself to smile. "It is Sunday tomorrow. I trust that you will be attending Mass?"

"Of course, Mary. I never miss Mass."

Hmmm. That's not what I have heard. "Then you will take Holy Communion with me? As we did when we were children." I turn my gaze to my father, and I do not blink. "Long before you became Queen."

Katherine smiles and fingers the long string of pearls around her neck. She looks awkward all of a sudden. I knew it! Her own words have poisoned her! I have suspected her of holding Lutheran sympathies from the very first moment that I returned to court; from the very first moment I heard her questioning my father's religious views so brazenly. If you ask me, she is doing so much more than trying to distract him from his woes . . . and it has not gone unnoticed by others either.

"Perhaps, Mary," she smiles. "I will give it thought."

I knew it! "You do not wish to eat the body of Christ?" Her words astonish me. She must be challenged. It is my duty to the Church.

"Mary . . ." My father, the King, speaks to me. His voice is low. Why has he interrupted me? I have asked a perfectly ordinary question, have I not?

The witch's child looks up at our new stepmother and speaks: "Katherine, how does bread turn into the body of Christ? I have always wondered. My tutor never makes sense when he tries to explain it."

My eyes widen in horror at her blasphemous insinuation and I take a sharp intake of breath. I stare pointedly at the child. It is as if the Devil himself has entered the room. I allow my eyes to bore into that face and I don't care who sees it; it is the face of the whore, of that Anne, who destroyed my family and killed my mother. I take a deep breath and try to keep my voice measured for the sake of the boy.

"The Church tells us that it is a miracle," I tell her firmly. "That is all you need to know. Some things . . . some things should not be questioned. They should be accepted, as they do not require an explanation. We should not hope to understand the ways of the Almighty." I cross myself slowly, holding her gaze. "Lord forgive your childish ignorance."

She looks away from me and towards Katherine for the reassurance that she does not deserve. I do not take my eyes from the girl. Her blasphemy will not go unnoticed by me or the Lord.

The King begins to chuckle. "Not *question?*" He looks at Katherine, who blushes like a silly girl. "Oh, we question everything these days, Mary. Just you ask my wife! Why, I don't think that she has accepted anything in her entire life!" He roars at his stupid joke.

The child laughs along with him. How dare they mock me!

"Why, be it the sun or the moon or sky itself, Katherine will question it!" He tousles the girl's hair and I feel my stomach turn in horror. "And it looks as though Katherine is not the only one, hmmm?"

The girl beams at him. She looks as though she is about to burst with happiness. Katherine looks at me hesitantly. I can see that she is embarrassed, as she cannot hold my gaze. Well, of course she can't. She knows as well as I do that the mysteries of the Holy Church are anything but a joke. God forgive them all.

"Your stepmother," he continues, smiling at the girl warmly, "is really quite an intellectual in such matters. She certainly keeps me on my toes! Listen to her, children; she will teach you all well!"

He reaches towards Katherine and takes her hand in his. I notice Katherine recoil slightly at his touch, I am sure of it. Did nobody else see it?

"She has been the making of me, children. The making of me! I am already a new man thanks to her! And this . . ." he gestures to us all, "would never have been possible without my wife. She has helped me to recognize the error of my ways as far as you are all concerned. What do you think of that, children?"

Disgusting. That's what I think. Far too little; far too late. "The error of his ways". Ha! How perfectly insignificant and forgivable when put like that. I purse my lips together angrily. Why does he need to continually rub salt into the wound? Does he think that any of us wishes to hear this? I look at Edward to gauge his reaction. This charade can hardly please the poor damaged child. And yet, he is looking up at Katherine adoringly as though he too has accepted her as his new mother. I shake my head in dismay. Are they all smitten by her? I notice that Katherine's smile is anything but genuine as she looks into the eyes of her husband; I can see right through it. I can see my old friend in that face, even after all this time. I can still see the frightened child that I knew as she prepared for her first marriage. I am not fooled. She does not like my father one bit.

Three months later . . .
Thomas Wriothesley,
26 May 1544, Whitehall Palace

The sight makes me sick to my stomach. That heretical woman tending to His Majesty's ailments and acting as though it were a labour of love. Ha! Well if you ask me, being a nursemaid is all that she is good for. She's certainly not fit to be a Queen, so God only knows why he chose her. I could have told him that the first moment I set my eyes on her nasty pinched face, for I knew that she was going to be trouble. Let her nurse him if it makes him happy, but her simpering ways and that stupid smile will never fool me. I will watch that woman with a cunning that a wily fox would be proud of.

I inspect the state of my hands; anything to take my eyes from this sickening display of wifely modesty. I frown at my imperfect nails. Well this won't do at all; perhaps I will ask Phillip to file them for me later . . . A smile creeps across my face at the mere thought of my manservant. Perhaps filing my nails is not all that I shall ask of him tonight.

I glance back at the King and his wife. Even from the other side of the chamber, I can see that he is looking better than he has in a long while. No longer is he propped up in his bed like an ailing, oversized cow, and nor is he wheezing or wincing every time he moves. At least he is now able to sit in a chair, with his back straight, as a King should. He appears really quite contented. His wife is kneeling before him, toying with his leg ulcers as though they were bejewelled pieces in an enchanting game. In the dim light I can see her simpering face as she dabs at his wounds with a wet cloth. I watch with horror as a dirty liquid trickles through the revolting mess of his leg and into the pot that rests beneath his foot. I sneer at her efforts. I am not fooled by her forgery; nobody can take the pleasure she claims from tending him as she does. Why does she have to do that now anyway? It is such a hideous sight. Not to mention the stench. She can do it as often as she likes, but she really ought to show a little consideration when it comes to the stomachs of important men like me.

Where is that damn Gardiner? There are urgent matters to discuss this evening. *She* had better hurry up too, so that we men can be alone and free from distraction. Affairs of state are certainly not meant for her ears. I frown, and try to think of how I might suggest to His Majesty that his wife should be excused. Lord only knows how to approach him, for he has never been one to accept instruction from others, and especially not when it comes to that woman.

It is strange how he is with her; at times he seems to forget himself and acts like an obedient puppy pleasing its master. It's only when he remembers that he is the man that he puts her back where she belongs: under his thumb. As he ought. From the way that he is humming and gazing at her, I would say that it is going to be difficult to persuade him to banish her in a hurry.

I sigh quietly and fold my arms, and try to enjoy the warmth of the fire that is rippling across my back. What is the point of being the Lord Chancellor if I cannot have control over matters as trivial as this? Queen or no Queen, she should do as I say. So why is it that I dare not utter a word to her in His Majesty's presence?

I watch them as they whisper to each other in hushed voices as though they are deliberately trying to exclude me. Damn rude! I drum my fingers impatiently against the fireplace and turn to look out of the window. I can see little of anything outside as it has suddenly grown dark. I instructed the Bishop to join us at a precise hour of the clock, and the delay in his arriving suggests more than impertinence. I cannot bear delay, especially now that I am forced to endure their intimate whisperings.

There is a sharp tap on the door and the Bishop is quickly ushered in by a guard. He is wearing the sour expression that he always wears. With his downturned mouth, his features are as joyless as ever. He strides towards the King, his scarlet robes billowing behind him, and kneels. The King acknowledges him with a quick nod of his head and his wife turns to do the same. The cheek of her, acting as though the display of devotion was for her! The Bishop rises and walks across the room to greet me.

"Sir Thomas. Or should I say *Lord Chancellor!*" he gushes fondly using my new title, and I dip my head in return. The Bishop and I are trusted colleagues. I would even go so far as to say that we are friends, and that is not a term I use lightly. The Bishop shares the same values and pious beliefs, and wholeheartedly endorses everything that I have sought to do, including my decision to watch that woman and record her feelings for a later date. As a result, I have a great deal of respect for the man. Now *that* is not a word I use often either. It is a great relief that finally the Kingdom is in the hands of good men such as myself and the Bishop, for it has been a long time coming. Not to mention painful. The people should think themselves very damn lucky indeed.

"I trust that she is not to remain?" He talks under his breath and jerks his head in the direction of Her Majesty. His jowls quiver with distaste. I glance at the repulsive sight and then back again at Gardiner.

"Your guess is as good as mine, My Lord Bishop." I shrug and sigh. "I expect that she will need to be *told* to leave, by one of us, no doubt. I think that His Majesty is in one of his affectionate moods."

We turn towards the couple and I try my best to contain my growing nausea. It does not look as though she is in any hurry to leave at all, and neither does it look as though His Majesty wishes her to. Perhaps I should take matters into my own hands? After all, I did not rise this high in court through indecision. I stroll across the room as casually as I can and bow to the King.

"Your Majesty," I gush, "forgive me, but as Bishop Gardiner has now arrived, we must attend to the important matters at hand. I do wonder, Your Grace, whether these are matters that are suitable for the delicate ears of a lady . . .?" I glance down at Katherine and smile widely, willing her to look up at me. I am certain that she will be clever enough to read the warning in my eyes and take the hint. She raises her head but she does not meet my gaze. She chooses to look at her husband instead. I watch as she smiles expectantly and waits for instruction.

"Nonsense!" His Majesty booms. "My wife shall be included in the discussions. The girl can debate as well as you and I can, Wriothesley!" He reaches down and clumsily tousles her hair. "Perhaps even better, eh?"

"Of course, Your Majesty." My voice is as sweet as honey. I turn my head to glance at Gardiner and screw my face up with disgust. He looks back at me with a noticeably defeated expression, and shrugs. It seems that there is nothing that either of us can do about this damn woman tonight.

"Get yourselves seated then, gentlemen, if you want to get started. There is no time like the present!" The King waves his arms towards the chairs and beckons for us to join him.

I grit my teeth with irritation. If we must discuss these matters in front of a woman then so be it. Let's just hope that she does not dare utter a word when I am speaking or she will be sorry. I look down at her, sitting on a cushion on the floor with her back to me, pawing at his revolting wounds. The King may choose to blind himself but I will not be fooled. And neither, I'm sure, will Gardiner.

But then ... oh foolish man! Perhaps I have misjudged the situation! If she *does* have a ready tongue and will use it in debate, then perhaps I can goad her into saying something that she might regret; and in front of His Majesty too! Now, the King does not know it yet, but each of the matters at hand concerns religion and religious heretics, and if she *is* a hot-headed reformist as rumour would have me believe then it is unlikely that she will be able to keep her thoughts to herself. Ha! And I know that Gardiner, ever astute, will be listening for any slip of her tongue, as he too will be keen to snap the snare shut at the first possible opportunity. Perhaps this will be more entertaining than I had first thought.

I pull my heavy chair to His Majesty's side, and carefully position myself so that I can watch

Katherine's face. If she so much as blinks then I will know about it. The Bishop pulls his chair across the room until it is next to mine. I take a deep breath, and try to proceed as I normally would; as though this were any other meeting in the King's presence chamber between men.

"Your Majesty, if I may begin?" I lean forward and raise my eyebrows expectantly for confirmation. He nods impatiently, as though it is I who have delayed matters.

"Your Majesty, it has come to my attention that a number of translated Bibles have been found in various residences across London. We think that we can identify the perpetrators, and so with your permission, Your Majesty, I would like to ensure that they receive a painful stint in the Tower as a just punishment . . . at the very least." The King strokes his beard and nods again.

"Seems reasonable, Wriothesley. Can't have these damn sympathizers taking religion into their own hands, what? Next!"

My, that was easy! I can't help but smile. I feel no small amount of pride when His Majesty shows me that he trusts my judgement. I open my mouth to announce the next topic, but I am suddenly interrupted by the high-pitched voice of that woman.

"Forgive me, Your Majesty." She looks at us all in turn before resting her gaze on me. "Sir Thomas, I cannot help but question the necessity of the punishment here, for I feel that everybody should have the opportunity to read the word of the Lord, should they not? God loves us all equally, I am sure of it, and yet there are only a few of us who are entrusted to read His words."

I open my mouth to respond, but she interrupts me before I am able to begin.

"I understand that a priest of the Holy Church is the best person to teach us the word of the Lord, but surely there are times when people may need guidance to remind themselves of the words of scripture when they are not in church, and perhaps are in their own homes. These people who you seek to punish, Sir, isn't this all that they have been doing? Is that such a crime? Surely, Sir, you do not seek to deny them of the right to remedy a poor memory and avoid the sin of erroneous belief, and wander from the teachings of the Church?

"Forgive my impertinence, but I cannot help but feel that this is a right that all men should be allowed to exercise freely for the sake of their souls."

I watch her face as she speaks with such passion. The Devil is in that woman! I do not respond, and neither does Gardiner. Neither of us had prepared ourselves for such an outburst! I almost laugh out loud as I wait for His Majesty to reprimand her for uttering these foolish words. I am certain that he will not allow her to get away with this. His Majesty begins to chuckle.

"You forget, wife, that we are talking about ordinary people here, and the ordinary people are illiterate! They would be unable to read the holy word of God even if it was available to all and sundry!"

I purse my lips to suppress my delight as I watch his wife lower her head in embarrassment.

"Not everybody is as educated as you are, my dear!"

I look up at the King in sudden disbelief. Has he just complimented her? He should be reprimanding her, for she has openly and unashamedly challenged the primacy of the Church in front of two of his most senior ministers. Her words are nothing short of Lutheran, for God's sake! What is the matter with the man?

She raises her head abruptly and looks him in the eye. "Perhaps that is true, My Lord."

Is she really still speaking? I cannot believe my ears. Isn't it enough that the King has just disagreed with her? I watch her with growing interest as the hole that she is digging for herself grows deeper and deeper.

"But there are many ordinary people who have a rudimentary grasp of the written word —"

"Oh yes! Yes, that is right!" He snorts loudly, rightly interrupting her. "Wriothesley, listen to this!" He looks at me and waves his fat hand in the direction of his wife. "A *rudimentary grasp*, no less!"

I laugh along with His Majesty, thoroughly enjoying the Queen's discomfort. It seems that she is not as intelligent as she thinks. His Majesty continues to chuckle and becomes more animated as the moments pass.

"Listen to this; I can just see it! Look, *there* he is! *Look*, Katherine! It's old Farmer Shit-tosser from the bogs of Devonshire. Can you see him, wife? Can you?" He pauses as he is barely able to breathe for laughing. "Let's watch him as he studies the Gospel or a letter from Saint Paul! Goodness, doesn't it make a nice change from pulling up his mangel-wurzles or fucking his pig!"

His great voice booms with laughter and he grabs his shaking belly with both hands. I glance at his wife, keen to gauge her reaction, hoping that she now feels as embarrassed and ashamed of her ridiculous assertion as she ought. I am dismayed, though, to see that she is smiling at the King, and it isn't long before she too collapses into fits of giggles. His Majesty roars even louder in response.

I try to chuckle along despite myself, but it is forced and unnatural. How dare they act as though the Holy Church is some filthy joke fit only for the lowest tavern? I glance at Gardiner, who is not even trying to pretend. His eyes are wide in astonishment and his mouth more downturned than ever. I sink back in my chair. It is no good; thanks to His Majesty's repulsive humour, Katherine's words are now forgotten. But we still have other matters to discuss.

"Your Majesty, if we may continue?" I ask politely as his laughter recedes to a rumbling chortle. He nods reluctantly but does not take his eyes from his wife; he continues to smile at her as though she is a prized foal. I force myself to ignore this revolting spectacle. "Your Majesty, about their punishment . . .?"

"Next!" he bellows. "I'm sick of this Bible nonsense."

I take a deep breath and quickly turn my attention to the next matter. "Your Majesty, the Church has rightfully requested that some of the riches stolen from the monasteries by Cromwell are returned to their rightful place." This should be straightforward. His Majesty frowns and rubs his beard again.

"Not as easy as that, man," he declares.

I look at Katherine, who is busily bandaging His Majesty's leg. Thank God for that. About time that foetid thing is hidden away. I wonder if she will dare speak her mind about this as well?

"The former property of the Church was sold, Wriothesley, as you well know, and much of the money has been spent fighting the damn Scots! And not to mention arming the troops for Boulogne, and building new ships."

Of course I knew that, but I am certain that the crafty Cromwell must have squirreled a large portion away for himself. But Cromwell is still a touchy subject with His Majesty even after all these years, and so I wonder if I should dare pursue the matter? Suddenly that voice pipes up again.

"Your Majesty, the actions of Cromwell were indeed so very wrong, but I wonder why it is that the Church needs such great riches when its function is to communicate with God. If there are riches that have not yet been spent, then I wonder if perhaps this should go directly to the poor? Surely, Your Majesty, the purpose of the Church is to guard the souls of the people and to ensure their safe passage to Heaven. I cannot understand why it is that they would need great riches for that. A wrong has been committed against them, that is for sure, but surely they will understand if we choose to spend their money on something more urgent?"

My mouth gapes open involuntarily at the sheer audacity . . .

"But, wife," His Majesty holds her gaze intently.

Hurrah! She is going to be put in her place at last!

"Our Church is a celebration of the Lord, and of our love and devotion to Him, yes? Then the Church has the right to celebrate using the wealth that they have collected! It would make a very miserable celebration if there wasn't anything nice to look at, now wouldn't it?" He raises his eyebrows questioningly, as if he wants her to debate the issue with him. Gardiner and I sit in stunned silence. This is *not* a debating matter! Katherine sits back on her heels and purses her lips.

"Communication with God should be a simple affair, My Lord. It should not be hampered by trinkets and gold."

I can't help but gasp. Who does she think she is, referring to the magnificence of the Church as such? Dismissing the donations of centuries! She must have heard my sharp intake of breath but she chooses to ignore it.

"Do you think that He would be impressed by opulent and unnecessary displays of wealth? Surely not! Did our Saviour not live a simple life? For what purpose were riches to Him?" Her voice begins to rise. "If anything, it cheapens His love for us!"

His Majesty smiles and places his hand on her shoulder to calm her. She needs a lot more than that if you ask me.

"My love, the poor and ordinary people like to see riches from time to time. Just as you do! It gives them an opportunity to escape from their miserable and mundane lives. I have always thought that it must offer them a taste of heaven itself!"

Gardiner and I smile at each other. His Majesty certainly has a flare for debate, and thankfully, when the need arises, he is more than capable of speaking sense. Well, sometimes . . .

"Forgive me, My Lord," she continues, with as much certainty as before, "but surely, all it does is remind the poor of how miserable their own lives are, and of what it is that their rents are spent on. Do you think that, while the people starve to death, they would be pleased to see the priests dining from golden plates and furnishing their rooms as though they are palaces?" She shakes her head. "If you ask me, the money would be better spent going straight to the poor."

Well no one *is* asking you, are they! I watch with growing dismay as His Majesty simply smirks and sits back in his chair. He looks defeated, but strangely not perturbed at being so. Taking this as a sign to end the conversation, his wife turns back to her task and finishes bandaging his leg. I try my best to ignore the satisfied look on her smug, ugly face. How can he allow her to get away with this insubordination?

I clear my throat and turn to Gardiner for direction. He nods gravely and gestures for me to continue. I cannot concentrate any more. Gardiner and I are worth a hundred of her, and we are being made to feel as though we are intruders on a private debate. I grit my teeth and will myself to continue as normal. The sooner this is all over, the better, as it is certainly not going to plan.

"I have heard talk, Your Majesty, of forbidden texts being read ... here in court, and without your permission." Surely this will get him riled. Surely he will want to take immediate and serious action if this is happening right under his nose. I look at him, a smile playing at the corners of my mouth. And if the rumours are true about her, and her own reading habits, then I expect that she is beginning to sweat a little by now.

"Hmph. Well I suppose there is nothing wrong with a little healthy debate, Wriothesley. Christ, man, any straighter and you'd be a plank of wood!"

I wince at this insult. I do not take kindly to any form of humiliation and especially not in front of an audience. It is very lucky that it is the King who has irritated me. Had it been anyone else then I would not have been able to contain my wrath.

"Your Majesty, forgive me but perhaps you have misunderstood my meaning. By forbidden texts, I mean forbidden religious texts. All dark sedition and wilful heresy. Surely you cannot allow this? They challenge the divine order of things and go against the teachings of the Holy Church itself! Anybody possessing such filth should be punished!" I lean forward in my chair and hold his gaze for emphasis. His Majesty returns my stare coldly as though I have insulted him by arguing this point. I bite down hard on my lip as Katherine suddenly looks up.

146

"My Lord, the Holy Church should not fear such words. They merely provide an opportunity to demonstrate the wiser council of the Bishops of Rome."

I hear Gardiner snorting at this, which he tries to disguise by coughing loudly. I desperately want to argue with her, but how can I do so without insulting the King? How can I reprimand her, as I should be more than entitled to do, for this diabolical and unholy talk? Besides, I should not *have* to. The King should do so himself. At the very least he should recognize her heretical words for what they are.

"Oh, I do not think that the Holy Church has anything to prove, dearest."

Thank the Lord, for finally he can see sense and is choosing to correct her. Finally, the man has developed a backbone.

She shakes her head. "But the Church seems adamant that they should stifle any kind of discussion, My Lord. How can we ever progress if we accept without truly understanding, and do not question or challenge anything? Surely that is the key?"

I listen to her with amazement. It is as if she truly believes that she possesses a superior intelligence and a divine right to challenge the most powerful monarch in Christendom. She is talking as though she is Saint Peter himself!

"Some in the Church have tried to stifle progress in all manner of things, My Lord," she continues. "In medicine and with science."

"Ah, but, my love, healing is the work of the Lord. It is a miracle! Why would the Church need to debate what should be a matter of faith?"

His Majesty gives a satisfied smile. I look at her pointedly, willing her to just shut up if she is not going to incriminate herself.

"The reason that the Church stifles debate is because of some fear that it will challenge their authority when it merely challenges their notions of the truth, and yet there *must* be alternatives! It is they who would keep us in a darkened and unenlightened state." She gestures to his legs again. "What have the priests done to heal you of your ailments, My Lord? Your ulcers are improving only through my perseverance, and my experimentation with the new techniques that I have dared read about in books that the Lord Chancellor will tell me are forbidden!"

I roll my eyes with impatience. Damn her for so openly trying to discredit me. His Majesty grunts in response and shakes his head. He does not respond and so I can only assume that he is unwilling to argue with her. I dig my nails into the palms of my hands in frustration. How can he not realize that if he does not control her unholy outbursts, then she will poison his mind and turn the Kingdom into a heathen mess of dirty Protestant filth?

I wonder whether there is any point in discussing the last topic on my agenda. Because of her presence we have been completely unable to resolve any of the other matters, and her outbursts have proven to be of little consequence either. I feel enraged by both her and the King, and defeated all at that same time. It is preposterous that I should feel this way at the hands of a mere woman! I turn to Gardiner with raised eyebrows. What does he think we should do now?

Suddenly Katherine rises from her position on the floor — where she belongs — and makes her way to the back of His Majesty's chair. She has finished tending to his leg, but rather than leave the room she chooses to remain, and rests her hands on his shoulders. I can't help but shoot her a look of disdain. How dare she stand above us? His Majesty moves his hand to rest on hers. I can see that she has no intention of going anywhere.

"Is that all, men? Haven't got all bloody night!" His Majesty suddenly barks, startling me.

Gardiner speaks in his deep, slow, rattling voice. "The matter of these texts is something that we must take very seriously, Your Maj —"

"Enough! We've spoken about that. It's undecided. There are arguments for and against discussion. You have heard them both, Bishop. Next!"

The Bishop sighs heavily and makes a point of rubbing his temples as if he is in pain. "Of course, Your Majesty. The final matter then. People have been caught eating meat on a Friday again. It has been going on for a while now, as you know. I think that you will agree that this is a grave breach of our holy customs."

We both look at His Majesty, keen to gauge his reaction. Nothing can challenge this sacred doctrine, surely? And nobody could get away with trying to either.

His Majesty nods. "Indeed, customs that are dear to the Holy Church should not be deviated from. I think that a very harsh punishment is in order here."

I cannot help but smile at this. Sense at last. Let her try to contradict him just one more time if she dares, for we all know that there is only so far that His Majesty can bend before he breaks.

"Forgive me, Bishop." She speaks again. "I can't help but wonder sometimes, for what purpose are these customs?"

"Your Majesty . . . " Suddenly the Bishop can hold his tongue no longer. "These are hollowed by time and the grace of the Church." His voice is undeniably grave.

"I can't help but think that they have no basis or justification these days."

She looks down at Gardiner from behind His Majesty. I do not like this position of power that she has placed herself in. She has done it deliberately.

"My Lord Bishop, I do not wish to challenge you, but why do you think that God would think this is such a great sin? What punishment could ever be justified for this small act when the world is already so full of evil and vile acts?"

"*Small* act . . ." I scoff. It is all that I can do not to laugh out loud at her impertinence. Why, if she were not damning herself so spectacularly then I would have to leave the room!

"Yes, Sir Thomas. Just think; if one were starving to death, and found a morsel of meat on a day that happened to be a Friday, do you think the Lord would punish him for eating it rather than insist that he die?"

Gardiner turns to me; his jaw has dropped in amazement at her affront. These are the words of Lucifer! Luckily His Majesty sees fit to interrupt before Gardener says anything that he might come to regret. He turns to look at his wife.

"Katherine, our Lord was crucified on a Friday. It is a day of fasting and prayer. Our customs are dear and sacred to the Holy Church. They keep the fabric of society together. They instil order and discipline in the lives of the ordinary people!" He pats her hand affectionately as though she is an unruly young horse that needs gentle persuasion.

"But, My Lord, for many ordinary people *every* day is a fast. They hunger so! Why punish them further for a custom? They are simple people. You said so yourself. How did you describe them? As *knowing* their pigs . . .?" She looks at all three of us as she says this but His Majesty is the first to respond.

"Nonsense! The Church is everything to the poor. It is their source of entertainment, it provides them with festivals and traditions, and more importantly redemption and salvation. Katherine, it offers charity and education such as they would never receive! Not everyone is subject to a court education as you once were! Many of the monks act as physicians in the rural villages. Is that so very corrupt? It is the main source — perhaps the only source — of support that they have, and these customs are an integral part of that."

He removes his hand from hers and folds his arms across his chest in anger. I try to suppress my growing smile. I can see that finally, he is well and truly tired of her ridiculous outbursts. Even so, she does not seem to be deterred in the slightest. Let her continue; let her go too far.

"The Church may offer temporal support and may distract them from the misery of their ordinary lives, My Lord, but it is too . . . controlling! It seems to me that the Church is quicker to threaten punishment than offer forgiveness. Punishing the poor for eating meat if they are lucky enough to find some is not Christian behaviour! It is not even justified!"

I sit back and run my hands along the length of my perfectly groomed beard. This is finally becoming interesting. On top of everything else, she is now daring to reprimand the King!

"You can leave us now, wife." He shrugs her hands from his shoulders. I watch with enormous satisfaction as her face falls and as her eyes well up with tears. Stupid girl. She curtseys to him and walks out of the chamber in haste.

Three months later . . .
HRH, Queen Katherine Tudor,
12 August 1544, Oakham Castle, Rutland

Edward gasps loudly with delight as the falconer carefully lifts the small, plumed hood from the bird's head, revealing a pair of bright and intelligent eyes. His hand squeezes mine with nervous excitement, and I find myself beaming with happiness. I can't help but feel blissfully contented today; it is as though I have become a different person overnight, with not a care in the world. Can anything surpass being outside, in the heart of the countryside on a beautifully warm summer's day such as this? I think not. Truly nothing at all! Oh how I have longed to be far, far away from the filth and the pomp of London for so long; far away from all those dreadful, deferential people, and back in the North where I belong! It is only a shame that it has taken a most savage outbreak of the plague and an unnecessary war abroad to permit me this brief and joyful respite.

"Where did the bird come from, Sir? Did you breed it yourself?" Elizabeth inquires, looking up at the falconer, wide-eyed and excited. Always so full of questions. I smile with pride as she wraps her arm around mine. Sometimes her agreeable affection makes me feel as though she is my very own daughter.

"He's from Holland, Your Grace. I travelled there myself to buy him several months ago. I've been working on him for the Earl, so that he can be ready for hunting when the season begins."

I hear Mary sighing with impatience from behind me and I try my best to ignore her. If only she could, just for once, try to enjoy herself; if not for her own sake then for that of the children. It is not often that we can be together like this, away from our duties at court, and it is not often that we can be completely free from the unpredictability of the King either.

★ ★ ★

153

I have been staying with the Earl and Countess of Rutland for the past two weeks in their castle in rural Leicestershire. Fortunately it has been possible to take my stepchildren with me, which has given me the opportunity to really get to know them, unhampered by court restrictions and etiquette, and without the risk of interference or unpleasantness. We are, of course, accompanied by a large train of staff, who are always at hand to minister to our every need, but this is nothing compared to the life that I have grown accustomed to back in London. Here, we are afforded a degree of privacy to be ourselves, almost as though we were any other family enjoying each other's company and making the most of the pleasures that the summer brings.

My husband set sail for Boulogne in early July to quell a French uprising against the English. He has been in much better health of late, and so decided that he would lead the army himself. Shortly before he left, he made the rather unexpected announcement that I would be Regent, and that I would be held responsible for making all of the important royal decisions in his absence. It was a most surprising and touching honour; one that I would never have anticipated and one that, for the very first time, made me feel as though I might actually want to be Queen. Naturally the Privy Council was suspicious, and doubted my competence and experience, but my husband was quite insistent.

Shortly after he set sail from Dover, there was a virulent outbreak of the plague in London. I needed no further excuse to leave the city, and so gathered all of

154

my most trusted staff together and set off for the safety of the country. And so with our cavalcade of heavily laden wagons we travelled north under my command and set up our own court there; almost as though we were embarking on our very own summer progress! As Regent, I was perfectly entitled to take my stepchildren with me. God forbid anything happened to any of them on my watch.

"What is that around its foot?" Edward inquires, pointing at the leather cord that binds the bird to the falconer's gloved hand.

"This is so he don't go flying off, young Prince, and —"

"Don't you *want* him to fly off?" interrupts Elizabeth forcefully, "and catch things?"

"Only when I say so, Your Grace."

The falconer walks a few paces away from us and towards a low perch in the middle of the lawn. He tips his hand and the bird jumps obediently down. The moment it settles, it turns its body and looks up at him expectantly, waiting patiently for instruction. We all watch in awe as the young bird remains exactly where it has been placed whilst the man returns to us.

"Ready, children?" he asks. "I shall call the bird, and all being well he will fly back to me, and not off into those trees over there."

"It can't fly off; it is tethered to you," Elizabeth protests. I try not to smile at her impatience and gently nudge her in the elbow so that she will remain quiet. I feel Edward's body tense in anticipation as the falconer turns to face his bird. Even I am excited to see how well

155

it will respond, and I have seen a falconer at work on many occasions.

He gives a long slow whistle, and the bird spreads its great wings and thrusts his body effortlessly into the air. Edward jumps behind me in fear as it silently swoops towards us and circles above our heads. I too can't help but jump a little at the quiet rush of its wing feathers as it glides elegantly past my face. The falconer walks a few paces towards the bird and raises his gloved arm. The bird swoops towards him, and with barely a jolt it lands squarely and effortlessly as instructed. We all clap with delight at such a graceful acrobat, and much to my delight I find that even Mary cannot help herself from joining in. The falconer lowers his arm until the bird is level with my waist.

"Your Grace, Sir, you can stroke him if you like?" He looks expectantly at Edward.

My eyes widen with concern at the thought of the future King of England being so very close to something that might harm him. I hold my hand out instinctively to keep the bird away. It is as if the weight of my husband's trust has suddenly descended upon me, and I feel foolish and irresponsible for allowing Edward to be so close to this dangerous beast. I look down at the great beak and at the long talons that pierce into the man's thick leather glove, and shudder. I shake my head at the falconer, refusing his offer, imagining the damage that could so easily occur . . . No, I cannot permit even closer contact. I cannot allow even greater risk.

"No, thank you," I tell him firmly. "That won't be necessary." I look down at Edward, who is standing behind me, peering around my side at the bird with a look of wonderment. He lowers his head to the floor the moment he catches my eye as though he has been scolded.

"Katherine, he wants to stroke the bird." Suddenly Mary finds her voice. "Father is in France. We won't tell."

"Oh, he's used to people, Your Grace," the falconer tries to assure me. "He's been through the manning period."

I smile politely in response, even though I do not entirely understand what he has just said.

"Oh, yes, Mother, do let him. He so wants to touch his feathers, don't you Edward?"

I look down at Elizabeth and find myself smiling. I do love to hear her call me Mother. Why, I would do anything for that child when she calls me that.

I lower my body until my head is level with Edward's, and sigh. He looks so small and broken all of a sudden; as though I have cruelly reprimanded him for wanting to do something that is so very normal. So perfectly childlike. I shake my head at his small dejected form and wonder what on earth has been done to him by those men who are entrusted to care for him. How have they managed to break his spirit so?

"Do you want to stroke the bird?" I ask him gently, trying to reason with myself. Trying to force myself to see sense. It is just a bird, for heaven's sake.

Edward shrugs his shoulders slightly as if suddenly he does not care. Still he refuses to meet my gaze.

"If you would like to stroke the falcon, my darling, then, if you are very careful, you may."

"But Papa . . .?" he whispers, looking up at me sadly.

"Papa won't know a thing," I whisper back. "It will be our little secret."

We all watch as he begins to smile. He looks up hesitantly, fearing that we might change our minds or that we might be toying with him. Carefully he reaches around me towards the bird and runs his small fingers across its long, smooth wing. His face is a picture of concentration; he is frightened of upsetting the animal by his touch.

"He likes that, young Prince," the falconer chuckles. "You seem to have a way with him."

Edward grins as though not a greater compliment could have been paid and places his hand in mine. He looks up and quietly thanks me. Poor little boy. I can't help but feel ashamed at my initial reluctance. Why, he looks happier than I have ever seen him; more like a child than a prince.

12 days later . . .
HRH, Queen Katherine Tudor,
24 August 1544, Greenwich Palace

If only we could have stayed in the country. If only we could spend every day riding in the clean fresh air, playing tennis and watching the falconer train his birds. But the plague has abated, which I know I should be grateful for, and so we had no other choice but to return. Wriothesley was the first to remind me in his patronizing way that I have a Kingdom to run and, as Regent, I knew that I could hardly argue with that.

Sadly, my dearest Edward has left us to pursue his studies among the men whom the King entrusts to care for him, but thankfully, Mary and Elizabeth have remained in my household under my care. I will miss my darling Edward more than I had ever imagined that I would, almost as though, in the short time that I have known him, he has become my own little boy. I would like to think that he enjoyed his time with me, and that in my care he felt a little less like a prince and a little more like a boy.

I do my best to find a comfortable position at my desk. As hard as I try to concentrate, however, I cannot help myself from gazing absentmindedly out onto the beautiful ornate palace gardens. Who put this desk here anyway? Stupid place! It is impossible to focus! It seems that no matter how hard I try to compose a letter to my husband, I cannot think of the words to write. Already, he has written two letters to me, and now I feel that I have no other choice but to reply. My reluctance makes me feel rather ashamed of myself; after all, he has been bravely fighting the enemy these past few months whilst I have been doing little more than indulging my own pleasures.

I sigh heavily and drum my fingers on the parchment. My husband writes such gushing and unnecessary words of love and devotion that he leaves me feeling uncomfortable and confused. It is as though he is writing to someone else; to a beloved sweetheart that I am most certainly not and never have been. Still he insists on demonstrating his love for me as his feelings intensify with every passing day; and still he insists on referring to me as "his most dear and beloved". For some reason he must feel that I have earned that praise.

I must admit that my feelings have changed towards him, but only insofar that once I was cold and bitter, and now I am merely cautious. Less terrified. But as for love . . . well, that is an emotion that I had never expected to feel for him and one that I am absolutely certain I never will. It would be quite impossible. I have without doubt softened towards him over the past year, there's no denying that, and I might even go as far as to say that at times I enjoy his company when he is in the right mood. He has a quick and lively mind, and an eager thirst for knowledge that I find appealing, but I could never fool myself into thinking that this is or ever could be anything that might resemble affection.

But still, he has made me Regent, and showers me with compliments and accolades that I do not deserve. How trusting of him to bestow such a privilege on me, and to allow me such complete responsibility for his own children — for his own beloved Edward. If only I could allow myself to soften a little more towards him; to care for him as he cares for me. Would that be so very hard to do?

I lean back in my chair and close my eyes, well aware that it can never be. My pride will never allow it. Not after everything that he stole from me. I have and I will continue to do my best to be a dutiful and obedient wife, and I will try to be a most *useful* Queen, just as my royal motto dictates. But never love ... No, that will not be an option, even if my heart was free for the taking.

I shall force myself to respond with gushing words or he will think me ungrateful. I do not want him to imagine that anything might be amiss. I must admit that despite my reservations I do not like to think of him on the battlefield, suffering with an unrequited love. It is strange because still I resent him so very much for choosing me as his sixth Queen, and I still feel that I owe him nothing. And yet, somehow, I feel utterly in his debt.

I grab the quill, and scratch the ink forcefully across the heavy parchment. I bite down on my lip as the insincere words flow from my pen in a torrent. I tell him that I miss him, that I love him dearly as only a wife could, and that I cannot wait until he returns. I tell him that the Kingdom is nothing without his being here, and that his children love and miss him as much as I do. I grit my teeth in shame as I tell him that I count the days until he returns, knowing all the while that his absence has given me the only happiness that I have known since the day that we were married. When I can think of nothing else to say I end my ramblings by signing my name in a flowery and childlike manner that I am certain he will like. I refer to myself as his *most dear and beloved wife* just as he has referred to me. There! Letter written. My undying love and devotion has been expressed without restraint. God forgive me.

161

Six weeks later . . .
Robert Caskell, Groom of the Stool,
5 October 1544, Whitehall Palace

I gulp heavily to suppress an urge to vomit. It is one thing helping His Majesty to do his business and dispose of it afterwards, but quite another to inspect it for the purposes of medicine. Still, anything to ensure that he is in good health, I suppose, and who am I to argue with science! Besides, who else can say that they are so trusted as to be given such access to the fruits of the royal bowel? Very few, that's who. Just me and the physicians. But even so, I can't help but wince as I reach into the chamber pot and wrap my fingers around the softly formed stool. It is essential that I do not to break it if I am to examine it properly.

I carefully lower it onto a small plate and lean forward to take a closer look. The physicians have told me exactly what I should be searching for. They are the real experts, and they have explained to me everything that I need to know in detail, as *nothing* they say, can describe a man's health better than his daily movements.

I can already tell just from the feel of it that the consistency is as it should be. Quite unlike some of the stools that I have had the honour of examining in the past! Why, in recent years His Majesty has evacuated all manner of horrors, from tiny hard black pebbles through to a nasty brown water; neither of which I would like to see again in a hurry! The poor man has had no end of problems in his fundament and I more than anyone can testify to that.

I frown as I try to describe the precise colour of the almost perfectly formed sausage that is lying before me. Chestnut brown, I would say. Or walnut brown, perhaps? It is essential that I describe it perfectly to the doctors. Perhaps it should be a shade darker? But who am I to grumble, for I have seen them as pale as chalk before, and even I know that that isn't good.

I hesitantly lower my head a little further and force myself to take a deep, lung-filling sniff, just as I have been instructed to do. Ugh . . . the smell is nothing short of offensive, but it is not the worst that I have smelt by any stretch of the imagination. I know the smell of infection by now, and thank God, this clearly isn't infected.

I brace myself and plunge my forefinger deep into the stomach of the stool. I wriggle it around a little until it is broken into small pieces. One by one I lift the chunks in the air, squashing them between my thumb and forefinger. Although, by anybody's reckoning, this is deeply unpleasant, I have been taught that it is vital if I am to properly inspect the consistency. Consistency is everything, apparently. Hmmm . . . it is a little lumpy, perhaps, in parts, but not horribly so, and it is certainly well formed. And the lumps are very small, which I can only assume is encouraging.

I raise my fingers to my eyes to inspect for any signs of undigested food. Bravo! There is not a single morsel to behold! Despite my revulsion, I cannot help but smile a little at the sight, for it seems that he is well and

163

truly on the mend; and if this isn't proper scientific confirmation of that then I don't know what is.

I can hear voices in the next room. His Majesty is in his bedchamber with two of his physicians. I expect that they are still busy inspecting his body. I do hope that their examination is as positive as mine! I am anxious that they finish soon so that I can report my findings to them. Perhaps I will ask if they would like to see the stool for themselves; after all, it is such a pleasant sight today. I wipe my hands and peak around the door.

Hmmm . . . perhaps it is best if I do not to disturb them for a while, as the drapes are still drawn around His Majesty's bed. I lift my hand to inspect my fingernails. Yuk! I will have to search for a small sharp twig later to dig out the muck. Best I do that as quickly as I can, for experience tells me that if I leave it to become ingrained then it will stay there for weeks. I hear the King chuckle and I smile instinctively. Things must be going well.

His Majesty has only recently returned from the war against the French, and he did so as a thoroughly victorious man! If rumours are to be believed, his army rampaged through those filthy Gallic towns and burned them mercilessly to the ground, just as they deserved! I grin at the thought. Nobody should dare risk the wrath of my master, not if they value their lives! Not unless they want their rotten old country put to the torch! Ha! Didn't the King show them! There is nothing quite like a war to bring out the best in a man. Simply splendid!

After a few moments the voices grow louder and I hear the sounds of footsteps tapping across the floor. I stroll casually into the bedchamber wearing a triumphant smile.

"Well, boy?" one of the doctors demands. He is the shorter of the two, with harsh features and an unpleasant, bossy demeanour to match. But he doesn't faze me in the slightest.

"Chestnut brown in colour, Sir, softly formed like a sausage, somewhat pungent in smell but certainly not alarming; soft consistency with a few small lumps, but nothing untoward." I reel off the facts with unwavering confidence and rack my brain in case I have missed anything. No, my description is flawless. There are no flies on me, thank you very much!

"Ah, excellent!" the taller, and more pleasant of the two announces, clapping his hands together, smiling at the King. "This is simply perfect, Your Majesty!"

I look at the King who is lying prostrate on the bed. He is grinning like a child.

"I bloody knew it! Haven't felt this good in years!" he roars triumphantly. "Now leave us; I need the boy to help me with my stretches." He waves a podgy hand at the doctors, who bow deeply and scurry away without question.

I hurry to his bedside to help him into a seated position, but he brushes away my outstretched arms dismissively. My, he is becoming more determined by the day! He manages to raise his great shoulders and sits before me triumphantly as though he has achieved another victory. He is semi-naked, dressed only in his

165

short black hose, with thick bandages covering his calves. I smile at him with encouragement and try not to stare at the flaccid breasts that sit across the many rolls of creamy-white stomach fat. I must admit that despite his mighty, unnatural bulk he does seem to have lost a little weight recently. It must have been all that fighting. There certainly seems to be a little less of him spilling over his waistband than usual, that's for sure. But even so, I can't help but pity him when I see him on show like this. He looks vulnerable and exposed, and desperately enormous. Even for a King.

His Majesty is still suffering greatly with his legs, which is to be expected, of course, as those deep wounds will not heal overnight. He is also suffering from pains in his groin as a result of his momentous bout of exertion. His Majesty has been largely dormant for years and so it is to be expected that the effort of being in the saddle for so many hours each day would take its toll. Goodness only knows how he managed to command an entire army to boot!

I have been helping him to stretch his muscles to ease the tension, and although exhausting, I do enjoy helping him. Even more so, I enjoy listening to the proud tales from the battlefield that he likes to regale me with and, of course, the lavish accounts of his own bravery and the gutless terror of the enemy. There are fewer things as exciting as a tale of war, and never more so than when it comes from the mouth of the most mighty and magnificent man in all of Christendom!

I sit in his bedside chair and reach across to his right leg. He places it on my lap and I rub his thigh vigorously to warm the muscles.

"Ouch!" He kicks his great leg in the air, narrowly missing my face. He laughs good-naturedly as I jump back to avoid the blow.

"Bruised knee, boy, took a bit of a bludgeoning! Fucking Frogs!"

"Oh, I am sorry, Your Majesty." I move my hands back to his thighs, taking care to avoid the sore patch.

"Ha! Small price to pay! But didn't I show them. They were quaking in their filthy French boots when they saw me coming." I watch with amusement as he catches my eye and shifts his weight onto one buttock and constricts the muscles in his face. I purse my lips and brace myself . . . Just when I think he won't manage it, the King releases an explosion that almost rips the sheets apart.

"Your Majesty!" I exclaim in mock disgust.

"Don't 'Your Majesty' me, my boy! There's many I've sent to the graveyard who would love to smell that!"

"I'm sure, My Lord! A most piquant and meaty bouquet!"

We both fall about laughing, and I prepare myself to respond in kind. After what seems an age, the King loses his patience.

"For God's sake, Robert, stop it or you'll mess yourself again! If I want a riposte to my salvo I'll fire my own shot, thank you very much!"

Smiling and admitting defeat, I sit back and slowly raise his leg and straighten it as far as it will go. It must weigh more than a hundred of mine put together.

"How does that feel, Your Majesty?"

"A little tight, boy, but keep going. I will say when I am in too much pain. My wife says this is good for me."

I struggle to raise his leg a little further, my hand cupped under his ankle, taking care to keep the knee as straight as I possibly can. His Majesty winces and so I decide to keep his leg still for a while, for it must be stretching nicely as it is.

"Definitely better than yesterday," His Majesty grunts before offering me his other leg. I begin the same process of rubbing and stretching whilst the King reaches his arms above his shoulders for an indulgent stretch. "I think that I shall pay a visit to my wife's chambers tonight!" he announces, chuckling like a boy.

"Excellent idea, Your Majesty!" Yes, I think that the Queen will be most delighted to receive a visit from her husband this evening. I am certain that she would much prefer his embrace to any more of that interminable political talk. She is a woman, after all. Romance not rows, that's what I always say.

"Yes, I feel the time is ripe to start breeding again!" he announces confidently, more to himself than to me. "I think that Katherine and I shall do lots more together now that I am in better health. I think that we will play a little tennis, or perhaps we will go and hunt some deer! Oh, how I have missed that . . . The sound of the hunting horn, the furious singing of the hounds. But it's not just the thrill of the chase, m'boy, oh no, it's

168

the thrill of watching my wife galloping fearlessly up and down dale on her mare. That's what I like! All dressed up in her long leather boots! Yes, I think that we shall ride first thing tomorrow morning as though our lives depended on it!" He suddenly chuckles. "That is, if we are not too exhausted from the night before!" He gives me a conspiratorial wink, and I snort with laughter. I can't help myself.

One month later . . .
HRH, Queen Katherine Tudor,
8 November 1544, Hampton Court Palace

"Je n'aime pas!"

Oh, for heaven's sake. "Bessie, she doesn't like it. Can you bring her something else, please?" I turn to the French Ambassador's wife, who is sitting in my chair in my privy chamber, tapping her foot impatiently. "Fromage, peut-être, Madame Dupont?"

"Non."

"Bessie, will you bring her some bread and some meat, please? Chicken or something." If she is hungry, then she will damn well eat it.

Of all the things that I dislike about being the Queen, this is certainly amongst the worst. I just do not understand why it is that the foreign ambassadors insist on taking their wives with them when more often than not they do not want to go. What is it about these ungrateful women? Part of my role is to entertain them, which is no easy feat as there are fewer things more difficult than trying to entertain someone who does not wish to be entertained.

Now this one, she will not even make the effort to be civil to me, for heaven's sake. Oh, this is going to be a very long day indeed. If she won't eat then perhaps we should try to discuss the evening ahead instead. All French ladies enjoy dancing and feasting, I am sure of it. She will have the perfect opportunity to show off the latest Parisian fashions, and will no doubt leave us all feeling most unattractive and grey.

Oh, but I still have so much to do, and yet here I am wasting my time on this woman! The King has instructed me to organize the festivities and to oversee the feast that lies ahead, and so all week I have been busy rushing from the kitchens to the banqueting hall like a mad woman, trying to ensure that everything will be no less than perfect. It is essential that the French dignitaries are made to feel welcome and valued, especially after the recent troubles. If we are ever to achieve a lasting peace then we must all be on our very best behaviour and show each other that we mean to be friends. Clearly, though, someone has forgotten to share that little detail with My Lady visitor.

I must admit that I am not particularly looking forward to this evening. I do not really enjoy these displays of excess, and the drunkenness and debauchery that tend to go with them. I didn't enjoy them when John was alive, when I was just an inconspicuous guest, and I enjoy them even less now that I am the centre of attention. Thankfully, my husband seems to have mellowed a little over the years, and so is not as insistent as he once was that each event should eclipse the last.

This evening we are to host a banquet for several hundred people in the name of improved Anglo-French relations. We are to entertain the dignitaries and our own great and good with music and magic and theatre. I have selected no less than twenty-seven separate dishes to be served, which I am confident will delight even the most seasoned courtier. Our chefs are nothing short of magicians themselves, and so I have left the execution of each dish entirely in their capable hands. I have told them that the crowd should be wooed, and that the tables should groan under the sheer quantity of their creations. I know that it is frivolous, but for my husband's sake, and for the sake of unity, this must be perfect.

Henry has been unwell again of late, and so I do hope that this negotiation business will not be too much for him to bear. He has suffered terribly with his megrims for years, but never as he does now. He was in much better health after his return from his French invasion, but alas, it was not to last. Already he has surrendered to the excesses of court life, and it has set him back tremendously. No one can forget how easily men are seduced by ease and indulgence, and my husband is no exception. Things here are so easy for him that he has become indolent and listless, and when he is listless, he becomes distressed, and when he is distressed he eats. He has already grown so very large that he can no longer do most of the things that used to make him happy.

Like most men, my husband has an irrepressible hunger for purpose, and when he has nothing to drive him, he feels worthless and empty, and struggles to occupy his time. Sadly, at home, he feels that he has nothing to strive for, and nothing to fight against. I know this for certain, as I too could so easily become indulgent and apathetic if I did not have my books and my writing to keep me busy.

In France he had genuine opposition; there he could not order the enemy to do his bidding. There, he had to fight; he had to make the right decisions and command his army properly if he was to win. There, he had to think, negotiate and compromise; he had to exert himself on the battlefield and think of others as well as himself. I do hope that he is a little better today, or his temper will be very short indeed, and I hope he can recognize that a successful friendship is something to strive for, and is just as important as defeating the enemy in battle.

I suggest to Madame Dupont for the second time that we take advantage of this unseasonably sunny day and visit the beautiful Abbey in Westminster. I explain to her with enthusiasm how we can take a barge along the river and how I can show her some of the splendid churches that we have in London. But she is having none of it. She tells me, in French, that she is bored and that she is tired, and waves my suggestions aside with a sweep of her gloved hand. Bessie places a large plate of bread and meat on a small table next to her chair. I can't help but smile at her efforts as she has prettied the plate with flower petals.

Madame Dupont glances at the food for a second, curls her lip in disdain and turns to look out of the window.

"Thank you, Bessie," I say on her behalf. One is never too grand for manners. "Please leave it on the table in case she feels peckish later."

"Où est mon mari?" she inquires. Always in French.

"Avec mon mari, le *Roi*." Yes, her husband is with my husband — the *King* — and probably behaving much better than she is. I make one last attempt to amuse her and ask if she would like to play a game or if she would like to listen to Elizabeth play a tune on her viola, but she refuses my efforts. Perhaps if she finds the English court so thoroughly disagreeable then I will ask Bessie to prepare a bed for her in one of the guestrooms so that she can excuse herself and lie down.

That afternoon . . .
HRH, Queen Katherine Tudor,
8 November 1544, Hampton Court Palace

I stand before the mirror and smile. I have made a great effort to make myself look like a Queen today, and I hope that I have succeeded. I feel that I owe my husband a tremendous debt after he made me Regent, when he could so easily have left me in the hands of the Privy Council. I want him to be proud of me, and to feel that he can show me off to the French. I know that

173

I will never be as attractive as the Parisian ladies, but I hope at least that he will find me pleasing.

I stroke the creases from the front of my deep red kirtle and adjust the padding around my hips. Bessie laughs as I twirl in front of her, and as my kirtle billows out beneath me. I still feel as though I am wearing clothes that were made for someone else.

"Kate!" We look up with surprise as Anna rushes into the privy chamber. She looks flustered. "The King wants you immediately! He is frightfully cross."

I turn to Bessie and roll my eyes. I had expected a tantrum from my husband at some point in the day.

She smiles warmly. "You are finished, My Lady. You look beautiful, now go!" She gestures to the door impatiently. We both know that I dare not leave my husband waiting for an instant.

With my skirts and my train gathered in my hands, I rush along the corridors to attend to the King. I can hear his booming voice long before I reach his presence chamber door. I find him standing in the middle of his privy chamber, dressed only in his hose, with one of his servants behind him, furiously trying to lace his great white corset. I watch my husband as he puffs and pants crossly like a bear, and I try to keep a straight face. I clear my throat to catch his attention and curtsey deeply, keeping my eyes to the floor so that I will not collapse into a fit of giggles.

"Kate! Good! You must help me decide what to wear. I want to show those bloody Frogs what's what!"

I purse my lips tightly and nod.

"Boy!" he bellows to his groom, Robert, who rushes into the chamber, struggling to see beneath a dozen colourful hats. "Help this idiot pull my corset in! I will not have those Gallic bastards thinking me portly, thank you very much!"

Robert throws the hats onto the bed and rushes to my husband. He catches my eye and grins as he pulls the cords behind his back with all his might.

"Well, did you find out what he is wearing, boy?" my husband demands, trying to look over his shoulder.

"Uhh . . ." Robert is heaving with the effort of pulling. "Breathe in, Your Majesty!" he cries before tugging the cords a final time. "There!"

My husband turns to look at him. "What is that fucking Frog wearing, boy? I won't have him outshine me!"

"He is wearing blue, I think —"

"*Think*? You bloody *think*, you idiot? Is he or isn't he? He'd better not be wearing gold, boy, that's all I can say or I will wear your fucking eyes as jewels. I will not have those arrogant French bastards trying to upstage me."

Robert darts to the cupboard and finds him a shirt. A golden shirt.

"Cod piece!" my husband shouts to nobody in particular. "Bring me the biggest fucking cod piece in the Kingdom. I'll show those greasy fuckers what a real man looks like! Make haste, you fools. There are only a few hours left to dress me!"

★ ★ ★

That evening . . .
HRH, Queen Katherine Tudor,
8 November 1544, Hampton Court Palace

"Fucking French pig-shits! They'd screw their own mothers and daughters if they weren't so fucking ugly!"

My husband is in a beastly temper. At least he was able to contain his rage until after his meeting with the Ambassadors. Poor Robert was forced to bear the brunt, but he didn't seem too bothered by it. Perhaps it is wrong, but on occasions I encourage my husband's outbursts. He is like a horse that needs a good hard gallop on the hunting field before he can be still.

God help us all if he is not still this evening. It has taken me some time, but I have learned when my husband's moods are to be taken seriously and when they are just grumbles. Today he is barking — growling, in fact — but I know that he will not bite. I link my arm in his as we walk along the corridor to the banqueting hall. I chide him good-naturedly by speaking only in French. Best for him to get it all out in the open now so that he can be civil again later.

"Absoluement, Henri! Continuez, s'il vous plaît!"

"Bastards! Filthy, fucking foreign bastards! Arrogant, stinking, lecherous, lying, greasy fuckers. The lot of them!"

"Très bien!"

Thankfully the meal is sumptuous, and the King, at last, is happy. We are dazzled by the explosions and the flames and the fantastical dishes that his guests have

176

come to expect. We are presented with swans with trotters, pigs with wings, birds with birds inside, sheep with beaks . . . it is really quite a sight, and our French visitors cannot help applaud each offering.

Personally I cannot bear the sight of these monstrous creations, but my husband is delighted, and that's all that really matters. I am unable to eat much due to the bones that are sticking into my ribs through my corset. Not that I mind, as the unnatural sight before me is threatening to turn my stomach. It isn't so much the look of the dishes as they are served, it is that when one cuts into them, one never really knows what might hop, crawl, fly or slither out. Goodness only knows how the King has managed; I can only assume that the knots in his corset have come undone or snapped under the pressure.

It isn't long before the musicians begin to play their instruments and the guests rise to their feet to mingle and to dance. There are so many people here that it will be impossible for me to address them all, but as Queen, I know my role and will leave the dais and make the effort that my husband expects of me. The King is engrossed in his conversations with the ambassador, and as Madame Dupont's temper has not improved in the slightest, I am more than happy to find any reason to excuse myself.

I make my way towards a group of gentlemen who have travelled from the French court with the Ambassador. They bow deeply as I approach and insist on kissing my hand. I exchange a few pleasantries with them in their native tongue: I ask after their families, they tell me that they are well; I inquire after their journey, they tell me that it was pleasant; I ask after the weather in France this autumn; they tell me that it is warm.

I move courteously from person to person, to the same greeting of: "Bonsoir Monsieur," to the same reply of "Enchanté, Madame La Reine." I hold out my hand; it is taken, kissed and released. I offer it to the next guest for similar treatment, and try not to appear too anxious to have it returned. It isn't long until my cheeks hurt from the smiling, my back hurts from standing so erect and my knuckles ache from the stubbly faces that have scratched them. If only I could put a stop to the interminable formalities of bowing and scraping, so that we could hurry this along and I could go to bed!

I walk towards a group of English nobles and offer them similar bland pleasantries. I watch them as they elbow their way towards me, and as they brush their wet lips across my fingers, dulling my rings. As I exchange a few pointless words with the Earl of Leicestershire I feel a hand wrap itself around mine. It has been a very long day and I am almost too tired to pull it away. I bid the Earl farewell and turn to face the person who has seized me. I breathe deeply and prepare myself for yet another pushy noble who is sorely lacking in manners.

Suddenly my heart stops. It's him. It's Thomas. It's my Thomas.

My eyes are wide and my jaw drops. It is him; he is standing in front of me. He has my hand in his. Oh dear God; it is him . . . What? How . . . ?

"Your Grace," he whispers. I cannot take my eyes from him. I cannot move. He is staring down at me with the eyes that I have never forgotten; with that unruly brown hair and with that beautiful full mouth. I feel suddenly faint. We hold each other's stare; neither of us knowing what to do. I stand like a statue, overwhelmed and afraid. Still he does not release my hand and I do not have the strength to pull it away. I feel my face and chest flushing, and my heart beating with such ferocity it is as though I am being struck repeatedly in the chest.

"Thomas . . ." I manage to whisper. I gasp and quickly snatch my hand from his. I am suddenly aware of *us*; of how I have been staring at him and he at me. It must have only been for a second or two, but it feels so much longer . . . and here; in front of everyone; in front of the King!

My eyes widen in horror and I look around frantically, searching for the accusing pairs of eyes that must be out there. Thankfully, I see no one. No one is paying us any attention. I turn to him and smile hesitantly. I am so very nervous. "Dear Lord, thank you," I whisper. "I feared that you were dead."

"No." He shakes his head. He does not take his eyes from mine. He reaches down and takes my hand again and draws it to his lips. He kisses me with an overwhelming tenderness. He looks so broken. "Can I see you? Away from here?" he whispers.

I shake my head forcefully. What is he thinking?

"Then can I write to you?"

179

I look at him with desperation. Is he mad? "No!" I hiss, trying not to move my lips. I look around again in fear. "My God, he will have us both killed if he even thinks that you and I have seen each other! What are you doing here? You shouldn't be here!"

Suddenly, a young woman with long fair ringlets and a pretty lace dress pushes through the crowds and wraps her arm around Thomas's shoulders. She startles the instant she notices me, and curtsies deeply. As I watch her lower her head I feel my heart break anew; this woman with her arm around my Thomas, with her youthful face, her worry-free eyes and her long, golden mane.

"It is a pleasure, Your Grace," she gushes, giggling like a child.

I turn to Thomas and try to blink away my tears. "Your wife, Sir?" I ask him, as lightly as I can. I know that it is unfair but I so desperately want him to tell me that she is not. He smiles and shakes his head.

"I have never married, Your Grace."

The girl giggles again and looks up at him expectantly. He does not turn to her. His eyes do not leave mine.

"I wanted to marry once," he tells me, gently.

I stare back into those big brown eyes that are so full of sorrow. "You did?" It is all that I can do to stop myself from sobbing; from throwing myself into his strong arms. If only he could hold me as he once did.

He nods slowly, keeping his eyes on my face. "To the most beautiful woman with eyes the colour of emeralds."

"What happened?" the girl asks, pouting with jealousy.

He drops his gaze to his feet as though he can no longer bear to look at me. "She married someone else. Someone far more important than me."

"That's awful!" she scoffs, shaking her head and tutting loudly.

Thomas looks up again and searches my eyes. I shake my head slightly, willing him to stop. I do not know if I can listen to him any further without weeping. I do not know if I will be able to stop myself from telling him just how much I still love him.

But he will not stop, and nor can I blame him. He must feel so wronged and in need of an explanation. "I would like to think that she loved me as I loved her, but I cannot understand why, if that were true, she would marry another."

I take a deep, shaking breath and try my best to smile. "Perhaps, Sir . . . perhaps she was made to marry this other man. Perhaps she had no other choice."

"But how could she marry someone if she was in love with me?"

I am forced to turn my attention to the floor in fear that my expression will betray me. His words make me almost too ashamed to look at him. "Perhaps she could not marry you. Perhaps she was not allowed to marry you . . ."

He shakes his head sadly. "I wonder sometimes if she loved me at all."

I look up suddenly. Surely he cannot doubt how I felt about him? How I still feel? How I will always feel? I

181

hold his gaze with wide, troubled eyes until he smiles slightly.

"No, no, I do not wonder that. I know that she loved me as I loved her, but sometimes . . . sometimes I ask myself if she loves me still, after everything that has happened."

I swallow deeply and lower my voice until I can barely hear myself speak. "Do you still love her, Sir?" I feel my face flushing as it once did all those years ago when we danced together in this very room.

He moves his head towards mine, just a little, but enough for me to feel his breath on my face. "I will always love her, Your Grace."

I shake my head with sadness. I know that I cannot stay here any longer. It is a miracle that we have not already been spotted. I hold my shaking hand aloft once again for him to kiss. He takes it gently and raises it to his mouth. I watch him close his eyes as his lips touch my knuckles. We lower our hands together; neither of us wanting to release the other's grip; neither of us wanting to say goodbye forever.

"Sir, I do not know this woman you speak of, but if I had to imagine, I would say that she loves you with all her heart. I would say that she has loved you from the first moment she saw you, and that it is by this love that she married another, in order to keep you safe; so precious are you to her." I release his grip and quickly glance around the room to check that we are not being watched. I take a step forward and lean towards him. I place my hand over my mouth protectively and hold my head next to his for a split second so that I can whisper in his ear. "I will always love you, Thomas. Not even the King can take that away."

I brush past him and hurry towards the dais. I rush to my husband, who is still talking with the Ambassador. I lower myself onto my seat and smile at nobody in particular. My face is still flushed, my heart is still pounding and my eyes are stinging from the strain of holding back my tears. I turn my head away from the guests in fear that I might see my beloved again. I cannot look at him. I should not have spoken to him.

I close my eyes bitterly and lower my head. Why has God chosen this path for me? What was so wrong with the one that I had chosen for myself? I clench my fists tightly in my lap with anger until my knuckles turn white, for I know that there can be but one outcome for us; I will never speak to him again; I will never look at him again; I will never think of him again. God has chosen my destiny, and for whatever wrong that I have committed in His eyes, I know that Thomas will never be a part of it.

CHAPTER
FOUR

Dark Words Whispered

Four months later . . .
Thomas Wriothesley,
14 March 1545, Whitehall Palace

His Majesty's health is deteriorating faster than I can find physicians to tend him. For the first time in my career I find that I am frightened. Suddenly my future is uncertain, for I do not know what will become of me or the Kingdom should God see fit to take him from us. One thing is for certain: *she* cannot be left in charge, and neither can any of her Protestant ilk. I shudder with loathing as I think of the Queen, and I quicken my step along the corridor.

I have received word that His Majesty is in particularly poor health tonight and so I must go to him. I only hope that his wife is not fussing over him as she often does. I can just imagine her in there now, telling him how she is going to do this, and how she is going to take care of that. The impertinent bitch! I must put a stop to this lunacy before she does any real damage.

I stride to the door leading to His Majesty's presence chamber and growl at the guards. "Stand aside!" They

184

know better than to even think about stopping me from entering. Both of them jump to attention, lift their halberds and allow me to push the door open. I make my way through the deserted room until I reach the door leading to the royal bedchamber. That stupid boy of his emerges from God only knows where and stands in front of the door as if to guard it. I smirk the moment I see him. One look at my expression should be more than enough to tell him that I am in no mood to be messed with today. And yet, strangely he does not move . . . he dares to stand in my way.

"I do not have time for games tonight, idiot."

He replies with a high-pitched quivering voice that any girl would be proud of.

"His Majesty is not to be disturbed, My Lord Chancellor. He is with the Queen."

"I don't give a shit if he is with the Pope himself. Do not dare refuse me entry, boy, or you will regret it! Who the hell do you think you are anyway, turd-sniffer?"

I grab his greasy doublet and shove him aside. I am in no mood for time-wasters. I enter the dimly lit bedchamber in anger and am greeted by the nauseating sight of the King and Queen together. His Majesty is lying on the bed, with his dear little wife sitting beside him, keeping vigil. *Vigil!* Ha! To the unsuspecting eye she looks quite the picture of devotion; all concern and wifely feeling. How very touching.

I narrow my eyes. On second glance something looks different. He usually has his great fat legs sprawled all over her, and they are either laughing together or she is rubbing his stinking feet, but strangely not tonight. I make my way to the bed and look down at his face. Good God, he looks rough. I cannot help but cross myself at the sight. His wife finally notices my presence, but not until I am just a few feet from the bed. She looks up at me as though I am a common intruder, a thief in the night. Bitch of a woman! I've been here far longer than she has, and if I have my way I will be here an awful lot longer, too.

I offer her the smallest nod of my head and turn my attention to the King. "Your Majesty, I am here to inquire after your health. I heard that you had taken a turn for the worse, and I could not overcome my grief." I speak over his wife's head. The King opens his eyes a little and holds my gaze, but he does not reply.

"His Majesty has a fever."

Katherine speaks on his behalf. Her irritating voice makes me wince. Who asked her?

"I am trying to keep his temperature at bay." She looks up at me pointedly. I don't care *what* she is trying to do! "He needs to rest, My Lord Chancellor."

I shake my head in response. Oh no! I am not going anywhere just yet, thank you very much! I watch as he lies on his side beneath a thin sheet. His massive frame heaves with each laboured breath, making the bed come alive. The woman is mopping his brow with a wet cloth. I frown at the sight of his sweating face as it is the ruddiest that I have ever seen it. This is not good . . .

I lower my head a little. Did he just mutter something under his breath? Is he delirious as well? God help us if he is. I wonder what she has been saying to him whilst he has been lying here, feeble-minded

186

and unable to defend himself. What vile poison has she been whispering in his ears? What foul act has she been trying to persuade him to agree to? Something tells me that in this state he would agree to just about anything. Best that I stay for a while, and keep an eye on her.

She looks up at me with an accusing expression before turning back to the King. She lowers the cloth into a small bowl of water and again places it on his forehead. I wince at the revolting noises that she is making as she sings to him; she is treating him as though he were a child. Wretched woman.

"Is there something the matter, Wriothesley?" His Majesty's voice catches my attention. It is barely audible. I don't think that I have ever heard him so quiet before. It is alarming. Disconcerting. He looks up at me through his half-closed eyes and I bow deeply.

"I . . . uh . . . I wondered if there is anything that I can do for Your Majesty?" What else can I say? There is no obvious reason for me to be here, other than to keep watch on that woman, of course, and to save the King and his Kingdom from corruption.

"There is nothing that you can do for me. Unless you can perform bloody miracles, that is. But since you are here you might like to listen to some of the plans that I have been making with my wife . . ."

I raise my eyebrows and assume an expression of expectancy. What in God's name has he agreed to?

"Katherine was just telling me her plans for some of the money that I had intended for the Church. You tell him, Katherine." He closes his eyes again. "It hurts to speak."

She glances up at me and smiles a little hesitantly, as though she fears my reaction. She had better fear me. As His Majesty's eyes remain shut I do not bother to return her smile.

"Well, I thought that I would open a small hospital in London. Perhaps a house for those poor souls who are cursed with a disordered mind."

How fitting! Who the hell does she think she is? *Poor souls?* The insane should be punished, not rewarded. I clear my throat. "That is certainly a bold idea, Your Grace, but do you really think that a hospital is a necessary expenditure when the Church itself can offer better medicine for the poor? This money was intended for the Holy Church. No doubt it came from the Holy Church in the first place. I wonder whether *they* should be the ones to best decide how the money should be spent." My argument sounds utterly sensible. It is the argument of an intelligent man and I am certain that even in his frail state, His Majesty will recognize this. I smile at her widely for I am confident that I will not be challenged.

She leans forward and brushes away a damp lock of hair from His Majesty's forehead. "I thought that we had discussed this, My Lord Chancellor. The money will not be going back to the churches." She turns to look at me over her shoulder. "My husband has entrusted me with the funds. He believes that I will do the right thing, the Christian thing, and that is exactly what I will do. And oh yes, I agree that it is a most bold idea, as it seems that nobody cares a jot for those whose minds have been so cruelly afflicted. Very bold indeed."

188

I grit my teeth. When in God's name did the King entrust her with money of all things? *Why* in God's name . . .? She can barely manage her own ladies. How does he think that she can possibly make a decision such as this? He knows damn well that she has no intention of spending it on anything of worth!

"Splendid," I mutter, and smile at the back of her head, just in case His Majesty should open his eyes.

Katherine turns to the King and places her hand on his shoulder. She lowers her head and after a few moments speaks to him quietly as if to exclude me.

"Have you thought any more about the children's tutors, My Lord?" she asks. I can't help but smile. This should be good. It is well known that she has been trying to poison court with Lutherans for some time, and now she is trying to infect his own children as well. It's a good job that I am here to witness this and to stop it. I am certain that His Majesty will thank me later.

The King moans and turns his head away. Come on, man! You are not too ill to let her get away with this!

"I have decided on Dr Baker," she tells him with certainty.

My jaw drops in amazement. I cannot believe my ears. Is she goading me? Did she just *tell* His Majesty who is to educate the future King of England? I don't care if the Devil himself educates the whore's child, but Edward is a different matter entirely. She cannot make this decision; it is not hers to make! I shake my head in sheer wonderment at her audacity.

"He comes highly recommended," she continues.

189

Highly recommended by the Antichrist, no doubt! I look at the King and will him to protest. But he remains silent. Is he even awake?

"Your Majesty . . ." I walk to the other side of the bed so that I can speak directly to the King. If His Majesty is too weak to prevent this unstoppable torrent of wickedness then I will be forced to do so on his behalf. "Forgive me, but I must question why it is that Her Grace has chosen a Protestant dog to tutor the Kingdom's most prized and precious possessions; His Majesty's most beloved children!" I lean across the bed until my head is close to his. "Your Majesty," I whisper, "I am confident that you can trust me to think of someone far more —"

His Majesty suddenly opens his eyes and roars like a great beast.

"If my wife tells me that he is highly recommended then so be it, man!" I jump back in fear at this unexpected outburst. This is her doing! She has corrupted him! I stand back as His Majesty blasphemes loudly and throws his left arm over his eyes. Katherine leans towards him and strokes his head again softly. I watch them in utter disbelief, completely unable to move. She has bewitched him!

I back away from the bed and try to contain my fury. How dare he allow this to happen? How dare he allow her to treat me like a common fool! After everything that I have done for him! There must be something that I can do to stop this? Something that I can say?

I turn and stare at her for a few moments and stroke my beard. Hmm . . . now, hasn't she come a long way in such a short period of time? My mind wanders to that day three years ago when I visited her in her late husband's home; to that day when we made an unspoken agreement that would change the course of both our lives. The corners of my mouth twitch involuntarily as I picture her then trying to hold back her tears. Perhaps I should remind the King of exactly who this woman is, who sits here mopping his brow with affected love and devotion. Perhaps he would like to know how she cried like a baby when I told her that she was to marry him, and how I had to threaten her with her own sister's life. Ha! He certainly wouldn't trust her if he knew how she really felt!

I turn my gaze to the great, useless behemoth and feel a sudden revulsion as it pants and wheezes. If it wasn't for his arrogance then he would have realized long ago that she doesn't want to be here. She doesn't love him at all. If truth be known, she detests him, just as I detest her. She may fool everyone else, but she will never fool me!

I am forced to turn my back to them as the sentences form so temptingly in my mind. I can feel them lingering on the tip of my tongue, willing me to utter them, to ease my own rage. I take a deep, shaking breath and bite down hard on my lip to stop myself. No. This is not the time; this is one card that I do not want to play unless I absolutely have to . . .

★ ★ ★

Katherine slowly rises from her seat so as not to disturb the King. She walks towards the door and beckons for me to follow her. Part of me so desperately wants to disobey her, to turn my back on her disdainfully, to dishonour and discredit her. But I know that I cannot. For better or worse, she is still the wife of the King.

"As you can see, Thomas, His Majesty is very unwell," she whispers. I purse my lips at her use of my name. The only person who has any damn right to call me that is the man lying on the bed. To all others I am Lord Chancellor! But I bite my tongue and keep my anger to myself. For now, at least.

"I'll thank you not to get him so worked up when he needs to rest, and to recover." She speaks sternly as if scolding a wayward child. It is all I can do not to spit with anger. How dare she speak to me in this way! How dare she tell me what to do!

"The country will not run itself, Your *Grace*." I do not attempt to hide the sarcasm in my voice. "I am merely trying to ensure that His Majesty's illness will not affect the decisions that he has to make. Important decisions. Decisions that should be left to the Privy Council." I lick my lips and lower my head until she can feel my breath on her forehead. I know how intimidating I can be to women.

She pulls away from me. "You are forgetting, Sir, that I was made Regent not so long ago. I think we both know that I am perfectly capable of acting on His Majesty's behalf when there is a need." She turns to leave, but I am quick to move. I block her way and move a step closer. I lower my head until my lips are mere inches from her ear.

"Do not get above yourself, Katherine. Remember that it was me who made you. And I can break you. You think that you have the ear of the King today? Well, what about tomorrow? What about the day after?" I snap my fingers in front of her eyes, making her jump. "His loyalties can switch in a heartbeat, and you would be best to remember that, for I am going nowhere. I have seen all his wives come and go, but I have remained steadfast. I will be here when he finally sees you for what you really are . . ."

She pulls away and looks up at me, suddenly afraid; and rightly so, for she should be afraid of me. She picks up her skirts and darts back to her husband's bedside. I stare after her with narrowed eyes, and exhale slowly. I am fired by a hatred that threatens to consume every bone in my body, and I will bring her down. I vow that I will beat her.

Six months later . . .
Mary Tudor, 12 September 1545,
Whitehall Palace, Royal Chapel

"Father confessor, in your presence I kneel before almighty God and all His angels and saints, ready to confess my sins and to cleanse my soul of iniquity. Mea culpa, mea culpa, mea maxima culpa." I cross myself solemnly, ready, once again to bear my soul and to seek His divine guidance.

"Speak, Your Grace. The Christ Lord hears you."

I know that He hears me, for He is my Saviour and my Salvation. It is He and no one else who has sheltered me and protected me during my difficult journey on this earth. I only hope that He will take pity on me once again and will light the uncertain path that lies ahead, for I fear that I am no longer strong enough to continue without His help. It is an unnatural and unholy fear that brings me to the confessional on this cold autumnal morning; a terror that threatens to devour me if I do not learn to control and to tame it. I am not here through habit or convention; I am here because I am crying out for His help and the help of His Holy mother.

I take a deep breath to steady my nerves and I choose my words carefully before speaking them. I do not want the priest to think of me as an hysterical and emotional woman.

"I must speak to you about my father," I whisper, "and his new Queen. And about my place in this family. I need you to help me so that I can understand God's holy will and His purpose for me among these . . . sinners."

The priest says nothing in response.

"I try to be a dutiful daughter, Father, but I am struggling, for I do not know how I am supposed to behave among these people. I find myself almost ravished by the bitterness that has been inflicted upon me for so many years, for I cannot forget the sins that were committed against myself and my dearest mother. God rest her soul."

I hear the priest sigh and murmur his agreement.

194

"I find that as hard as I try I cannot feel pity for my father at his time of great anguish. My heart has become cold and hard towards him, as if infected by the same terrible disease that eats away at his legs. He is weak and has been bed-bound for many weeks, and yet, despite this, my heart does not soften. I do not know what to do or how I should act towards him. Those around me shower him in kindness and warmth as though they are oblivious to the terrible acts that he has committed against his own kin. Should I also do this? Should I help ease his pain, or harden my heart still further? I need to know, Father, whether his suffering has been inflicted on him by the Almighty Himself . . ." I lower my voice ". . . to punish him for his great sins."

I can hear the priest breathing, but still he says nothing in response.

"Every time I see him crying out in agony I think of the pain that was endured by my poor mother at his hands. I did not see her pain, Father, for I was not there. I was kept far from her, as I'm sure you know, but I have been told how she suffered. And unlike my father, she was denied the support of those she most loved, and so she suffered all alone."

I shake my head to ward away the tears that threaten to consume me.

"Of course she had the Lord with her, but she was denied the love of her only daughter; she was denied the human kindness that my father now has in abundance. And yet that did not seem to matter to him, for never did he visit her, and never did he visit me or permit me to go to her!"

I inhale deeply, and the cold morning air rushes into my nostrils. I concentrate on the scent of the incense so that I do not lose myself to my emotions. I cannot allow myself to cry. Not even here in the privacy of the dark confessional. I do not want anyone to think of me as weak.

"An eye for an eye, Father," I tell him urgently. "Is that not the lesson that God teaches us? Is this not the law of retribution? Divine retribution? Is He not punishing my father as my father punished my mother? It is written, is it not: 'Whatever he has done must be done to him'? Leviticus, Father, Leviticus! Why would we dare to thwart God's will? If the Lord wishes him to suffer then we should not offer succour. Should we? It was God's will for my mother to suffer, was it not? And no one intervened to help her! No one." I halt my outburst the moment I hear my voice beginning to shake.

Despite my pain, I know that I must continue my confession. I must face my darkest fears for I no longer know how I should act and what I should do. I once thought that I was strong, but I am beginning to question my resolve as though I were a child again; unable to cope with the strange, conflicting emotions that seem to stem from even the simplest of occurrences. I know that I have no other choice but to seek the Lord's assistance, for no one else can help me now. No one else can help me understand this confusion and the dark, unremitting anger towards the King that is beginning to eat away at me like a plague.

196

Still the priest says nothing. I squint against the dark, wooden slats that separate us. I can see that he has bowed his head a little as though he is deep in thought.

"Part of me so desperately wants to help him, Father, to pray with the others and to tend to his wounds as his new wife does. Would that be so very wrong? Did Saint Peter and Saint Luke not speak of compassion? Are we not told in the book of Job that we should show pity for the afflicted?

"And yet . . . something is stopping me. I have a burning within my stomach, Father, that festers; it fills my blood with an unnatural hatred towards him as though some dark force is lurking within my soul and controlling my very being. I cannot find forgiveness no matter how hard I try! I cannot excuse his vile actions and nor can I understand them. To me, Father, he is an abomination against God and His Holy Church!" I manage to control my rising voice. "I just pray that my father has confessed his sins so that He can forgive him, because I fear that I cannot."

I close my eyes and picture my father lying on his great bed with his infected leg resting heavily across Katherine's knees. I see his face wince in pain as she unties the bandages that hide his great shame from the world. I lower my head and feel my emotions soften despite my anger. "And yet, when I look into his face I see a shadow of the man whom I so adored all those years ago, with his full red beard and his eyes that crinkle at the sides whenever he smiles. And when I see that man, Father, I find that I cannot bear to see him suffer. It is as if a part of me dies with each new wave of agony that afflicts him, and I want to throw myself into his arms as though I am a child again. And yet still, I hate him."

I swallow heavily as my rage threatens to rise to the surface; it is always so desperate for dominance these days. My face darkens with anger as my thoughts return to my poor mother.

"But he does not deserve my pity! He sent me away, didn't he? I was just a child, for heaven's sake! He sent us both away! And for what? For that whore, that's what! And I can never forgive him for that. Never."

I lower my head with exhaustion. I must resolve these conflicting emotions or I will go insane!

"But Holy scripture says that we should forgive, doesn't it? But it also speaks of a just and righteous punishment for those who walk in wickedness. What shall I do, Father? Tell me, what does my Saviour expect me to do?"

"We cannot hope to understand the ways of the Lord, Your Grace."

I sigh deeply. This is just the sort of response that I had feared.

"The answer is within your heart," he continues, softly. "It is not for me to tell you what is right and what is wrong. It is for God to show you what you must do."

I shake my head with frustration as the confusion builds like a torrent. I can barely see beyond the complex jumble of thoughts and painful memories.

"And still I do not know how to be towards the Queen, Father. You must help me understand what I should do with her for she, too, is troubling my mind! As much as I will always care for her, I will never accept her presence here; for I know that she lives a lie! Their marriage is nothing short of a sin. It is adulterous! What did Saint Matthew say? He told us that he who divorces his wife without good cause, and marries another commits adultery. Is that not what he said? Is adultery not a sin? Never did he have good cause to marry another."

"But your father was a widow, Your Grace. Your late, sainted mother had departed this world when he married your brother, Prince Edward's, mother. And she herself is dead. And as for the other two — the whores — well, they don't count. So you see, my child, he was free to marry again without committing that sin."

I rub my eyes wearily. Suddenly I see my dearest childhood friend whom I loved like a sister, smiling up at me with her kind, green eyes trying to ease the pain that was caused by my father.

"In truth, I still don't know what she is doing here. I don't know why she married him, for she hated my father almost as much as I did. She saw what he did to me and my mother all those years ago. Oh, we were so very close then. But she has changed. Something dark has happened to her soul. I listen to her talking to my father, and it is at times as though a heretic is speaking through her lips. She says that she argues with my father just to make him feel better and to take his mind from his pains; she says they debate religion because he is passionate about his faith and that he is always keen to discuss it and defend it . . . but I do not know. Why would she want him to defend it? And from what? Lies? Untruths?"

I move my head to the wooden divide and lower my voice, forcing the priest to move his head closer to mine so that he will not miss a word.

"I suspect that at the very least she sympathizes with the Protestants, Father, or why would she continually discuss them with him, and with such passion? Perhaps she *is* a Protestant? I don't know. Do *you* know, Father? Has she confessed to you? Does she even attend confession any more? She has always been a good person so I cannot believe that she has truly turned from Rome.

"Perhaps she is just trying to help him?" I feel my cheeks burn. "But that still does not excuse her from using such irreverent and unforgivable words! Why, I have heard her trying to persuade him not to burn Protestant heretics who have been spreading lies against the Holy Church, of all things! God forgive her, but I even heard her arguing that their devotion to Christ is no less than ours and that they should be spared. I cannot tell you just how much I hate having to listen to the poison that spills from her mouth! It is like bile . . . a rancid, noxious bile that could infect unwary souls.

"But not me, Father. Never me. I will not be polluted or turn away from the true faith. But for all her talk, I cannot forget that it was she who called me back; it was the Queen who persuaded my father to allow me to resume my rightful place at court. If it wasn't for

Katherine then I cannot deny that I would still be so far away; forgotten and discarded as though I was nobody."

I grit my teeth as my thoughts become ever more clouded and jumbled. Contradiction after contradiction . . .

"I confess that she has been nothing but kind and generous since I have returned. She cares for my father as no one else does, and she has even been quite saintly towards the Boleyn child. Somehow, she has even managed to soften *my* heart towards that girl. Oh Father! Is that not Christian?"

The priest mumbles something that I cannot understand. I lower my voice further and move my head until my lips are almost touching the divide.

"I have to tell you that I have heard talk that the Privy Council is concerned about her." I grasp my hands together in my lap to stop them from shaking. "They believe that the Queen may, in truth, be trying to corrupt my father and undermine his return to the Holy Church. I do not know what to do. I do not like the thought of the Council becoming involved or being anywhere near her for that matter for I know exactly what they are capable of. She needs to be chastised, Father, that is for sure, for it may be that her intentions are malicious. But I fear for her and I do not want to see her hurt.

"Pray for her, Father, please pray for her and forgive her for her sins, for somehow she seems unaware of the darkness that looms ahead. And pray for me, Father, please. Pray that the Lord helps me to understand what I should do. Pray that He lights my way and that He reveals to me my chosen destiny in these dark and uncertain times."

Five months later . . .
Thomas Wriothesley,
13 February 1546, Whitehall Palace

"Harder, boy. I said massage my shoulders! I don't want you to stroke me; I'm not a puppy, for God's sake!"

Phillip kneads the back of my neck with all his strength. I can honestly say that I don't think I have ever felt quite as tense as I do today. True, I am often worked up about one thing or another, but I am feeling the strain right now as I never have before. Thank the good Lord for Phillip and his capable hands, for nothing can ease the tension as much as good hard rub from the boy. I close my eyes and try to enjoy the sensation as his oiled hands push against my skin.

I am sitting in my tall desk chair with my shirt off, and my head hanging forward. Philip is standing behind me, tending to me as he often does. It is the middle of the afternoon, although one glance outside at the stony grey clouds and one would think that it is already evening. I have so much to do today, but I am capable of nothing, for I can barely see beyond the pain that thunders through my head.

I pinch the bridge of my nose with my thumb and forefinger and close my eyes tightly. Dear God, how did it all go so very wrong? To think that I almost had her . . . I move my fingertips to my throbbing temples and circle them gently over my skin. It is hard to believe it was only yesterday that I was so close to bringing her down; so close that I could almost taste the sweetness of success. But alas, it was all for nothing, for I am no closer now than I ever was.

Phillip threads his fingers through my hair and massages my scalp. As far as this blasted megrim is concerned, his efforts are proving to be almost entirely wasted. In all honesty, he might as well stab me repeatedly in the head with a pitchfork for all the good that he is doing. I groan with frustration as my mind drifts back to that woman.

"Is everything alright, My Lord Chancellor?"

"Does it bloody well look like it?" I can't help but snarl at him. I know this isn't his fault, but I don't care. It amazes me how slow-witted he can be sometimes, with his stupid, pointless questions.

Phillip leans towards me and whispers in my ear. "Can I do anything else to make you feel better?"

I don't have to look at him to know what *that* question means and I can just imagine the face that he is pulling behind my back. Dirty boy. Normally this would arouse me, but not today; I am not in the mood for anything right now unless it brings me any closer to ensnaring that woman.

"You can place our divine Queen Katherine's head on the block for me if you really want to help!" I utter the words with conviction, but I cannot help wincing as I hear them spoken aloud. Perhaps I should not be so open in front of the boy. It is hardly a secret that I suspect her of heresy, but even so, I must watch my tongue, for I could so easily be accused of treason myself. I am quite sure that Phillip knows better than to betray my confidence, but it is best to be on the safe side. Trust no one; that is what I have always said.

"Don't speak a word of this to anyone, boy. Understand? I was jesting." I make my voice as menacing as possible, which is not at all difficult.

"Of course! I would never!" Phillip shouts as if I have insulted him.

"Be sure that you don't." There. That has put an end to it.

As Phillip moves his hands to the tops of my arms, my thoughts turn to the King. He is not in a good way right now; that's for certain. Not by a long stretch. Not with his leg, nor with his perpetual megrims. Well, if his pain is as dreadful as mine then he really does have my pity. And on top of everything else, he has that damn wife of his to contend with; trying to corrupt him and the entire court with her Lutheran ways.

A heretic Queen is the last thing he needs, but does he see that? No, he does not! I thank the Lord that the doctors have managed to persuade her that it is in his best interests that she stays away from him for a few days, to give him some peace. That is something we can all be grateful for, at least, for God only knows what poison she is mind to whisper into his fevered ears. How long she will stay away, however, is anybody's guess. He may be blind to her many ills, but I most certainly am not, and I will see to it that she does not get away with her blasphemies, even if it takes me a lifetime! Ha! To think that I was making such progress in my quest, and to think that everything seemed to be coming together so nicely.

Oh, what to do about that blasted Askew woman! For a Protestant she is certainly bearing up better than I had thought, and has kept her silence after everything that I did to her. After all that pain . . . To think that she could have spared herself such suffering had she just opened her mouth and sung to my tune. Ugh!

I close my eyes and picture her rotten face. I expect that she is curled in her cell this very moment, lying among the filth and the rats. Such a waste of my day, thanks to her stubborn stupidity. Well, I just hope that her dear Queen is worth it, that's all I can say, for I would bet every penny I own that Katherine would never have endured the same for her.

I sigh as Phillip leans his body forward and rubs his hands across my chest. His breath is hot on the back of my neck, and despite my fury I cannot help but feel a little aroused. But now is not the time. I must try to think further on this Askew creature, for there may still be some other torment that will make her talk and secure the ruin of her precious Queen.

I cast my mind back to just two days ago, to the royal stables, when this all began. I was inspecting my daughter's pony, for the damn thing had gone lame once too often for my liking. I had a quick look at it and ordered the groom to slit its throat then and there. Best thing for everyone, despite the tears to come, for I was in no mood to continue to pay for a damaged nag.

I remember hearing footsteps from behind me, and turning to find Bishop Gardiner scurrying across the courtyard like a man possessed. I can still see him as he ran to my side and how he rested his hands on his knees in an effort to catch his breath. I recall staring down at his great bulk with pity and thinking that a man of his stature really shouldn't exert himself so. How inexplicable the things that we remember!

"My Lord Chancellor . . ." he finally managed to utter. "We have arrested a woman!"

I can picture myself frowning at him. That was hardly news, and certainly nothing to exert oneself over.

"A Protestant!" he went on to tell me. "A woman who could barely stop herself from blabbing her heathen views to every last soul in London!"

Again, I shook my head in confusion. Why was he telling me this? After all, we arrest heretics all the time these days.

"Not just any woman, My Lord Chancellor, but the wife of a noble!"

Well, that caught my attention. Arrests are always so much more fun when you know the assailant.

"A woman named Anne Askew!"

The name meant nothing to me at all and I admit that I felt a little disappointed. But Gardiner's excitement did not waver in the slightest. For some reason he appeared to be taking great delight in his revelation.

"No, I don't think that I know her either, My Lord Chancellor, but . . . she used to be one of the Queen's own ladies! It was a few years ago now, but even so!"

I remember gasping at the news. I might have even covered my mouth as I was in such shock. What luck! A known heretic from the Queen's own household! I can still see Gardiner's excited face lit up like a beacon with the widest of smiles. I knew precisely what he was thinking, as I was thinking the exact same thing.

"She is at the Tower now. She has already been questioned and has not only confessed to her own crimes, but has implicated others; two of whom are ladies in the Queen's current household . . . She is saying that they are heretics as well!"

I could barely contain myself. "Who? Tell me, Bishop!"

"The ladies Lane and Tyrwhitt!"

I think that I crossed myself then and there and thanked the good Lord aloud for this unexpected gift. I know these two ladies; they are close to the Queen and would certainly be privy to her views!

The Bishop grinned. "I think that this Askew woman is so scared of being tortured that she will admit to just about anything!"

I could hardly believe our fortune. Why, if she was prepared to denounce members of the Queen's own household, then God willing she might even be prepared to implicate the Queen. This, from someone who used to be in her household would be more than enough to convince the King that his dear wife and the other ladies should be questioned. And then she would well and truly be mine . . .

It was certainly good fortune that Gardiner had seen fit to tell me of the arrest, for I was the obvious choice to take over the investigation. I had the real questions to ask, and the stomach to ask them. I was more than certain that the mere sight of the rack would be all that was needed to give me exactly what I wanted. But, alas, God did not choose to smile on me, for this dazzling ray of hope came to precisely naught. For when I went to her, when it was my turn, the stupid woman barely uttered a single word. Despite her previous revelation, she said nothing in my presence to incriminate herself or any of the Queen's ladies.

I bang my fist on my desk with frustration and grit my teeth with rage as I picture her obstinate face. Damn that Askew! And damn that Katherine! Phillip takes his hands from my shoulders in fear and hovers behind me like an annoying fly. Damn him as well. I rise to my feet in anger and turn to face him; I suddenly feel an irrepressible desire to vent my irritation. He looks up at me a little hesitantly.

"Phillip, my boy, have you ever witnessed someone being tortured?" My voice is quiet. Reserved. He suddenly looks afraid. He forms a small circle with his lips, contemplating what to say next. I quickly put him out of his misery — not that he deserves it. "I am not going to torture *you*, fool! Just answer the damn question."

"No, Sir, I . . . I have not."

"I need you to help me with something." I grab him roughly by the arm, making him squeal, and drag him to the bed. Perhaps he can help me to understand where I went wrong? And if not, then at least it will make me feel a little better.

208

"Let's imagine that this room is a torture chamber."

Phillip is already panting in fear. Damn soft, this boy; God help him if he ever does encounter anything like this.

"Imagine that this bed is the rack, boy. Now imagine somebody lying naked on top of it and screaming for mercy. Imagine their limbs as they pop from their sockets."

My voice becomes louder and more animated as I stare at the bed and picture the satisfying scene. "Imagine that you can see and hear their body being stretched like dough in Cook's fat, hungry hands." Phillip fidgets nervously and tries to free himself from my grip. "Imagine that the stench of piss and sweat fills your nostrils until you can barely breathe, and imagine, Philip, imagine that the air is thick with the ghosts of men who have been torn to bloody shreds by my own fair hands." I know that I am scaring him but I don't care. I want to scare him.

Phillip's top lip is glistening with sweat. I grip his arm tighter in anger. "So tell me, Phillip, if you were being tortured like this, would *you* tell me what I want to hear?"

"Y-yes, Sir!" Phillip nods his head vigorously. Of course he would. He has no courage. No resilience.

"Imagine that you are suspected of the worst possible crimes, and that I desperately need information from you. But for some ungodly reason, Philip, you will *not* talk! You choose to hold your stupid tongue! Why do you do that?"

He shakes his head in fear. "I — I wouldn't —"

"But let's say you did, Philip. Let's say that you wanted to protect yourself, or protect someone else. Someone important to you. Can you imagine that? What, pray, do you suppose I should do?"

"Um . . ." Phillip shakes his head, confused.

"Come on, boy! What else can I do to you?" I release his arm gruffly and push him away. He stands a few feet from me, looking up into my eyes like a beaten dog that does not know what his master wants him to do.

I am so enraged. What else *could* I have done to her? No person could endure that sort of pain without talking. I look at Philip again and shake my head. He is dabbing at his eyes with a small lacy kerchief. I wonder . . . is he really capable of imagining the terror of being on the rack? Even after the scene that I have described? I curl my lip at him in disgust. I doubt it; not with his limited mind. Perhaps I will make it even more real for him. Perhaps I will make him understand what it is that some people have to go through and what it is that I have to do in the name of good. I point at the bed and order him to lie on his back. He hesitates and so I angrily push him down. He should know better than to defy me.

"Spread your arms and legs," I bark fiercely. He looks up at me in fear, but he does exactly as I ask. "Now imagine that I am binding your wrists." I lean across him and trace my nail roughly along the soft skin of his wrists before squeezing them tightly to imitate the binding. "And your ankles." I reach down and squeeze his right ankle, and smile again as his leg

210

flinches beneath my touch. *Now* he is beginning to imagine the horror. "You cannot move, Philip, for you are tied so very tightly. You cannot move a muscle. You have no choice but to lie here and wait for me to show mercy . . . should I choose to. You can only pray that God takes pity on your wretched soul. But I will not, Philip; I will show no weakness. I will wind that wheel with my own bare hands until the rack stretches, until I can hear the sinew in your arms and legs tearing beneath your skin!"

I walk to the end of the bed and turn an imaginary wheel very, very slowly. Philip cries out in fear. "It is almost unbearable, isn't it? Your head is swimming, your nerves are screaming, and as you writhe in agony you empty your bowels like the bursting of a dam. And the screams that you can hear . . . they are your own. And then, suddenly . . . *pop*! Your legs don't work any more! *Pop*! Your arms are no longer part of your body! You know that you cannot help yourself any more, Philip, and you know that you may not even survive this. All you can do is watch me as I turn this wheel, and wonder if, dear God, if I will ever stop!"

I raise my head and smile at him. His tears tell me that I have conveyed the scene very nicely indeed. "*Now* would you tell me what I need to know? After everything that I have done to you; after everything that you have endured, after all this pain, would you talk?"

Phillip opens his mouth to speak but he makes no sound. He quickly nods his head. I look at his face with a sudden repulsion; his bottom lip is trembling and his cheeks are wet. He is more of a woman than the heretic is. I sigh heavily and shake my head. For what use is this demonstration anyway? It is not making me feel any better and it is hardly providing me with the answers that I need. *She* did not break; that is all that really matters. She is made of sterner stuff than Philip. It can only be the Devil in her.

"Oh, get up," I tell him impatiently before marching across the room towards the window. Phillip rushes from the bed and scurries towards me.

"Did you torture somebody, Sir? Did-did it not go to plan?" His voice is still very shaky.

"Ha! So you do have a brain after all, boy!"

I take a deep breath and look out onto the rain-splattered courtyard. I know it is wrong, but I enjoyed every moment torturing Askew. I was so confident that she would talk; that she would incriminate the Queen.

"I tortured somebody, all right," I mutter. "And it was a woman. I stretched her bony little body until her legs were broken, and her arms were plucked from her wretched shoulders. I tore the skin from her stomach, Philip, and I laughed as the blood spilled over the edges of the rack." I turn to face him. "But the stupid bitch kept fainting. We had to revive her before we could inflict any more pain. It took a long, long time, Philip. And it happened again and again. Can you imagine how frustrating that was? When we knew that she had the answers to our prayers at the tip of her heathen tongue?" I shake my head in anger. "Do you know what happened then? After we revived her for what must have been the fifth or the sixth time? Well, those gutless fops at the Tower refused to participate any further with the interrogation. Can you believe that? They said that I had done too much already. They spoke as though I was doing something wrong!"

My voice rises as I recount the scene. "But we *needed* that information, Phillip, and I was not going to allow her fainting fits to get the better of me! And I didn't care if we killed her in the process, either." I spit on the floor. "So I continued to turn that wheel myself. I bloody well knew that only she could seal the fate of the Queen, and I was determined to get exactly what I wanted."

I grab Phillip by the wrists and hold his fingers close to his eyes. "Her hands were so constricted that blood poured from her fingernails!" I squeeze him as hard as I can. "But still she would not speak! Tell me, Phillip, what else could I have done? Used fire, or cut her open and placed rats in her belly?"

"I don't know, Sir." He tries in vain to tug his hands from mine, but I do not relinquish my hold. "Please, Sir, you are hurting me." I snort with disgust before letting him go. He looks as pitiful as a wounded deer.

"Oh fuck off then and make yourself useful elsewhere if you refuse to help me. This is the thanks I get for everything that I have done for you. Get out of my sight!"

I storm back to my chair and lower my aching head into my hands. This damn headache just will not go! Perhaps I am being too hard on myself? Perhaps there was nothing else that I could have done? If she had Satan on her side then she could have stood the torment of hell, and nothing could have changed that. Well, if that is the case then I will see to it that she is sent back to whence she came. I will see to it that she is burned at the stake for dashing my hopes. Nobody will make a fool of me so lightly.

One month later . . .
HRH, Queen Katherine Tudor,
9 March 1546, Hampton Court Palace

The harder I try to sleep, the more alert my mind becomes, and it seems that the longer I lie here with my eyes closed, the more frustrated I feel. I was awake before the birds; I was awake during their morning song and I am still awake now that they have settled. If only I could be more like them and live a simple life, uncomplicated by the stresses of men. If only I could rid my mind of these terrible fears, and sleep, for I am so very, very tired.

My husband is bed-ridden again. Or so they tell me, for he has not called for me in five days. I am beginning to think that I must have done something to upset him, for it is unlike him to not want to see me. It would not concern me in the slightest if this silence were because he had found himself a mistress. In fact, I would be rather pleased, as it would remove the worry that I might be called to his bed, and it might also help to improve his mood. But even so, why has he not called on me, at least to minister to his leg? Surely he would not ask another woman to tend to those poor wounds?

No, that is quite absurd; infected ulcers are hardly the things to woo pretty young ladies.

I grab my heavy pillow and place it on top of my head to block out the morning light. If only I could rid my mind of these exhausting fears for just an hour . . . But I know that I cannot. I cannot rest whilst so much is going on that I do not understand. Why is it that I cannot think rationally when I lie in my bed and will myself to sleep? Why do my fears seem so much worse when I am alone at night with just my imagination for company? Why is it that my thoughts so easily darken and intensify to the point where there seems to be no possible resolution?

Things are changing at court. I cannot deny it. I only hope that my husband's distance has nothing to do with it. I have heard dark words whispered around the corridors of the palace; words that are so cold that they almost extinguish the heat from the spring sun. I have been privy to the most dreadful talk about a young woman who was in my household a year or so ago; and of how she has been sent to her death. I barely knew her, and if truth be told I cannot even recall her face, but despite this, I am left feeling shaken and uneasy. I hear that she was executed for treason under Wriothesley's direct orders in a most cruel and brutal manner, for simply expressing her Protestant beliefs. I find it shocking that he has become so confident in his barbarous crusade that he is now targeting people who are known to His Majesty. It suddenly feels far too close to home for comfort.

It sounds to me as though a terrible injustice has been committed, but even so, I know that I must hold my tongue in the current climate, in case I too am labelled a heretic. I do not know if this murder is the reason, but I have observed a distinct change in the behaviour of several of my ladies, for many of them seem to be turning away from me as if I have done something wrong. They are becoming more and more distant with each passing day, as though they are suddenly afraid to be near me. I have watched them struggle to hold my gaze, and I have heard them make their excuses to leave my company to find work elsewhere in the palace.

I can't help but feel that something terrible has infected my chamber. Anna and Joan have told me that some of my ladies are frightened that they too will be labelled a Protestant and treated in the same way as that poor woman. But why do they think that they will be so accused just for spending time with me? Do they feel that because I have expressed my opinion on a few matters of faith that I will be accused of heresy, and they by association? Dear God, do people think that voicing my concerns about the injustice and corruption within the Church makes me a Protestant? Do they think that I have committed treason by simply reading texts that question the notion of truth, and for encouraging a little free thought?

I pray to Almighty God that this is not the reason for the King's silence, for if he thinks that I am a Protestant then I am surely damned. But how could he think so? He is not simple like some of my ladies; prone to hysteria and paranoia and swayed by the latest gossip. No, he is an astute and free-thinking monarch, which is the reason that I have dared to discuss these issues with him in the first place. I search my mind trying to think of what it is that I might have said or how I might have acted to displease him, but I can think of nothing.

It suddenly feels very hot under the pillow and so I force myself to sit up, and I fan my face frantically with my hand. I do not know whether it is the warmth of the sun flooding into my chamber or the sudden fear of the unknown that is making me sweat. I lower my head again and pray that this terrible suffocating sensation is for nothing.

Three days later . . .
HRH, Queen Katherine Tudor,
12 March 1546, Hampton Court Palace

I walk with as much purpose as I can muster along the narrow stone corridors that separate my husband's chamber from mine. He has not called for me in eight days and I am really beginning to worry. If his illness is worse, then I do not want him to be tended to by those witch doctors. I want to oversee their actions and decide for myself what should and should not be done. They may have their diplomas, but I am the only one who can really make him feel better. And I do not want those wretched rodents from the Privy Council anywhere near him either; particularly if he is feeling poorly. They are self-serving tyrants, each and every one of them, with a view to their own advancement and nothing more. God only knows what they might persuade him to do if he is not in his right mind.

As I turn the corridor I catch sight of the two guards standing at his door. Without warning I simply freeze. I have seen them a hundred times before, standing perfectly still with their eyes forward and their halberds crossed before them; and yet this time the sight of them leaves me feeling afraid. Suddenly they cease being my husband's servants, and become powerful men with the ability to constrain me and control my actions. What will I do if they refuse me entry to my husband's chamber? I haven't prepared myself for this . . . I swallow heavily and march towards them with my head held high. What else can I do?

Thankfully, they do not challenge my demand to enter. They simply raise their halberds as they always do and I walk into my husband's chamber, trying my best to suppress the feeling of rising panic. I pause the moment the door has been closed behind me and try to gather my thoughts.

Am I going mad? What on earth did I think they were going to do? With some relief I look around the room and see the King alone, lying prostrate in his giant bed, despite the hour of the day. I can only assume that he is suffering with another of his megrims. I tiptoe quietly to his bedside and lower my body until my eyes are level with his head. He is sweating and looks ghostly pale as though his doctors have been bleeding him again. Damn them!

I gently reach out to touch his cheek and notice how drawn and sallow he is. Have they not been feeding him? I move my hand to his forehead, and sigh with sadness. He is burning, as though on fire. Suddenly he raises his hand to his face and grasps my wrist with a strength that surprises me. I gasp as his fingers wrap painfully around my skin. His eyes open wide and lock onto mine, and we hold each other's gaze.

I force a smile but my heart races in panic as he stares at me coldly. It is as though he no longer knows me. Time passes, and slowly he loosens his grip on my wrist and his expression softens. His face changes and he smiles warmly and without reservation. Without warning, my eyes fill heavily, and I lower my head. I could fill an ocean with my tears at the sight of that smile.

"Katherine, my love. It is so good to see you."

Strangely, it is good to see him again too. It is certainly wonderful to see him so calm and unguarded.

"I have been quite ill," he whispers. His voice is craggy. He sounds as though he has not spoken for some time. "Did you know?"

"Yes, and I wish that you had called for me. The doctors said that you needed to rest alone, but I was terribly worried, and so I decided to ignore them and come here uninvited."

He holds his arms out to me and I lower my head to his chest. He is like a giant warm bear, and I, for once, find myself not minding his touch at all.

"I am so pleased you did ignore them, you unruly wench!" he teases, wrapping his arms around my shoulders. "They told me that I needed to be quiet and that I was better off without any female company."

I raise my head so that I can look at him. I am quite amazed that they could think such a foolish thing. I take his hands in mine and squeeze his fingers affectionately.

"Well, it sounds to me as though they were very much mistaken then, doesn't it? For who will care for you as I do?"

"No one, my love!" The King begins to chuckle as though he has been told off.

"And who can make you forget your pains as I can?"

My husband's smile widens. He takes his right hand from mine and points one of his fat fingers at me. "That is exactly what they are talking about."

I frown at him. "What is? What are you talking about?"

"Oh, those silly old fools on the Council. They say that a talkative woman is not the best person to care for me when I am ailing."

I continue to frown at him. *Talkative?* What on earth is he saying?

"They say that you talk too much about too many things when I am poorly and that you confound my poor brain and upset my humours. I need my rest, apparently, so that I can get better, and all your *chit chat chit chat chit chat* is making me tired. At least, that's what they say."

I smile at such foolishness. "What nonsense, my love, that's what *I* say to all that! Now, if it pleases Your Majesty, I would like to read to you from a book that I am writing, and I should very much like to hear your opinion." I pull sheets of rolled parchment from my deep pocket with a growing excitement. I really am keen to share my latest endeavour with him.

My husband grins widely in return and shifts his weight a little so that he can focus his attention on me properly. I notice that already some of the colour has returned to his cheeks.

"What is it called? This book that you are writing?"

"Well, it is just an idea at the moment, but I am thinking of calling it *The Lamentations of a Sinner*. Doesn't that sound grand?"

Henry laughs loudly in response. "What sins do they commit? Saucy ones, I bet!"

"My Lord, please, it is a spiritual book; a journey into the soul, and a quest for obedience, and freedom from sin."

"Are you the sinner, Kate?"

"We are all sinners, My Lord."

"Then tell me, what are you lamenting?"

"It is not just about me, My Lord. The book concerns everyone. It is about how we all struggle from time to time to be good and decent God-fearing people. It is about how we should conduct ourselves in the eyes of the Lord and in the eyes of our masters. I have brought a section that I thought you might like." I smile mischievously as I leaf through the pages of the unfinished manuscript. "It focuses on Saint Paul and his assertion that wives should be obedient to their husbands."

Henry almost chokes upon hearing my words. He laughs uproariously and for much longer than is necessary in my opinion. Of course, it is nice to see him smile, but honestly! "You should read that bit to Wriothesley! He would like to hear that!"

I raise my eyebrows in surprise, and my smile falters at the mention of that creature's name. I very much doubt that Wriothesley has any difficulties when it comes to spousal obedience. I do not know his wife, but I would imagine that the poor woman is terrified of the brute.

"And Bishop Gardiner for that matter!" he adds forcefully. "You should read that bit to him as well!" He lowers his voice and beckons for me to move my head closer to him. "They would be surprised to hear the word *obedient* coming from your fair mouth, wife, for they think that you speak . . . how was it they put it? Ah yes, you speak 'out of turn to me,' apparently. They think that you have forgotten your manners and that you have forgotten that you are but a mere woman!"

My breath catches in my throat. Dear God, what else have they been saying about me? I try to keep my voice level as my mind fills with terrifying thoughts.

I lower the parchment slowly until it rests on my lap, and look into my husband's face. "What exactly have they said?" I can feel my heart thumping painfully in my chest. Are *they* the reason that my husband has not called for me? Are they trying to keep us apart? Why . . . why would they do that?

"Well, they think that you are rather outspoken with your views."

My husband is smiling widely as though this is nothing more than a joke to him. Dear God, is he not aware of the damage that they can do with these insinuations? If he were ever to believe them . . . "They think that you try to teach *me* about religion and they have even suggested that you act at times as though you are a priest in Holy Orders and are permitted to discuss such things!"

I feel the blood drain from my cheeks at the mention of the word religion. I can almost see Wriothesley's reptilian face dribbling this poison in my husband's suggestible ears. I brace myself and take a deep, shaking breath. "And what do you think about that, My Lord?"

Henry scoffs and brushes his hand in front of him, keen to dismiss the idea as fantasy. "Well, I told them to mind their own business and that I enjoy talking to you. Ha! I said that I didn't choose a woman with a keen mind for nothing! That told them!"

He leans back until his head is resting on his pillow and sighs heavily. I watch with concern as the smile slowly disappears from his face. "But I would be lying if I said that their concerns didn't worry me a little . . . for once or twice I have felt rather challenged by you. Now that is all well and good, and quite right when we are discussing some matters, but you must admit that you have taken certain liberties, and in front of others —"

"I have not!" My voice rises loudly in defence as I feel my panic rise. "What rot, My Lord!"

He holds his hand in the air to stop me from speaking. "You are taking liberties now." His expression becomes stern and I can almost see his thoughts twisting and turning as he watches me. I lean back and gaze weakly at him as he slowly works himself into a temper. "You have even been known to correct me on more than one occasion, which has been more than embarrassing —"

"I would never —" I cannot help myself from interrupting.

"You. Just. Have!" He bangs his palm on the bed three times to emphasize every word. "You just *have*, Kate." He places his hand over his eyes as though his megrim has suddenly worsened. "I do love you, and I love how you care for me with such kindness. But I must admit that they are right about some of this. I hadn't realized it until they brought it to my attention, but I have been thinking about it whilst I've been lying here. I have had little else to do these past few days. A wife should be there to produce heirs, not to challenge her husband."

My eyes widen with amazement and I stare at him in disbelief. How can he dare mention an heir when he is as guilty as I am that we have no child of our own? These words can only have come from Wriothesley's foul mouth, for in the three years of our marriage, never has he spoken to me as though this is my fault.

"It pains me to admit," he continues, "but you do criticize me and you do discredit my opinions in public, and frankly I do not like it. And, Katherine, I do not approve of all this religious talk either. I do not like the insinuations that people are starting to make."

224

He turns to me and raises his hand aloft again the moment I open my mouth to challenge him. He holds my gaze rather coldly. "I ask that you refrain from doing it, that's all."

With an almighty effort he rolls himself onto his side so that he is facing the opposite direction. His heavy snorting tells me that he is still angry with me and that he is stewing in his own self-pity. His ridiculous words have opened a brand new wound, and it is entirely of his own making. Or of Wriothesley's making. Right now it is clear that he has no desire for me to tend to that injury, or to any other.

"Now I am sorry, Katherine," he mutters into his pillow, "but I must sleep. We will go through your sinner book at a later date."

One month later . . .
Robert Caskell, Groom of the Stool,
12 April 1546, Whitehall Palace

I hug my arms across my chest, and shiver violently. It doesn't matter that it is raining outside and that it is bitterly cold in here, for once again His Majesty is burning with an almighty fever. Sometimes I wish that I had a fever too; anything to ward off the terrible cold that bites into my fingers and toes like a dull blade. I watch him as he sleeps atop his sweat-drenched sheets, oblivious to my plight, and I try to warm my hands with my breath. It is such a shame that Her Grace no longer tends to him as she used to. She would make him better for certain.

There is an unexpected rap at the door and His Majesty stirs.

"Who is it? Robert?" His lips move but he does not open his eyes.

My face falls as the Lord Chancellor enters the chamber uninvited. He stands at the door looking at us, sneering whilst tapping his foot impatiently. It seems that he is always here these days, pestering His Majesty to agree to this or to that whilst he lies in his sick bed. If you ask me, the rogue is taking advantage of His Majesty's weakened state. He marches towards the bed, holding a sheet of parchment; no doubt another document for the King to sign.

"I am sorry, Sir, but His Majesty needs rest," I tell him, rather feebly, for I know that he will not listen.

"I am well aware of what he *needs*!" he snaps. "He needs to be protected. Why, if it wasn't for me then he would have all manner of unwanted distractions here bothering him, and then he would never rest! Now would he?" He shoves me out of the way. Surely he cannot mean the Queen? Surely he has nothing to do with her absence? "Now, away with you, boy! I have urgent business with your master."

He lowers himself into the chair next to the bed. "Your Majesty, the latest arrests have been served." He speaks before he has even introduced himself. He does not even bother to inquire after the King's health. His Majesty sighs but does not respond.

Wriothesley leans across the bed and lowers his voice a little. "The ladies Lane and Tyrwhitt have been taken in for questioning, Your Majesty. Earlier today, in fact."

My eyes widen in surprise at his words. What in the devil . . .? These are two of the Queen's ladies . . . I wonder if the Queen knows? I lower myself into a dark corner of the chamber and hug my knees to my chest for warmth. It is quite strange how the room seems even colder now than it was before.

"And? What have you found?" The King is suddenly alert. I look at him and frown; did he know about these arrests? Surely he did not condone them?

"Well, nothing conclusive yet, Your Majesty, but it appears as though they have indeed been reading suspicious texts . . ." A heavy silence descends upon the room. Wriothesley looks at the floor as if he is suddenly embarrassed.

"And?" His Majesty demands. He is growing impatient.

"Your Majesty, I fear that these texts have been shared among . . . among . . ."

"Yes?"

"Well . . . all the ladies."

"*And?* Are you going to arrest them all, Wriothesley?"

"Well, forgive me, Your Majesty, but when I say *all* . . . I fear that this may also include Her Majesty . . ."

My eyes widen in fear. Dear God, did he just mention the Queen? I watch the King fearfully and will him to say something but he simply sits still and stares at Wriothesley as though he does not know what to say.

Wriothesley takes a deep breath. "I cannot help but feel that Her Majesty should be, at the very least . . .

questioned so that she can demonstrate her innocence, and stop the rumours spreading."

"Don't start with that again, Wriothesley. I won't bloody well have my wife questioned by anyone. Certainly not by the likes of you! I don't like any of this, man. I don't like where this is going. I don't know what it is that you are trying to achieve."

The King raises his voice in anger; it is the first time that I have heard him shout in many weeks. "Now, what have you done to these women? I am no idiot, I know your ways. I know what you can get people to admit to. You better not have laid a finger on them!"

"Your Majesty, I have simply spoken to them at this stage. Nothing more. But these are grave matters of utmost importance and I urge you to reconsider. They are withholding information, I simply know it." He speaks quietly, but not so quietly that I cannot hear him. "I am certain that they are trying to protect others in the Queen's household. If you would only allow me to question them properly . . . as I see fit —"

"No. Remember who you are talking about, Wriothesley. They are ladies; they are not criminals. They are my wife's ladies."

"Then allow me to simply question the Queen, based on the information that we have."

"You have nothing!" His Majesty's face is flushed and I can see that he is having trouble breathing. If only Wriothesley would stop this terrible onslaught and leave him alone! "You do not have an accusation from either of them, do you? I bet they haven't even *mentioned* my wife!"

"But we have arrested people suspected of far less than this in the past. As much as I love my Queen deeply, we cannot allow these suspicions to fester and poison your court any further. Past experience has taught me that."

His Majesty does not respond. Wriothesley takes advantage of the silence. "Your Majesty, forgive me, but I feel that the Queen is trying to make a fool of you. I have heard her arguing with you on many occasions, and I cannot help but think that some of the things that she says are ... well ... alarming! I struggle to understand where she gets these foreign ideas from!"

"Not this again, man. You have told me all this rubbish before!"

"But the *way* that she speaks to you, My Lord. It pains me to hear her disrespect you so. Her forcefulness and lack of modesty; it is unnatural, especially for a woman. My Lord, I feel that there is something powerful driving her and I can only assume that it is of these texts that we speak. The texts that we know her ladies have been reading . . ."

"Do you know that she has been reading them too?" His Majesty growls.

Wriothesley strokes his beard thoughtfully. "I cannot be certain of that fact, Your Majesty, but for a woman so clever there can surely be little going on in her household that she is not privy to. Perhaps even little going on without her say-so. Your Majesty, we must question her for the sake of your most Catholic heirs. That is all I ask." There is an urgency in Wriothesley's voice that frightens me. He is desperate for this.

"My wife reads all manner of things. She has never hidden that from me. She is a scholar! I have read fairy tales, man, does that mean I believe in dragons?" His Majesty shakes his head and turns away. "Robert, show the Lord Chancellor to the door. I am tired now."

Wriothesley lowers his head and sighs. He looks suddenly defeated. I rush to the door and escort him into the presence chamber. Thank God he is going. He walks past me with a dark, seething expression.

"I will see you tomorrow, boy," he whispers.

"Uh, Sir, His Majesty should rest —"

He ignores me and continues speaking as if I have not even opened my mouth.

"And if need be, I will see you the day after and the day after that and the day after that. I will keep coming, boy, you mark my words. And when he finally chooses to see sense, *then* I will let him rest."

CHAPTER
FIVE

Lamentations of a Sinner

Three weeks later . . .
Mary Tudor,
3 May 1546, The Corridors of Whitehall Palace

How many guises can a simple piece of parchment take? I hold it in my hand and slowly run my fingers over the elegant letters that decorate the page. How strange that when I hold it this way with my eyes half-closed I can almost see a noose . . . How strange that if I hold it that way I can make out the shape of an axe . . . and if I close my eyes completely, I can imagine how such a thing as this could ignite the flames of a heretic's candle . . . It is nothing less than unimaginably queer how the mind works; how a few brushes of a simple quill carrying nothing more than a little black ink can convey so much more than a pretty pattern.

Is this sheet of parchment that I hold a message from God? Is it the sign that I have been waiting for, telling me what it is that I should do? I read the words again carefully and ponder what force directed my feet along this very corridor at this particular moment. Had I

231

chosen a different route back to my chamber from the chapel this morning, had I not passed the chamber of the Lord Chancellor, then I would not have seen this parchment lying where so many others might so easily have discovered it.

I take a few steps back until my spine presses against the cold stone wall. I tilt my head back and close my eyes. It is as though I am on fire. I take a deep breath and force myself to read the words once more. It has been penned by Wriothesley, and it has been signed by him and by my father. My hands begin to shake until I can no longer see the words. No, I am not mistaken. This *must* be a message from God; it is His way of telling me that I must act now in His name. Finally, He has spoken to me . . . but His words are unclear. I know that He is testing me, for He has placed into my hands the fate of my new stepmother. I am the chosen one; I will act on His behalf and judge her for her crimes. No one else.

I roll the parchment into a tight tube and place it deep within my pocket. I have never been this close to an arrest warrant before . . . in fact, I do not think that I have ever seen one. I certainly have never seen anything that speaks of *interrogation for extreme Protestant sympathies.*

Ten minutes later . . .
Mary Tudor,
3 May 1546, Whitehall Palace

With a shaking hand I rap against the door of the Queen's privy chamber. A maid opens it and I walk slowly inside. It is, strangely, very quiet in here today. My stepmother is sitting next to the fire on her comfortable chair, engrossed in her knitting. My half-sister Elizabeth is at her feet like a faithful little dog. A number of Katherine's ladies are also in the room. Katherine looks up as the door opens and smiles warmly the instant she sees that it is me. She beckons for me to approach her.

"My dearest Mary! How lovely it is to see you. Would you like to join us?" She seems so pleased. "We are all trying our best to knit!" She giggles and holds aloft a long, misshapen rectangle. "Do you believe it, but I have been working on this for a whole week!"

I frown at the strange blue thing that she has in her hand. "What is it?" I ask quietly. I don't know what else to say.

She smiles broadly. "Well, it is supposed to be a lovely thick scarf, but as you can see it is none of those things! Hours, I have spent, Mary! *Hours*! It is for your father, to keep his neck warm. He gets jolly cold and nothing seems to keep the chill out. So I thought that I would take matters into my own hands!"

I look at her open face and feel my heart begin to race. It is so very hot in here.

She smiles even more broadly and holds one corner of her labours towards me to inspect. "This . . . this is supposed to be his initials. I managed to find the most wonderful golden thread, but I fear that it has been wasted on me entirely! This bit here, this is supposed to be an 'H', but as you can see, it looks more like an 'N'!" She shakes her head before gesturing to one of her ladies who is smiling sympathetically. "I should have left it to Joan, but I just couldn't resist having a go, and I so desperately wanted to make something for your father." She sighs and looks up at me. "Something tells me that he is not going to like it at all."

As her ladies protest I walk towards her. I do not smile. "Katherine, I need to speak with you." I look at the others pointedly. "There is no time for this pointless chatter."

Katherine senses my urgency, and quickly ushers everyone else from the room. She insists that I sit next to her on a high-backed chair that she has dragged from the other side of the chamber. She ignores my insistence that I stand. She doesn't realize that this is a deeply formal matter. I still do not know what it is that God wishes for me to do. I think that I should be here, but I am uncertain as to what I should do next. How can I know His will? I close my eyes and offer a silent prayer to the Blessed Virgin before I look Katherine directly in the eyes. I do not return her expectant smile.

"Please tell me the truth when I ask you this, for it is very important to me." I grab her hand. She cannot lie to me. "Are you a Protestant?"

Katherine is immediately taken aback and stares at me with wide, unsettled eyes. She holds my gaze for a few moments as though at pains to choose her words.

"No. No, Mary, I am not a Protestant . . . But I will be honest with you; I have my doubts about the wisdom of some of those in our Holy Church. Grave doubts. I am open to new ideas, you know that, and I have wondered if there are simpler and more direct ways for the people to learn to love our Lord. I have never lied to you, for I respect the devoutness of your faith, and recognize that, unlike me, you have not chosen to question established practice. But I have never tried to hurt you or to involve you in my discussions, for I deeply admire the strength of your beliefs and I would never try to change them."

I cannot help but smile slightly. Her words trouble me greatly, but despite this I am touched by her sincerity. I am also touched that she has not asked the purpose of my question. I take my hand from hers and place it in my pocket. I brush my fingers along the end of the roll of parchment. Lord, please tell me what I am to do . . . She has admitted that she has doubts about the Holy Church . . . grave doubts. That is a sin, and anyone else would be punished for it. I clench my hand into a tight fist. They *should* be punished.

I take another deep breath. "Do you love my father?"

She opens her mouth to speak but the words seem to stick in her throat. This answer does not come as readily. Her eyes move rapidly around the room as she struggles to find the answer. After a few moments, she sighs and rests her gaze on the scene outside her window.

"Your father is a very complicated man, Mary, as you know. I am very fond of him. He has been a good husband to me these past few years, and I have tried to be a good wife to him. And a good Queen."

I shake my head. She could have told me anything. She could have sworn an unquestioning faith in the Church and all its Bishops; she could have said that she loves my father as she has loved no other. But instead she has chosen to tell me the truth. She has decided to trust me with her confidence and not to dismiss me or treat me like a worthless child. My hand instinctively reaches into my pocket again. What to do with this thing . . .? Should I return it to my father? It is his, after all, and it is his right to challenge or to question whomever he sees fit.

I hold her gaze. She is looking into my eyes, trying to read my thoughts. She looks so very troubled. But if I return this thing then what in God's name will they do to her? Will they understand her as I do when she speaks so honestly to them? I take a deep breath.

"Katherine, do you love and fear the Lord? As I do?"

Her face brightens without hesitation and fills the room with happiness. "Of course I do! The Lord is my Saviour, Mary; I love Him with all my heart and soul, for He is my entire reason for being!"

There is no denying her sincerity yet again. She places her hand over her heart for emphasis. "You do know that, don't you? Mary?"

236

I hold her gaze until my eyes unexpectedly overflow with tears. I take my hand from my pocket and reach out to embrace her. I know at this very moment, without hesitation that she is my dearest and most treasured friend. I could not allow myself to acknowledge it before, as I was so consumed by my own bitterness, but I know now that she will always be the girl whom I loved and adored as a child. The girl who tried so hard to help when the odds were against my mother and me. I suddenly know what it is that He wants me to do.

I quickly untangle myself from her surprised embrace and sit back in my chair. I wipe my eyes and look at her with a great urgency.

"Then we must act fast." I pull the warrant from my pocket and place it in her hands. "Katherine, do not panic, but there is a conspiracy against you." She stares at me in alarm; her eyes are wide with fear. I gesture to the parchment.

"This ... this is an arrest warrant for you, Katherine. It has been signed by my father. He has given his permission for Wriothesley to question you about your religious beliefs." My words flow fast and urgently from my mouth, as I know that time is short. "God knows how that dreadful man did it, for he has persuaded my father that you should be interrogated."

She drops the unread warrant on the floor and throws her hands over her mouth in horror. I watch her with a terrible anguish as she rises to her feet and begins to pace around the room. She starts to whine as if in great pain. I rise to my feet and go to her, but I do not know what to do. She shrugs me away and continues her pacing. I watch aghast as her moaning becomes louder and more pained as it escapes through the gaps in her fingers. I try to place my arm around her shoulders to calm her, but again she shrugs me away.

Suddenly, she stops moving and leans over the bed as though she is about to vomit. She takes her hand from her mouth and breathes rapidly. I stand at her side with my hand on her arm and watch her with utter terror. What is happening to her? Her brow is already drenched with sweat and her face and chest have become red and blotchy. I put my arms around her waist in fear as it looks as though she is about to faint.

Still she takes short, panicked breaths. I help her to sit on the bed and I wrap my arms protectively around her shoulders. She is heavy as though the effort of breathing has drained all of her strength and she can no longer support herself. I rock her gently and dab at her sweating brow with my kerchief. We sit in silence for a few moments; neither of us able to find the words to say.

Suddenly she pulls away and turns to me. "I am going to die!" she spits out. "He will kill me! Your father will kill me as he killed the others!"

"No! No!" I protest emphatically. I cannot believe that even he would allow this to happen. "He loves you! This is not his doing! This is Wriothesley! He has taken advantage of my father in his weakened state and has made him sign. It is the only possible explanation."

"I am going to die," she repeats, whispering it over and over again. "I always knew this would be my fate! I have done everything he has ever asked of me, and yet it has meant nothing!"

She rises to her feet again and paces the room. "This is history repeating itself all over again, Mary. Just like the others, I will go to the block and I will lose my head! And for what?" She drops heavily to her knees and clasps her hands together in prayer. "God help me," she cries. "Have I not suffered enough? God take pity on my soul!"

"No, no, no!" I pull her forcefully to her feet. "God has ordained that you will be saved, Kate, I swear it, for He allowed *me* and no one else to find this warrant so that you could be warned —"

"What good is being *warned*, Mary?" she demands, interrupting me. "The die has been cast! I now just sit and await my fate!"

I grab the parchment from the floor and unroll it in front of her eyes. "No, look! The date is for tomorrow. You will not be arrested until tomorrow!"

She throws her hands in the air. "So I have until tomorrow! So what? So what do I do, pack my bags and leave in the dead of night? Shall I go and live on the streets? Shall I seek alms? Shall I live like a pauper in some back street dive?"

"No! You *go* to my father! You explain how sorry you are!"

"For what cause? He has already decided. Look!" She points repeatedly at the warrant that I hold in my hand. "He has signed it! He agrees that there is *just cause!*"

I shake my head for I am certain that the Lord will not allow this to happen. "Tell me, Katherine, why do you think that he has signed this? Do you think that *he* thinks you are a Protestant?"

She looks at me questioningly through her tears and shrugs. "I don't know. I don't think so. He has always encouraged me to discuss contentious issues with him."

"Then why did he sign this warrant? Why is it that he would allow you to be interrogated? There must be a reason. You *must* have upset him somehow? Think!"

She holds her head in her hands in frustration. "I don't know!"

"Think!"

"I don't know, Mary!"

"Katherine, think! You must have an idea! An inkling!"

"The only thing that he doesn't like is the *way* that I argue with him. But that makes no sense! You can't arrest someone for that! Not for *how* they argue . . ."

"What makes you say that?"

"Well, only that he told me a few weeks ago that he doesn't like me . . . what was it he said? *Contradicting* him. *Challenging* him in front of others. But that can't be it."

I smile bitterly and shake my head at the repulsive arrogance of my father. I can almost hear him saying it: "*She challenges me! Her husband, Lord and King!*" I can quite see him worrying himself into one of his rages

240

in his high dudgeon because his own dearest wife is not subservient enough. It really is pitiful.

"Then go to him. Tonight! Go to him, and let him speak of religion. And for God's sake, this time you are to be the demure, impassive wife that he wants you to be! Bow to his apparent better judgement; acquiesce to his stubborn will. If this is the only cause for his signing this damn thing, then God willing, you have the opportunity to change it."

We sit together on her bed; side by side as though we were girls all over again, trying to make sense of an impossible situation. I take her hands in mine and speak to her softly.

"You may think that you know my father, but you do not, for never has there been one so arrogant as him. You have gone too far without recognizing it, for you are so very innocent in all of this. But thank God, there is still time for you to save yourself."

That day . . .
HRH, Queen Katherine Tudor,
3 May 1546, Whitehall Palace

Was Mary right when she said that she should replace that warrant where she found it and that I should say nothing of this to the King? But he is my husband, so perhaps I should just take it to him and ask what it is that he suspects me of? Does he not think enough of me after all that I have done for him to realize that this is an unholy mistake, and that I have never, ever meant to embarrass him or shame him? Would he not take pity on me if I told him the truth?

I cannot bear the thought that I may have misjudged him or that I had wrongly thought he had changed; that he had softened as a person. I cannot accept that I have been wrong all these years and that he is still the tyrant I loathed for so long. It is with a heavy heart that I realize how complacent I have become, and I fear that I may have softened my heart towards him to my detriment.

Oh, why did I ever fool myself into thinking that I would not suffer the same fate as the others? Why did I think that I was so different? What makes me so damn special? Oh Lord, in my desire to be a good and just Queen I have forgotten that this man collects wives as though they were jousting trophies and then replaces them on a whim. This is the man who sent two to horrible deaths as though they meant nothing; banished another into obscurity and shunned the fourth for not pleasing his eye! Damn him, and shame on me for being so utterly stupid, for it may have cost me everything.

I know what I must do, and it begins here in my chamber. Though it pains me, Mary was right. I must gather together every last book and paper that questions the Church; every last shred of evidence that could be used against me by Wriothesley and his brutes. I instruct Bessie to stoke the fire as though her life depended on it, and I rush around my chamber, gathering the tomes, for not a moment is to be lost. I find the *Ninety-five Theses* of Martin Luther and bitterly fling it into the flames as though it has meant nothing to me. How I have enjoyed reading his enlightened words. I throw open the drawer to my bedside table and pull out my translated Bible. I hold it to my heart and close my eyes. This is the copy that John and I used to read together. I drop it onto the glowing coals and cross myself solemnly. I pray that John will understand and will forgive me for this sin. I walk to my desk and pick up the pages of my manuscript, my *Lamentations of a Sinner;* the fruits of so many evenings' labour. Is *this* treasonous? I gather together the many sheets of parchment and walk slowly to the fire as if in a trance. I lower my shaking hands to the flames but I cannot release my grip. I watch as the ink becomes clouded by my tears. No. Not this. I will not sacrifice my work for any of those disgusting men. I will give it to Bessie and ask that she stores it away safely for me in the hope that I might, by some miracle, survive this horror.

What else to do? I search through my remaining books and select those that Wriothesley could claim are controversial, and brutally cast them to the flames. Bessie and I search every last drawer, every possible hiding place for anything that I might have forgotten, but we find nothing. There is nothing else.

That evening . . .
HRH, Queen Katherine Tudor,
3 May 1546, Whitehall Palace

I sit at my husband's side in silence as his tailor fusses around him, measuring his great shoulders and the length of his arms. His Majesty is quickly losing his patience. Why oh why does the tailor have to do this now? Of all the opportunities that he has, he chooses this one. If Mary's plan is to work then I need my husband to be agreeable. My life may depend on it.

It is early evening in my husband's privy chamber and we are joined by Stephen Gardiner, the Bishop of Winchester, the most hated Wriothesley and the repulsive Francis Ballard. They have joined us to discuss Council business, and each of them pulls up a chair around the large oak table. My husband and I sit a little away from them on our identical chairs. Wriothesley shuffles his papers and catches my eye. The sight of the parchment in his long, bony fingers makes me feel dizzy and afraid. I know that it is stupid, but I feel as though each sheet is another warrant for my arrest; each more accusing than the last, and all demanding my death. He looks at me with a contemptuous smile. This time I cannot hold his gaze. I have no defiance left in me.

"Enough!" the King snaps, making us all jump. The tension in the room is oppressive. "This can wait, boy. Now take your fucking measuring stick and piss off out of my chamber. I am not in the mood for this tonight."

I look down at my hands and close my eyes. He has barely said a word to me all evening, nor I to him, and now that he is in such a filthy mood I fear that our silence towards each other will go unbroken.

"If Your Majesty permits, we can move on to the next matter ..." Wriothesley sighs as though he is bored. The King grunts and nods his head. I sit without moving as they discuss the arrogance of the French King, the impertinence of the Spanish King, an uprising in Flanders and the plague in Milan.

How long must I sit here like a dumb animal having to listen to their prattle whilst they act towards me as though nothing were amiss? Tomorrow I will be arrested if the King does not change his mind, and yet so far I have said and done nothing at all to save myself! I feel my cheeks redden and so I focus all my attention on the giant painting of my husband that adorns the larger part of the wall next to his bed. I don't know why I choose to look at it, as I do not like it at all. It was painted by the German, Hans Holbein, and was clearly designed to flatter. It is unnatural to have a painting that big. "Life-sized" they call it. Well I do not like its dimensions, and neither do I like the way that he has painted my husband. He could not have made him look any more menacing or intimidating if he had tried. Naturally the King adores it.

"What do you think, Katherine?"

"I'm sorry?" The King has caught me off guard. How stupid of me to allow my mind to wander at a time like this!

"We are back to that old matter: Protestant insubordination again."

Wriothesley clears his throat and smiles. "Rearing its ugly head just about everywhere I fear, Your Grace." I watch him with a sinking sensation in my stomach as he exchanges a knowing look with Gardiner. I could be sick.

"Well, Your Grace . . .?"

I look at their faces in turn. They are watching me with hungry expressions, waiting for me to say something to prove their suspicions. I grasp my hands together so tightly to distract myself from the enormity of my task that my knuckles begin to sting. With the greatest effort I manage to smile and turn to face my husband. What would Jane Seymour have done? What would Jane have said? *She* never spoke out of turn; *she* would never have dared voice her opinion.

"I would be more interested to hear your thoughts, My King."

"My thoughts?" He looks suspicious. "Why? What are *your* thoughts?"

I try to laugh lightly in response but I stop the moment I hear the ridiculous noise that I am making. They all turn to me.

"It does not matter what *my* thoughts are on this matter, My Lord, or indeed on any matter, unless, of course I am guided by your better wisdom." I swallow heavily and lower my eyes as demurely as I can manage. After several moments I glance hesitantly across the table at Wriothesley who is studying me with one thin eyebrow raised.

"But I want *your* opinion, wife. Tell me what you think! What should we do about these wretched heretics?"

I turn to him again and smile. I reach across and touch him gently on the arm.

"My Lord, I would not dare to tell you what to do in matters so grave. I am but a woman, and it is for you to instruct me."

He is looking at me and frowning. He appears confused. "And why, pray, would you not tell me your opinion? It has never mattered before that you are only a woman, so why would it matter now?"

He is toying with me. He is trying to catch me out. He is bright enough to know that I am playing with him.

I glance across the table hesitantly at our audience. I can see that they too are perplexed. I think back to my conversation with Mary and try to remember the words that she told me to say. "My Lord, I have been giving this matter a lot of thought of late, about what it is to be married; of how women should conduct themselves in the eyes of the Lord and the presence of men." My voice is shaking but I will myself to continue. "My Lord, I have been reflecting on the teachings of our most Holy Church, and realize that it is my most sacred duty to submit myself to you, my husband, as I would to the Lord."

My husband frowns. "You should know the word of the Lord by now, Katherine. Scripture has not changed. You are saying that you did not know this already? Pah, wife!"

I smile and lower my eyes again. "I am always seeking to become a better Catholic, My Lord, and one can never become complacent. There is always something new and wonderful to learn from our Church. Does it not teach that the husband is the head of the wife, just as Christ is the head of the Church?" I shake my head. "I cannot hope to understand the word of God as you do, My Lord. I struggle, and would risk grievous error if not for your great wisdom. Daily I thank Him for your guidance in the knowledge that it is you who will keep my soul from straying."

My husband shifts his head to one side and ponders my words. He is no longer smirking at me. "Go on."

"I have learned through the teachings of our most learned priests that just as the Church submits to Christ, I should submit to you in everything that I do and say, and that pride has no place in a marriage." I look him directly in the eye and squeeze his unmoving hand.

I recognize that this is my moment and so I take a deep breath for courage.

"My Lord, I realize that in trying to pretend that my wisdom is as yours that I have acted in ways that are unbecoming to a wife. If I have sinned against you, my beloved husband, it has only been so that you might think me cleverer than I am, and love me the more. But now I see that all I have done is raise myself above my position and caused you pain. My Lord, I most humbly apologize, for I know that no one is as wise and as learned as you are. No one. I apologize in the presence of these esteemed men and —"

"Your Majesty," Wriothesley interjects forcefully, cutting through my words. I close my eyes with a heart-wrenching sadness the moment I hear his voice overpower mine. He can see what I am trying to do, even if it seems my husband cannot. *He* will never allow me the opportunity to save myself. "Perhaps we should ask Her Grace for her opinion on how we should deal with these heretics? These people who deserve to be punished to the fullest extent of the law."

I look away. What in God's name can I say to this? I cannot agree that we should torture and kill Protestants if they think that I am one, for I will be condoning my own arrest and death. But neither can I disagree, as this alone would prove a further act of defiance against my husband.

"Silence, man!" the King shouts, interrupting my thoughts. I look at him with a desperate longing. Has he chosen to hear me over Wriothesley? He turns his body to me and raises his eyebrows. He is allowing me to continue. Dear God, thank you! He wants me to continue.

I take a deep breath and look at him and only him. "I want you to know, my most beloved husband, that I defer to you in all things. Your knowledge is greater than mine; greater than all of us in this room. You are not just a man; you are a King and I am both privileged and honoured to have you as my husband and as my master to correct my foolish thoughts and to help me become a better Christian and a better wife."

I continue to look into my husband's eyes and pray with every fibre of my being that he believes me sincere,

249

for if he doubts me for even a single second, I know that he will have me taken away and I will never hope to see the light of day again. "My Lord, know also that I love you and I fear you as I love and fear God."

We sit in a terrible silence for a few moments. There is nothing else that I can say. He continues to stare at me; his expression is a picture of confusion. I look into his face and will him to believe the wife who has cared for him so diligently and with affection. I pray that he sees me for the woman who has done everything in her power to be as good a wife and as good a Queen as she can be; the wife who has brought his family back together again, and who, despite herself, has grown very fond of him.

Suddenly his eyes crease at the corners and his face breaks into a wide smile. He holds his arms out and beckons for me to join him. I close my eyes with relief and finally allow myself to exhale. I rush from my seat with a great enthusiasm and throw my arms around his neck. He chuckles and bounces me on his lap.

"I cannot tell you how happy I am to hear those words, Kate," he tells me, kissing me on the cheeks. "For I admit I have had my doubts. You have tested me in no small measure! But now I know that we are perfect friends, and I am the happiest man in the Kingdom."

He pulls me close and embraces me once more, almost squeezing the wind from my chest. I submit like a cloth doll in his arms for I have no more strength left in my body.

★ ★ ★

As I lay my head on his shoulder I catch a glimpse of Wriothesley's rotten face. He appears both appalled and amused by my words but does not look at all beaten. He shakes his head very slowly the moment he catches my eye, for he knows that regardless of tonight, there is still the signed warrant with my name on it. The King has said nothing to revoke that. There is still tomorrow.

One day later . . .
Thomas Wriothesley,
4 May 1546, Whitehall Palace

I close my eyes against the easterly wind that blows across my face and ripples through my hair. But I am not cold. The weight of my impending task consumes my body and leaves no room for weakness. I have never wanted anything so much in my life, and now, finally, the time has arrived. Finally, justice will be served and the Kingdom saved from Protestant corruption at the highest level. We will return to the Catholicism of old, as it was under the Spanish Queen, and it will all be thanks to me.

I look around at the soldiers gathered at my command. Forty of them to be exact. All of them in perfect formation and in perfect dress. All of them bearing polished swords and serious expressions. A true reflection of the gravity of this holy day. Standing here in the royal courtyard, with the might of these guards behind me, I have never felt so alive.

It won't be long before the King and the heretic ride through the palace gates on their horses. He will be returning home, whilst she will just be starting her journey to a very unpleasant place. Oh, the thought of her face when I serve the warrant is making me giddy with excitement! I cannot wait to see her as her pride turns to despair. It will make a most edifying picture: me, striding towards her with forty armed men in my wake, and the King's warrant in my hands. Will there be tears? Will she plead and beg and throw herself on the King's mercy? Oh, I certainly hope so!

That wretched performance last night in the King's chamber has changed nothing. She is beaten and soon she will know it. I felt sick to my stomach watching her drool over His Majesty like that, feeding him such lies; it was an insult to his intelligence. Who does she think she is? Does she take him for a fool? I could see that he wasn't taken in, for he is too wily to allow the deceits of a woman to get the better of him. So he played along, I am sure of it; he lulled her into a false sense of security. He made her feel as though her years of heresy and wicked impertinence could be all forgiven in an instant! I can't help but laugh, for only a woman would believe that possible!

Now, I'll give it to her: she certainly chose her moment for a display of such penitence. I wonder what led to it? She can't have learned about the warrant; too few of us knew, and those who did were more than aware that I would rip out their tongues if they dared to whisper even a hint of it. Did she finally realize that she had gone too far with His Majesty, and exhausted his patience once and for all? Or was it the demise of the Askew woman that warned her? Well, whatever her motives, it was too late; the arrest warrant had already been signed by her own husband, and is due to be served in just a few moments! It is almost too hilarious to comprehend!

I tighten my hand around the warrant. It is such a precious document to me, and to all good Catholics. To think that it was so nearly lost! I grimace at my own carelessness. Stupid fool! Thank the Lord that Phillip found it outside my chamber, where I must have dropped it. To think how easily it could have gone wrong if someone else had found it! I doubt I could have persuaded His Majesty to sign another so easily! The Lord was certainly smiling on me yesterday for I am sure that He watched over it. Oh, how His angels will sing when we finally cleanse this Kingdom of the poison that flows through its veins.

A few of the men begin to fidget and mutter under their breath. They are growing impatient, but that is no excuse.

"Be quiet. Be still, you dogs!" I hiss through my teeth, which silences them. Nothing can go wrong today, everything must be perfect. I cast my eye over each of them; dressed to perfection in their red and black doublets and hats; they are indeed a sight to behold. Let her see this force of strength behind me! Let her see the might with which I shall bring her down! Oh, I can hardly contain myself!

★   ★   ★

The distant sound of horses' hoofs causes me to jerk my head back to the gate. They are coming! My heart begins to race with a nervous excitement and I feel my forehead dampening with sweat. This is it, the moment that I have longed for! I stand perfectly still and wait for them to come into view. Part of me wishes that she was not on horseback; I hate the thought of her looking down on me from that height. But if she thinks that she has any power over me — *ha!* — I have forty men behind me, and a warrant from the King! I'll have her torn down from her nag, and dragged to the Tower like the traitor that she is.

I watch them with baited breath as they trot up to the gates and slow their horses to a walk. His Majesty is on a ridiculous great carthorse, and that accursed woman, a puny black mare. What a pitiful sight they are! I can just make out their expressions. They are laughing together; she does not have a care in the world. Well, let her laugh; let her make the most of this moment, for it won't be long . . .

I try to suppress a grin as it dawns on me that this might be the last time that she will ever laugh. I draw myself up to my full height and stand squarely in front of my men. They will notice us soon enough and they will have no choice but to ride towards us. Straight towards her downfall; towards pain and destruction and the King's Salvation!

It is the woman who notices me first. She catches my eye and gasps. She pulls the reins with such force that her horse throws its head back in anger.

His Majesty follows her gaze with concern and halts when he too sees me. The two of them sit perfectly still and watch us for a few moments. They do not say anything to each other. The woman looks terrified. Somehow she understands that my presence here with all these men is no accident; she knows that we are here for her. I watch with amusement as she looks around; the colour draining from her face. I can't help but smirk. There will be no escape today, Your Grace . . . no escape at all. But I dare you to try, to run, to ride far away, for I will hunt you down, load you with chains and drag you back through the filth.

For some reason, His Majesty seems confused. He is staring at me with his eyebrows raised. He can't have forgotten? I tilt my head to the side and stare back. I cannot understand his expression; he knows full well the reason that I am here. He knows that today is the day that I am to arrest his wife; after all, he is the one who signed the warrant!

I decide that I will not move. Let her come to me. It will prolong the delicious moment and prove to her who holds the power now. The King digs his heels into the sides of his horse and plods slowly towards me. The woman hesitates, but follows. They ride onwards; their faces are grave. I take a pace — a single pace — to meet them. I can't help but look at her triumphantly as they approach. I twitch the warrant in my left hand, not much; just enough to catch her attention. She does not see it. I twitch it again. Her eyes linger on the parchment . . . She has enough sense to be afraid.

I clear my throat; I want to deliver my words loudly and clearly so that all will hear and remember. I take a deep breath.

"I have a warrant for your arrest, Your Grace. I am to take you to the Tower with immediate effect and to question you for matters of a religious nature."

She gasps and throws a hand to her mouth.

With the speed of her movements, the horse is panicked and it spins on the spot. It leans back and throws its front legs in the air. I quickly step back for my own safety and watch the woman grab for the reins. She stretches her arms around its neck and leans forward in her saddle to stop it from falling backwards and crushing her. I watch eagerly as its back legs teeter under the weight. *Fall back . . . fall back . . . .* It continues kicking for a few seconds, but does not lose its balance. Instead it lowers its front feet to the ground and snorts loudly. Oh, how sweet a fall would have been today; to have had her at my feet where she belongs! I notice that the woman is breathing rapidly and that her face has flushed a deep pink. She looks very afraid, as she ought.

I take another step back as the horse throws its head around and stamps its front feet against the ground. Its ears are flat against its head, and its eyes are rolling back until only the whites are visible. I have to stop myself from laughing as it spins around again and struggles to free the reins from her hands. It is all that I can do to contain my amusement as she stretches out her arm to stroke its lathered neck. *Throw her and trample her!* The stupid, weak woman!

His Majesty sits and watches from atop his mighty brute but for some unfathomable reason he looks terrified as the woman's horse spins and rears. Why does he care? Should he not be enjoying this as I am?

"ENOUGH!" the King roars, and I turn to him in surprise. The mare startles and comes to a halt. He reaches across and grabs the woman's reins, dragging the two horses close together until they are both still. He does not look happy. Have I spoiled the moment? Was my delivery at fault? I decide that I will finish this business as soon as possible, and take her away as we agreed. I realize that this must be difficult for him; another failed marriage . . . not a harlot this time, but a heretic. Poor man. I take a deep breath and step towards her. I hold the warrant aloft. I am calm. It is important that everything is done correctly.

Before I can speak, a sharp burning pain consumes my left hand. I look up in horror and see that His Majesty is holding his whip high in the air, and is glaring at me. Dear God, has he just struck me? I look at his face, aghast, my mouth wide open. What in the hell . . .? His expression is angry and his knuckles whiten around the handle of his whip. What in God's name did he hit me for? I have done nothing wrong! I glance down at my hand and see that it is already throbbing and pink. I gasp with horror. My hand is empty . . . The *warrant*! The force of the blow must have knocked it from my grip. I quickly bend down to retrieve it from the ground. Has the King lost his mind? No, it was a mistake; he meant to strike *her*.

I quickly rise with the warrant in my grasp once more, ready to serve it. As I look up I am suddenly struck again; this time across the head. The blow is so hard that it sends my hat flying across the courtyard, and almost knocks me to the floor. I stagger a few paces back and look up at the King in confusion. He is holding his whip above his head again, menacingly. There is no doubt any more. I know that he meant to strike me this time.

"Your Majesty . . .?" I raise my hand to my face instinctively. Dear God, is that blood that I can feel trickling down my forehead? He is staring at me with dark eyes. He looks so enraged! I glance across at the woman, who is stroking her mare's neck. I turn back to His Majesty who is red-faced, and snorting through his nose like an angry bull. There is spittle on his beard. "Your Majesty, I don't understand —"

"How dare you accuse my wife? And here of all places, in front of all these people! What on earth do you have an army for, you idiot? What in God's name did you think that she would do?" His horse suddenly takes a step towards me, and I raise my hands above my head to shield myself. His Majesty snorts with laughter.

"Afraid of a horse now are you, Wriothesley? Hear that, Titan? He's afraid of an old boy like you!"

I hear sniggering from behind me, but I do not turn to reprimand them. My face burns with embarrassment. How dare His Majesty ridicule me like this in front of that Protestant bitch, who should be in chains by now, pleading for her own life! With shaking hands,

I uncurl the warrant and hold it above my head defiantly.

"Your Majesty will recall signing this warrant for the Queen's arrest." My voice becomes louder and I turn to face my men. They will see for themselves that he is at fault; not me! "Signed by His Majesty, the King no less!"

I turn back to the Queen; I am eager to read her expression when she realizes that he has betrayed her! She looks at the King with a frightened expression. "This is a legally binding document," I tell her, "and it is my duty to see —"

"My wife, your Queen is no heretic!" the King spits out loudly, interrupting me. "You tricked me into signing that thing. I was ill with fever and not in my right mind. She will never be arrested!" He points at me accusingly. "I should have *you* arrested, you fucking imbecile!"

He turns to his wife and smiles gently. "Do not fear this louse, my love. You will always be safe with me."

My head pounds and I taste the blood from my cheek as it finds its way to the corner of my mouth. How could this have happened? Why in God's name is he going back on his word? He could not have been taken in by last night's performance?

"But . . . the warrant?" I hold it up and wave it in the air.

"I'll show you what you can do with your fucking warrant!" The King reaches forward and snatches it from my grasp. He throws his whip to the ground and

259

tears the parchment into tiny shreds. He smiles at me contemptuously before hurling the remains in my face.

"Now take your warrant, Wriothesley, and fuck off!" He kicks his horse in the ribs and together they rush past. I scramble out of the way and watch with a feeling of hopelessness and rage as she follows behind. I glare at her. She does not turn to look at me but I know what she must be thinking. I know that she thinks she has beaten me. My face darkens and I clench my fists in anger. I never thought it was possible to hate her more than I did before, but I was wrong!

"She did not want to marry you!" I scream to nobody in particular. My eyes widen in horror and I throw my hands over my mouth to stop myself from saying more. Dear God, what have I just said? His Majesty stops his horse. He stares ahead for a few seconds before turning the beast so that he can face me.

"What did you say?" He speaks very slowly. His face is darker than I have ever seen it.

My heart races in fear. I had never really meant to tell him, but I was so consumed with rage . . . What have I done? What will he do to me? I look up at him and smile weakly. Perhaps I should just tell him and get it over with.

"She didn't want to marry you," I repeat quietly. "I *made* her marry you. I had to threaten her sister." I shrug my shoulders. I feel utterly defeated and I barely know what I am saying any more. "She wouldn't have married you otherwise." I watch as his jaw drops slightly in disbelief. He turns his horse a little more so that he can look at her. He stares at her for a few seconds and searches her expression for answers. He looks desperate. The corners of my mouth begin to twitch and I am suddenly aware that there might yet be a chance . . .

"Katherine, is this true?" he asks.

I study her face; I am certain that she will not lie. Not about this. She will not refute me for she knows that I have Ballard, and he will confirm my story. She has no one.

A coldness enters her eyes and then her face softens. "No," she says quietly.

I gasp. She *is* lying to him!

"No, My Lord. This is not true. I always wanted to marry you. He tried to threaten my sister, because that is the kind of man he is. But there was no need. I would have married you anyway."

He sighs and smiles warmly at his Queen. The delusional, arrogant, fool of a man.

"I will deal with you later, Wriothesley," he growls viciously. "Make no mistake about that."

As they ride away, hand in hand, I feel the presence of my men once again. How must I look to them? I spit on the ground and walk purposefully towards the palace gates, not yet knowing my destination but certain that I must leave immediately. I do not give them orders; I no longer care what they do. I no longer care what anyone does. This court is a den of corruption. It has been tainted by evil and they, too, are part of it. I am a man of God but I am fighting devil after devil and I am beginning to think that I will never win.

CHAPTER
SIX

Let Him Sleep

Five weeks later . . .
HRH, Queen Katherine Tudor,
8 June 1546, Whitehall Palace

I don't think that I will ever really get used to moving from palace to palace each season. It is such an upheaval for everyone. It always feels as though just as I am finally settled in one set of chambers, we are forced to uproot and move on to another. It feels so transitory that I am rarely settled, and never do I feel as though I am truly at home. Not that I ever have, in all honesty, but that's by the by now. If I had my way, we would stay at Hampton Court Palace all year long and not just for summer, for that is my favourite. Whitehall is so gloomy in comparison, and Greenwich is sprawling and brash.

There is something magical about Hampton Court, I have always thought so, and it is not just because it was there that I first met Thomas. It is magnificent without being showy, it is sumptuous without being vulgar and its ornate gardens can lift my spirits at *any* time of the year. But of all the palaces, this summer, due to my husband's deteriorating health, we are to stay at Whitehall.

"Ready, Your Majesty?" There are four guards in the King's chamber dressed from head to toe in their black and red uniforms. Two of them approach my husband with some hesitation. Dr Wendy, the physician, is here, waving his arms around like a mad man and bellowing orders to anyone who will listen. My husband is sitting on the edge of his bed, dressed in scarlet finery and ready for Mass. His bandaged legs are dangling uselessly over the edge, and his face is red. He has hardly said a word all morning and so I am relieved that Dr Wendy is filling the room with his silly, whining voice, even if it is to talk nonsense, for I cannot bear the weight of my husband's silent rage.

There is a large, velvet-covered chair just outside the open chamber door. Although he knows that it is there, I do not think he has actually seen it yet. Neither do I know what he will say when he does, for it is no ordinary chair. I look at it sidelong with a degree of scepticism; at the plush cushion and the ornate back, and at the long wooden poles that have been bound to the arms so that it can be lifted at all four corners the moment he is seated. I watch my husband as he stares at the floor.

Now he *has* consented to being carried, of course, but if you ask me, the mere sight of that chair with those great batons may be too blatant a reminder of his terrible ailments. God knows how he will feel once he is sitting in it and paraded in front of everyone like an invalid. I take another glance at the large, odd-looking contraption and shudder. Dear Lord, please let it hold his weight.

★   ★   ★

I know I am not a physician, but I think that my husband's sudden deterioration reflects the demons in his mind. I for one have always strongly believed that worry and agitation can affect the body as readily as any sickness. In my opinion, the Lord Chancellor and his cronies should be horsewhipped for all the stress that they have caused him, and boxed on the ears for what they have done to me. Wriothesley, more than anyone, should think himself lucky that he escaped with his life. I am not sure why it is that my husband so readily pardoned him given how he cruelly pursued me, and I am quite sure that I would not have been that fortunate had his plan succeeded.

In recent days, my husband has changed. His mind has hardened towards some as quickly as his body has weakened. Perhaps it is unsurprising that he has become so suspicious? He trusts no one; not his Council, not his servants and, despite the fact that he came to his senses at the latest hour, he does not seem to trust me either.

He is ready. He frowns and grunts at the guards, who are waiting next to the bed. They stand at either side of him and lower their bodies until their shoulders are level with his. I can't help but grimace as he raises his arms and pushes his fingers into their shoulders. They wrap an arm around his wide back, brace themselves and slowly rise to their feet. I turn my face away in case my husband notices the worry in my eyes. The guards shuffle forwards and drag him towards the chamber door while his legs dangle weakly beneath him.

"Careful!" the doctor screams. "Remember who you are carrying! Don't crease him!"

I look up for a second as they pass, and notice that my husband's eyes are fixed on the ground in a determined manner and that his mouth is pursed in anger. The guards manoeuvre their way through the door and gently lower him into the waiting chair. I hold my breath for a few moments as he shuffles around and makes himself as comfortable as he can. Still he does not make a sound, which is not a good sign. He brushes a few specks of dust from the arms of the chair and roughly grabs the wooden poles to test them. Thank God they do not move. The four guards crouch in silence at each corner of the chair and keep their eyes facing forward. They have wrapped their hands around the poles in readiness and are waiting for instruction.

"Are you ready, Your Majesty?" Dr Wendy inquires, rushing into the presence chamber and fussing around my husband.

He looks up in anger. His face is flaming red and his eyes are flashing. "Does it look like I am fucking ready, you mincing shit?"

The air is tense, and so I quickly decide to speak. "To the chapel, please." I dismiss the doctor with a nod of my head. "You lead the way, please, My Lord."

I recognize how ridiculous my words must sound, but it is all that I can do to make him feel less useless. I stand aside and wring my hands together anxiously as the guards lift the chair. Dear God, please let this go smoothly . . . all they have to do is carry him to the chapel without dropping him.

Six months later . . .
HRH, Queen Katherine Tudor,
3 December 1546, Whitehall Palace

The heady scent of woodsmoke fills the King's chamber, and the fire spits and crackles beneath the weight of the giant logs. Despite this, it is still bitterly cold. We sit at my husband's bedside in silence on our gilded chairs, with our gloved hands, and our thick, fur-lined bonnets pulled down over our ears, and wait patiently for the moment he wakes.

I look down at his sleeping face and purse my lips, wishing that I were somewhere else. This waiting is interminable. He is sleeping for longer and longer these days, which means that we must wait for an age to tend to him. He insists that we are here when he wakes, but goodness only knows when that might be. In all honesty, it is not the waiting that we object to, for when he sleeps, he is bearable.

The windowpanes rattle violently against a sudden rush of wind. The noise startles me and I hold my breath for a moment. I watch him intently. He does not stir. His eyes continue to flicker rapidly beneath his pink, damp eyelids. I wonder what is going on in that mind of his. Let him sleep for longer. Let him not trouble us for once. I exhale slowly and turn towards Mary, who is absorbed in a small book that she holds in her gloved hand. I feel my face redden a little. If only I could distract myself so. If only I could contain these unchristian thoughts towards my own husband . . .

Shame on me, for he is not a well man. He cannot help himself.

I turn my attention back to the sleeping mass before me and rub my hands together in an effort to warm my aching fingers. I cannot blame him for resenting his terrible ailments . . . I cannot blame him for being angry . . . but if only he would not choose to take his frustration out on those around him as though we are the cause of his pains. I sigh quietly. It is so hard for us to bear, for we do *everything* that we can to help him. With the lightest touch I turn a page of the book of psalms that rests in my lap. But despite this I do not bother to look down; my mind is too preoccupied to read.

It is unsurprising that after everything that has happened this year I have become frightened of my husband. I am especially wary these days in case I forget myself and say or do the wrong thing. I cannot risk incriminating myself again as I almost did during Wriothesley's watch for I know that the King will not be so understanding a second time.

Because of my near arrest, my dreams have been plagued by terrible images of my own death. I watch myself from afar as I am made to kneel, and as I place my trembling head on the block, waiting for the axe to strike as punishment for a terrible crime that I have not committed. I dream that the executioner is my husband and that he is laughing behind his mask and jeering at me for being so stupid.

My life has changed immeasurably since the day that Mary brought me the warrant, and has worsened still with the deterioration of my husband's health. No longer do I feel free and able to act as I once did. It took several years for me to become accustomed to this life and to the moods of my husband, but now I am back to where I started: frightened, alone and unsure.

In recent months he has changed towards me, and I now see little of the love that he professed in the days that followed my near arrest. For then he was so sweet and protective that he seemed more like John than he did the King. But now I am afraid; I cannot sleep, and my appetite is not as it was, for the sight of food leaves me nauseous. I can hardly read any more in fear that I might read the wrong thing; I cannot calm my mind to write and I do not want to make any decisions about anything in case they are wrong. I trust almost no one. Everywhere I look I see people with a grievance; people who — like Wriothesley and Gardiner — might wish to bring me down. Even here, in this room I see enemies! The guards, the doctors, the advisors . . . I do not even want to spend time with my ladies in case they too turn against me.

My husband mutters something in his sleep. Mary and I look up and watch him with the intensity of hawks. His breathing quickly settles and we exhale slowly in unison. Neither of us speaks a word. Perhaps it is to be expected that I can no longer enjoy his company as I once did now that I know what he is capable of. Before he became ill and before my near arrest, we would spend many hours together, arguing and debating the most contentious of issues. And to think that I believed that he enjoyed our discussions as much as I did!

But now I fear being near him; talking to him; being alone with him, and yet I know that I have no other choice, for I cannot risk him being with anyone else in case they too try to poison his mind. More often than not, I take Mary with me when I visit the King. Just as today. Despite everything that he has done to her. Like me, she forces herself to endure the waiting and the temper tantrums. I know that she does not do it for him, for I suspect that she bears him little love. More than anything she helps me to retain my composure and bridle my tongue when I am around him. She ensures that I remain in character at all times, for despite all that has happened, I sometimes forget myself. It is not in my nature to pretend, and so I struggle to play the role of a different woman.

How long I can keep this up, I do not know, for it is so very difficult. Especially when I am forced to listen to my husband and his Privy Council talking such utter drivel to one another. Sometimes I can barely hold my tongue when I hear them condemning the common people to the most terrible punishments for the most meagre of crimes. I am desperate to intervene as I used to, for the sake of the poor innocents of this wretched Kingdom, but I know that I cannot, not if I value my life. These days, when I am near my husband, I know that I must remain gagged.

Mary frees her right hand to turn a page of her book. Her olive skin is quickly hidden again beneath her fur-lined glove. Mary's deep wounds have had longer to fester, and unlike Elizabeth, she has not been shielded from the grim realities of her father's decisions. I do not think that Mary will ever find peace with her father, and in all honesty, I no longer blame her. It wasn't so long ago that I thought *I* might achieve a contentment with him; that we would strike an unspoken agreement of loyalty and friendship . . . but I now know that I misjudged him, just as I misjudged myself. He will never be more to me than the man who forced me into marriage; the man who put a crown on my head and stole me from my true love.

My husband wrinkles his nose like a pig and thrusts a bare, pink foot out the side of the bed. I gently pull a sheet over him so that he does not catch a chill. I wrap the sheet around his toes with as much care as if I am securing a bandage. Still he does not wake. Mary catches my eye and smiles kindly. For better or worse, he is still my husband, and he is still her father, and so I know that we will never refuse to do what is expected of us, no matter how he behaves.

My hand brushes against the mottled skin of his ankle. It is so red and swollen and sore that I can't help but pity him. If only I could understand why his body is deteriorating like this and with such speed. I lean back in my chair and wrap my arms around my chest for warmth. He is as ill as I have ever seen him. He flitters between delirium and lucidity; he is bed-ridden for much of the time; his head burns in fever almost continuously and his mouth and eyes fester beneath thick, weeping scabs that we struggle to banish.

271

Lord forgive me, but if I did not know better I would think that he has been struck down with the plague. Although it would be treasonous to mention it, I can only assume that death must not be too far away. Mary tells me that this is his punishment from God for betraying me, and for all his other crimes, but I will not allow myself to entertain this, for I am more enlightened in my thinking than she is. But even so, his deterioration seems almost unnatural and does leave me unsettled. I do not know how to feel about his worsening state for I do not wish to see him in pain. And yet when I think of his death, I feel a relief washing over me that is as real as water. I would never wish him ill, but I wonder how much longer I can continue to live in this perpetual state of fear.

One week later . . .
Robert Caskell, Groom of the Stool,
10 December 1546, Whitehall Palace

I can hardly bring myself to look at him; can hardly believe the sight that lies before me. I cannot accept the pitiful state that His Majesty has been reduced to, and I don't want to, either. It has been several weeks since the poor man was last able to leave his chamber, or for that matter, do *anything* for himself, and it is just so desperately unfair! Each day I watch him fade, and each day I pray with all the strength in my body that he might somehow defy the expectations of us all, and recover. I can hardly believe that it was only a few months ago that we thought he was on the mend, for he was walking with a noticeable spring in his step as though he had not a care in the world. And now this . . .

He is now so weak that he can barely raise his head from his pillow, and it seems that there is nothing that anyone can do to help him. I cross myself and grit my teeth with frustration as I make my way slowly across the chamber to his bed.

Of course, we dare not mention aloud what we are all thinking, for to even allude to the King's passing would be treasonous, and quite right too. But everybody knows, of course. How can they not? There are few fools here. One look at the faces of the physicians who tend to him day and night speaks more plainly than their hollow words of cheer ever will. And if nothing else, how are folk to explain His Majesty's noticeable absence from court? That alone is enough to raise suspicion in everyone's minds. If you ask me, people are afraid. They do not know how to behave or what they should or should not say, and so they keep their heads held low and they speak only in whispers and try to keep their worries to themselves. What else can they do?

The King sniffs loudly and stirs, but does not open his eyes. I shake my head with sadness. The poor, poor man, reduced to this; lying helplessly in his giant bed, no longer able to muster the strength to even feed himself. He cannot keep his eyes open for more than a few minutes at a time, and is barely able to speak above a painful murmur. I feel a lump rise in my throat as I bend over his huge, useless body and look at his pale, grey features. However did it come to this? However did he fall so very quickly? I can't help but think that if this *isn't* from God, then why on earth *hasn't* He intervened? What has His Majesty ever done to deserve such pains, and for so very long? It just doesn't seem right to me. Punishments like this should only be for really bad people.

I swallow and will myself not to cry. "Time to change your sheets, Your Majesty," I whisper. He grunts and opens one heavily bloodshot eye, just a fraction.

"Robert . . ." he whispers.

I drop to my knees before him. "Yes, Your Majesty?" My voice catches. Just to hear him speak my name aloud is almost too agonizing to bear. He opens his other eye and holds my gaze for a few seconds. He does not smile.

"There is something I need you to do." His breath is rattling and there is a faint gurgling from deep within his throat. He speaks so quietly that I am forced to lower my head to hear him.

"Robert, listen carefully. Please summon the Council to my bedside early tomorrow morning. There must be no further delay." He narrows his eyes with a sudden urgency. "I would like to dictate my . . . my *will*, Robert, and to announce the succession."

His words startle me and I pull away in surprise. I had not prepared myself to hear him — or anyone else for that matter — say such dreadful things. Not yet, anyway. I force myself to smile and I shake my head

274

defiantly. I do not wish to disobey the King, but *this* is not necessary!

"My dear boy." He smiles kindly and lifts his swollen hand from beneath the covers and places it in mine. His hand is hot and damp despite the coolness of the room. "You have been so very good to me. You should know how much you mean to me."

I turn my head away and blink rapidly to contain my tears. He gently squeezes my fingers. In all the years that I have served him, he has never once sought comfort like this; not once has he reached out to me as he is now.

"Now listen carefully, Robert. I need you to ensure that everybody is present tomorrow. The Privy Council must be there, of course. Even Wriothesley must be present. And summon the Archbishops too. It is imperative that my will is heard by *everyone* that matters. There can be no room for misinterpretation, God forbid. I know what those bastards are like, Robert. They will try to twist everything for their own selfish gain." He coughs violently and gasps for breath. "We cannot allow that to happen. Don't trust a soul, Robert."

"But Your Majesty, we will make you better. *Please* don't talk like this . . ." My voice finally breaks and I can no longer hold back my foolish tears.

One month later . . .
Mary Tudor, 12 January 1547,
Whitehall Palace, Royal Chapel

"Father Confessor, in your presence I kneel before almighty God and all His angels and saints. I am ready to confess my sins and to cleanse my soul of iniquity."

"The Lord hears you, Your Grace."

I cross myself and sigh. "Father . . . *my* father, the King, is going to die."

The gasp from the priest is audible. "Hush, Your Grace! *Please!*"

"No, Father, it is true. It must be said."

"But it is a sin. It is treason to even *think* that the King might —"

"Are people not thinking it, Father? Are *you* not thinking it?" My question is met with silence. "My father . . . he *is* going to die." This is the first time that I have uttered these words aloud. I close my eyes and wait to feel something. Anything. But I feel nothing.

"I once came to you, and I asked you to show me the righteous path. I asked for God's guidance in a most painful and delicate matter, for I did not trust my own judgement. I was starved of love, and driven by the painful memories of my youth."

"Did the Lord answer your prayers, Your Grace?"

"He did, Father. He made me look anew, and softened my heart. He opened my eyes to the kindness of my stepmother, and then trusted me to save her when she was in the greatest peril." The smile falls from my face. "But as a consequence, my heart has turned to

276

stone. For I saw just how wicked and corrupt men can be. My father has proven to be so vain and contemptuous. Even in his dotage, Father, he showed that he could not be trusted, for I learned that he was prepared to sign his own wife's death warrant."

I can almost hear the priest's mind pondering my words. Of course, he knows nothing of this. I doubt he believes me. "But she is not dead, Your Grace . . ."

"No, thanks to *me* she isn't. Thanks to *God* she was saved. Through God's revelation I now despise my father more than I ever did."

"People are complicated, perhaps our Lord was trying to show you that."

"Complicated? Of course. But a complicated man is not necessarily an evil man; but that is who sired me! An evil man who commits evil acts time and time again without just cause. I had hoped and prayed that my father would repent. I had hoped that God could help me to find forgiveness in my heart, but by His revelation I despise the King all the more. I can only assume that He must feel as I do, and that frightens me, for I would not wish His vengeance upon anyone. Even him."

"Your Grace, you cannot know how our Lord does and does not feel, and He does not choose our emotions for us. We are free to choose for ourselves."

"I can believe that it is through divine will that my stepmother will soon be a widow. I once asked you if his ailments were a punishment for his wickedness, and you couldn't answer me. I still ask myself the same thing, but I *do* know this: the Lord feels that the world would be a better place without him in it. What does *that* tell you?"

"I cannot answer that either, my child. It is not for us to guess. He is not just a vengeful God or He would not have saved the Queen as you say."

"No. I think you are right. I do not think that God is cruel, as my father is. For everything that my father has done, for every wrong that he has inflicted upon others, the Lord saw fit to save Katherine for *his* benefit too. Because of God, my father's pain in his final days has been softened. *That* tells me that He has a merciful side. I cannot imagine anyone tending to my father with as much compassion and patience as she does, even after all that he has done to her. *That* cannot be by chance, Father?"

I picture Katherine's gentle expression. "My gratitude runs deeper, Father, for I will always be grateful to God for bringing her to our troubled home. Thanks to her, my father has been reunited with his family. It is a comfort to me, Father, as I have spent so many years in exile, without anyone to love me. And thanks to her, I am back in the line of succession. The Tudor throne might one day belong to me and mine, Father, and with it, a chance to restore our most Holy Church to its rightful glory, and cut out — once and for all — those poisonous doctrines that threaten our faith."

"Amen to that, Your Grace. God has smiled on you."

"Yes, He has. But still, my emotions are torn. Do you know with whom he plans to be buried? No? Well I will tell you, Father: with *Jane*! Jane Seymour! Not with my mother. Not with the one true Queen, oh no! He has even decided on the effigy that he wants engraved on their tomb; he wants them described as 'sweetly sleeping,' or some such nonsense."

I resist the urge to spit in anger. "*Sweetly sleeping . . . .* Even in death he will dishonour my sainted mother!" I cross myself again. "But, Father, I am scared about the future. Despite my father's idiocy, for the first time since I was a child I have found stability, and the thought of even greater turmoil is almost too much. I do not know what will happen when my brother is crowned. He is so young! I feel as insecure as I always have! I ask myself, Father: Will I live here? Will I live with Katherine? I do not know if I am strong enough to face the future uncertain and afraid, *again*."

"I will pray for you, my child. Know that our Lord is listening to you and is guiding you. You will find your place *and* your purpose."

CHAPTER
SEVEN

Only by Love

One year, six months later . . .
Katherine Seymour,
12 July 1548, Sudely Castle

There is a familiar *tap tap tap* on my chamber door that distracts me from my sewing. I can't help but smile. I know who this will be. Several strands of unruly brown hair appear a moment before the smiling face beneath it. My visitor searches the room with his eyes until he finds me. He lingers on my face for a few moments before his eyes move to my belly. My smile broadens in response and I too lower my gaze.

"I have missed you this morning," I tell him. "I was beginning to think that you were starting to prefer that new stallion of yours!"

His mouth twitches at the corners. "Well . . . it was a *very* difficult decision!"

He is wearing his riding clothes and looks dishevelled. He has caught the sun on the bridge of his nose, and as he walks closer I can just make out a scattering of freckles on his cheekbones. He lowers himself to his knees and gently kisses my swollen stomach through the layers of my gown. He smells of leather and horses, just as he always has. I close my eyes and find myself laughing out loud. I cannot help myself. I still cannot believe that it is Thomas, my husband, here with me.

"Do you know what day it is?" I ask him.

Thomas frowns. He does not remember and I do not blame him.

"It is the twelfth of July, my darling. I married the King on the twelfth of July." His smile drops a little at the mention of my late husband. I wrap my arms around him and pull him close. "I only mention it as it is five years to the day that he and I were married. It just feels, I don't know, like something that happened to someone else."

I hold him tightly and close my eyes. I can feel the warmth of the sunshine on the back of my neck. He rests his head against my belly again and smiles as our unborn child kicks his cheek. How I want Thomas to know how happy I am, and how five years ago I did not believe that I would ever be happy again!

I turn my head a little and look beyond the small black panes of my chamber window and out onto the quiet grounds of our beautiful home. *Our home*. Another kick from our unborn child brings me back to the present and reminds me that it will not be long until we two become three; a proper family; an ordinary, uncomplicated family no less, bound not by duty or obligation, but only by love.

Epilogue

Katherine's happiness was nearly shattered when Sir Thomas, true to his infamous ways, was rumoured to have had a romantic encounter with the fifteen-year-old Princess Elizabeth, whom Katherine had taken into her household following the death of her father. However, the besotted Katherine chose to dismiss the rumours, and on the 30 August 1548, realized her dream and gave birth to a healthy child; a daughter. A cruel irony followed, when just six days later, Katherine tragically succumbed to the puerperal fever.

Henry and Jane Seymour's son, the nine-year-old Edward, was crowned Edward VI upon the death of his father. He ruled for just six years in name only; the Kingdom being governed by the Regency Council until his death in 1553.

Thomas Seymour was executed for treason on the 20 March 1549, following his unsuccessful attempts to further his career by unduly influencing the young King. Mary stayed faithful to her Catholic religion during her brother's reign, and worshipped privately in her own chapel. She ruled as Queen Mary I of England and Ireland from 1553 until her death in 1558. During her reign, "Bloody Mary" as she became known restored the Kingdom to strict Catholicism. Elizabeth, the daughter of Anne Boleyn, became Queen after the death of her half-sister, and ruled successfully for fifty years. As "Good Queen Bess" she proved that Henry did not need a son to continue the Tudor dynasty.

Thomas Wriothesley was created 1st Earl of Southampton in February 1547. One month later he was deprived of his chancellorship and excluded from the Privy Council. He was never brought to account for his attempts to defame Katherine.

Katherine was buried in Sudeley Castle, and her tomb remains there to this day with the original inscription:

KP
Here lyethe Quene
Kateryn wife to Kyng
Henry the VIII And
last the wife of Thomas
Lord of Sudeley high
Admyrall of England
And onkle to Kyng
Edward the VI
Dyed 5 September
MCCCCC XLVIII

Author's Note

It would seem that a few Christian names were extremely popular in Tudor England. In order to make the book less confusing for the reader, certain liberties have been taken with the names and spellings of some of the characters. For example, Henry had three wives, all by the name of Katherine, and so I have used three different spellings to distinguish between them: Catherine of Aragon, Kathryn Howard and of course, Katherine Parr.

Katherine's sister Anna was christened Anne, yet to avoid confusion with Anne Boleyn and Anne of Cleves, she is referred to as Anna.

Bessie is entirely fictitious, as are the various grooms and lower office-holders. We know that someone performed these functions but not who.

Wriothesley and Gardiner were both chillingly real. Although much is known of the public lives of these and other characters in the book, the chronicles are largely silent on their personal affairs, thus granting the author a good deal of licence.

We know that Katherine was alerted to Wriothesley's attentions as it has been well documented that the warrant for her arrest was found and shown to her. Whilst we do not know who performed this brave act, why should it not have been Mary . . .?

The Concubine

Norah Lofts

"All eyes and hair" a courtier had said disparagingly of her — and certainly the younger daughter of Tom Boleyn lacked the bounteous charms of most ladies of Court. Black-haired, black eyes, she had a wild-sprite quality that was to prove more effective, more dangerous than conventional feminine appeal.

The King first noticed her when she was sixteen — and with imperial greed he smashed her youthful love-affair with Harry Percy and began the process of royal seduction . . .

But this was no ordinary woman, no maid-in-waiting to be possessed and discarded by a king. Against his will, his own common sense, Henry found himself bewitched — enthralled by the young girl who was to be known as the Concubine . . .

ISBN 978-0-7531-8330-4 (hb)
ISBN 978-0-7531-8331-1 (pb)

Crown of Aloes

Norah Lofts

Isabella of Spain was a great woman, a great Queen. *Crown of Aloes* is presented as a personal chronicle. Within the framework of known fact and detail drawn from hitherto unexploited contemporary Spanish sources, a novelist's imagination and understanding have provided motives, thoughts, and private conversations, helping to build up the fascinating character Isabella must have been. Her fortunes were varied indeed: she knew acute poverty, faced anxiety and danger with high courage, gave much, suffered much, lived to the full. At the end she was mainly aware of her failures. It was left to others to realise how spectacular her successes had been.

ISBN 978-0-7531-8834-7 (hb)
ISBN 978-0-7531-8835-4 (pb)

Eleanor the Queen

Norah Lofts

Eleanor . . . young, high-spirited, supremely intelligent, heiress to the vast Duchy of Aquitaine — at a time when a woman's value was measured in terms of wealth. Her vivid leadership inspired and dazzled those about her. And yet, born to rule, she was continually repressed and threatened by the men who overshadowed her life.

This is the story of a brilliant, medieval figure — of a princess who led her own knights to the Crusades, who was bride to two kings and mother of Richard the Lionheart. It is the rich, incredible story of Eleanor of Aquitaine.

ISBN 978-0-7531-8328-1 (hb)
ISBN 978-0-7531-8329-8 (pb)

The Duke & I

Julia Quinn

After enduring two seasons in London, Daphne Bridgerton is no longer naïve enough to believe she will be able to marry for love. But is it really too much to hope for a husband for whom she at least has some affection?

Her brother's old school friend Simon Bassett — the new Duke of Hastings — has no intention of ever marrying. However, newly returned to England, he finds himself the target of the many society mothers who remain convinced that reformed rakes make the best husbands.

To deflect their attention, the handsome hell-raiser proposes to Daphne that they pretend an attachment. In return, his interest in Daphne will ensure she becomes the belle of London society with suitors beating a path to her door . . .

There's just one problem, Daphne is now in danger of falling for a man who has no intention of making their charade a reality . . .

ISBN 978-0-7531-8040-2 (hb)
ISBN 978-0-7531-8041-9 (pb)

Perdita

Joan Smith

Governess Moira Greenwood's beautiful young charge, Perdita Brodie, is a high-spirited chit. Indeed, she rebels against her stepmama's choice of mate and manages to get Moira and herself positions in a not-quite-shabby travelling acting troupe.

While Moira cooks, her lovely cousin sings, attracting the very insistent attentions of the cold, handsome rakehell Lord Stornaway — who takes the pair for lightskirts!

Although Moira explains the truth, the self-satisfied lord believes not a word; he's positive the two are ladies of ill repute. Moira finds him the most rude, uncivil of men and tells him so. Still, there is something about him she can't quite define that is not completely loathsome . . .

ISBN 978-0-7531-8294-9 (hb)
ISBN 978-0-7531-8295-6 (pb)

ISIS publish a wide range of books in large print, from fiction to biography. Any suggestions for books you would like to see in large print or audio are always welcome. Please send to the Editorial Department at:

ISIS Publishing Limited
7 Centremead
Osney Mead
Oxford OX2 0ES

A full list of titles is available free of charge from:

Ulverscroft Large Print Books Limited

(UK)
The Green
Bradgate Road, Anstey
Leicester LE7 7FU
Tel: (0116) 236 4325

(Australia)
P.O. Box 314
St Leonards
NSW 1590
Tel: (02) 9436 2622

(USA)
P.O. Box 1230
West Seneca
N.Y. 14224-1230
Tel: (716) 674 4270

(Canada)
P.O. Box 80038
Burlington
Ontario L7L 6B1
Tel: (905) 637 8734

(New Zealand)
P.O. Box 456
Feilding
Tel: (06) 323 6828

Details of ISIS complete and unabridged audio books are also available from these offices. Alternatively, contact your local library for details of their collection of ISIS large print and unabridged audio books.